PENGUIN CLASSICS

CAPTAINS OF THE SANDS

JORGE AMADO (1912–2001), the son of a cocoa planter, was born in the Brazilian state of Bahia, which he would portray in more than thirty novels. His first novels, published when he was still a teenager, dramatize the class struggles of workers on Bahian cocoa plantations. Amado was later exiled for his leftist politics, but his novels would always have a strong political perspective. Not until Amado returned to Brazil in the 1950s did he write his acclaimed novels *Gabriela, Clove and Cinnamon,* and *Dona Flor and Her Two Husbands* (the basis for the successful film and Broadway musical of the same name), which display a lighter, more comic approach than his overtly political novels. One of the most renowned writers of the Latin American boom of the 1960s, Amado has had his work translated into more than forty-five languages.

GREGORY RABASSA (1922–2016) was a National Book Award–winning translator whose English-language versions of works by Gabriel García Márquez, Mario Vargas Llosa, Julio Cortázar, and Jorge Amado have become classics in their own right.

COLM TÓIBÍN's novels include *The Master* and *Brooklyn.* Tóibín worked as a journalist in Latin America in the 1980s. He is the Irene and Sidney B. Silverman Professor of the Humanities at Columbia University.

T0200926

JORGE AMADO

Captains of the Sands

Translated by
GREGORY RABASSA

Introduction by
COLM TÓIBÍN

PENGUIN BOOKS

PENGUIN BOOKS

Published by the Penguin Group
Penguin Group (USA) Inc., 375 Hudson Street,
New York, New York 10014, USA

USA | Canada | UK | Ireland | Australia | New Zealand | India | South Africa | China
Penguin Books Ltd, Registered Offices: 80 Strand, London WC2R 0RL, England
For more information about the Penguin Group visit penguin.com

Translation by Gregory Rabassa first published in the United States of America by Avon Books,
a division of The Hearst Corporation 1988
This edition with an introduction by Colm Tóibín published in Penguin Books 2013

Copyright © Grapiuna – Grapiuna Producoes Artisticas Ltda., 2008

Translation copyright © Gregory Rabassa, 1988
Introduction copyright © Colm Tóibín, 2013

All rights reserved. No part of this product may be reproduced, scanned, or distributed in any
printed or electronic form without permission. Please do not participate in or encourage piracy of
copyrighted materials in violation of the author's rights. Purchase only authorized editions.

Originally published in Portuguese as *Capitães da areia*
by Livraria Jose Olympio Editora, São Paulo, 1937

LIBRARY OF CONGRESS CATALOGING-IN-PUBLICATION DATA
Amado, Jorge, 1912–2001.
[Capitães da areia. English]
Captains of the sands / Jorge Amado ; translated by Gregory Rabassa ;introduction by Colm Toibin.
pages   cm.—(Penguin classics)
Previously published: New York, N.Y. : Avon, c1988.
Translated from Portuguese.
ISBN 978-0-14-310635-7
I. Rabassa, Gregory, translator. II. Title.
PQ9697.A647C373 2013
869.3'41—dc23   2013000991

Printed in the United States of America
1 3 5 7 9 10 8 6 4 2

Contents

Introduction

In his book on Nathaniel Hawthorne, written in 1879, Henry James offered a list of what New England could not offer a novelist: "No sovereign, no court, no personal loyalty, no aristocracy, no church, no clergy, no army, no diplomatic service, no country gentleman, no palaces, no castles, nor manor, nor old country houses, nor parsonages, nor thatched cottages, nor ivied ruins; no cathedrals, nor abbeys, nor little Norman churches; no great Universities nor public schools—no Oxford, nor Eton, nor Harrow; no literature, no novels, no museums, no pictures, no political society, no sporting class—no Epsom nor Ascot." But James understood, at least some of the time, that such a lack could, in a strange way, be as much a gift as a problem for a novelist. "The American knows," he wrote, "that a good deal remains." Seven years earlier, in a letter to an American friend, he had suggested that the richness of Europe was something perhaps the American novelist did not need: "It's a complex fate being an American, and one of the responsibilities it entails is fighting against a superstitious valuation of Europe."

In his efforts to root his fiction in a world of settled manners, however, James understood that he would have to possess the old world rather than embrace the new one. Since he believed in structure and form in the novel, and in the orderly and stately architecture of fiction, he lived merely with the shadow of what "the American knows" and feasted instead on the substance of what England, France, and Italy offered him. He relished in his fiction a thousand years of slow progress, a sense of order and continuity.

In listing what was absent from the world that Hawthorne inherited, James was suggesting a kind of wilderness, a place where nothing orderly, including an orderly novel, could easily grow. He did not wish to write disorderly novels.

As James was working, however, literacy and literary culture began to spread in places where civility was merely a rumor, or a sour joke. In such countries as Ireland and Brazil, for example, as poverty and social disruption reigned, and respect for form and continuity was sorely missing, the novel took on a new and strange shape.

This caused unease, to say the least. It took more than eight years, for example, for *Dubliners*, James Joyce's first collection of stories, to find a publisher willing to take the risk of bringing out a book with stark and relentless images of the sexual and social underside of a city. So, too, it took more than a decade for Joyce's *Ulysses*, after its initial publication in Paris in 1922, to become freely available in the English-speaking world. The enemies were not only the censors but also snobbish elements in the literary community itself, including Professor Mahaffy of Trinity College Dublin, who said: "James Joyce is a living argument in defence of my contention that it was a mistake to establish a separate university for the aborigines of this island— for the corner boys who spit in the Liffey." Or Virginia Woolf, who noted in her diary that she found *Ulysses* "an illiterate, underbred book . . . the book of a self-taught working man." Or Henry James's friend Edmund Gosse, who wrote of Joyce: "He is of course not entirely without talent, but he is a literary charlatan of the extremest order."

The year after Henry James published his book on Hawthorne, the Brazilian novelist Machado de Assis (1839–1908), a close contemporary of James's—Elizabeth Bishop, in her book on Brazil, ranked him and James as the two greatest novelists of their age in the Americas—began his novel *Epitaph of a*

Small Winner with a chapter called "The Death of the Author." The novel begins: "I hesitated some time, not knowing whether to open these memoirs at the beginning or at the end, i.e., whether to start with my birth or with my death. Granted, the usual practice is to begin with one's birth, but two considerations led me to adopt a different method: the first is that properly speaking, I am a deceased writer not in the sense of one who has written and is now deceased, but of one who has died and is now writing, a writer for whom the grave was really a new cradle; the second is that the book would thus gain in merriment and novelty."

This tone seems a century away from James, being close to the tone of certain, and indeed uncertain, playful texts produced in both the eighteenth century and the twentieth century by such figures as Laurence Sterne (whom Machado de Assis had read) and Flann O'Brien or Jorge Luis Borges. What *Epitaph of a Small Winner* lacks, of course, is what Machado de Assis did not have as his hinterland—a world of manners and morals that had developed enough to give characters choices and chances, or a sense of time itself as something that brought easy progress and gradual change, or a sense of a structured and ordered society in which a character could grow and develop and in which a narrative could grow too to satisfy a large and leisured readership.

Machado de Assis and other such Brazilian novelists as João Guimerães Rosa (1908–1968), Jorge Amado (1912–2001), and Clarice Lispector (1920–1977) came to play with language and tone and structure rather than offer representation for the same reason that such writers as Joyce, Flann O'Brien, and Samuel Beckett in Ireland set out to destroy the line in narrative and replace it with the circle or the jagged form. Fiction for them was broken glass, a cracked mirror, a way of reflecting and engendering distortion rather than offering a window on the world or creating a mirror in which the readers could see their own world in the world of the characters. As Terry Eagleton has pointed out, language in Ireland "is weapon, dissemblance, seduction, apologia—anything, in fact, but representational." The same is true also in Brazil, where the language of fiction has been a high-wire performance rather than a way of stabilizing the world below.

In a 1932 essay called "The Argentine Writer and Tradition," the Argentine writer Jorge Luis Borges attempted to formulate what this disruptive tone in fiction did, or where it came from. The South American writer, he wrote, by virtue of being both close to and distant from the center of Western culture, had more "rights" to Western culture than anyone in any Western nation. He compared this enriching sense of proximity and distance to the position of Jewish and Irish writers. "It was enough," he wrote, "the fact of feeling Irish, different, to become innovators within English culture. I believe that Argentine writers, and South American writers in general, are in an analogous situation; we can handle all the European themes, handle them without superstition, but with an irreverence that can have, and does have, fortunate consequences."

Thus Jorge Amado inherited the full tradition of European literature and felt free to do as he pleased with it. His social vision and his membership in the Communist Party meant he had no interest in dramatizing or inventing the lives of the fragile middle classes in Brazil. In his novel *Captains of the Sands*, he took what he needed from Charles Dickens and used also the form of the folktale, the picaresque novel, and the documentary novel. Like many novelists from the eighteenth century, and like his predecessor Machado de Assis, he did not bother too much with character development or a seamless structure. He wrote as a storyteller might speak. He used episodes rather than chapters. He merged a tone that was almost naive with a social vision that was challenging with a form that took its bearings from collage as much as from the orderly house of fiction.

Amado also set out to take the glamour away from Salvador de Bahia. Bahia was the first capital of Brazil, the place to which slaves were brought from Africa as early as 1535. It was around Bahia that the plantation system first grew. As Claude Lévi-Strauss wrote: "The world, gorged with gold, began to hunger after sugar; and sugar took a lot of slaves." Many of the slaves had skills, and some were literate, and much of the culture they brought from Africa survived in hybrid form into the twentieth century. The beautiful old colonial city, with its waterfront life and its magnificent baroque architecture and many churches, survived too. The capital was transferred to Rio in 1763, and slowly, as São Paulo became the coffee capital, there was no more reason to build in Bahia. Thus its architecture was preserved, and so, too, its folk art, its quasi-religious folk traditions—*candomblé, macumba, capoeira*—and its exotic feel.

Part of the drama in *Captains of the Sands* arises from Amado's refusal to romanticize, to evoke the city of Bahia in all its exquisite beauty. The novel is not written for tourists; it is written to give substance to shadows, to re-create the underlife of the city, to offer the dispossessed and reviled an inner life. There is a lovely, hard materialist vision at the heart of the novel; it veers between sociology and mythmaking. There is a battle going on within it between Amado's mission and his art; at times the mission wins a skirmish as his characters emerge golden and good; at other times the poverty of their lives diminishes any real possibility of choice or chance or development for them. Yet at other times their individuality emerges with artistry and sympathy.

Amado was writing to save his country's soul. His characters are the poor, the abandoned who live from stealing. The novel's hero, Pedro Bala, who is the leader of the group of youths at the heart of the book, is given a powerful sense of who he is and what he has inherited from the father he never met, who died leading a strike. But he is one of the few in the novel who is given a personal history. The rest of the Captains of the Sands inhabit the present tense, but with a sense always of the story of slavery and past cruelty as an essential, if mixed-up, part of their lives. Their motives are often grubby, their instincts mean, but there are also moments when their mission in the world is exalted, as when they set about rescuing Ogun the icon from the hands of the police. They believe in magic and in an older justice, one that came from Africa with the slaves. They also have talent, a talent for loyalty and love, as much as for robbing and deceiving. One of them, the Professor, even has talent as an artist.

The form that Amado chose for the book is close to fable, or to unstructured storytelling. The gravity of the book arises from his use of elemental forces, not only good and evil, wealth and poverty, the body and the spirit, but also the wind and the sea, the stars and the night, and indeed God or a force beyond and above the dull, repressive forces that seem to control the streets of Bahia during the day. There are passages where Amado draws what happens to his waifs in broad outline, but in other sections he manages a sort of razor-sharp realism. The scene where Pedro Bala is condemned to solitary confinement and begins to suffer from thirst is one of the most memorable and best-rendered accounts of being in prison we have in any literature. So, too, the scenes where smallpox and fever take their toll have a genuine edge of pain. Also, the scenes where the Captains of the Sands manage to fool the rich of the city and get away with it would have made Henry Fielding or Charles Dickens proud.

It is interesting that in his postface, written in Mexico in 1937, Amado writes, "I tried to set down the total life of my State," echoing Joyce, who wrote of his alter ego Stephen in *A Portrait of the Artist as a Young Man*, "I go to encounter for the millionth time the reality of experience and to forge in the smithy of my soul the uncreated conscience of my race." In both cases the writer came from a world that lacked the richness and the textures Henry James outlined in his book on Hawthorne. Both writers had to invent their textures and the forms that would display them best to the world. They used age-old systems of storytelling, replacing heroes with figures who were down on their luck; they used the shabby underside of a once-great city as though it were the very center of the universe; they both, in creating new and hybrid forms for the novel, offered the novel a new energy. They set about making the periphery the center of the known world while remaining true to its darker and stranger contours.

COLM TÓIBÍN

*For Aydano do Couto Ferraz, José Olímpio,
José Américo de Almeida, João Nascimento Filho,
and for Anísio Teixeira, the friend of children*

Matilde:
We used to play games of forfeit.
We used to ride in an ox cart.
We lived in a haunted house.
We chatted with girls and magicians.
You found Bahia huge and mysterious.
The poetry in this book comes from you.

Captains of the Sands

LETTERS TO
THE EDITOR

CHILD THIEVES

THE SINISTER ADVENTURES OF
THE "CAPTAINS OF THE
SANDS"—CITY INFESTED BY
CHILDREN WHO LIVE BY
STEALING—ACTIONS URGED
ON THE PART OF THE
JUVENILE JUDGE AND CHIEF
OF POLICE—ANOTHER
ATTACK YESTERDAY

Several times now this newspaper, which is without a doubt the organ of the most legitimate aspirations of the Bahian people, has carried news of the criminal activities of the "Captains of the Sands," the name by which a group of assaulting and thieving children who infest our city is known. These children who have dedicated themselves to a frightful career of crime at such an early age have no set abode or, at least, their abode has not been located. As has not been located either, the place where they hide the product of their attacks, which have become daily, calling for immediate action on the part of the juvenile judge or the chief of police.

This gang that lives off crime is made up, as far as is known, of more than 100 children of the most varied ages, from 8 to 16. Children whose parents neglect giving them even a few Christian feelings in their upbringing, are naturally given over to a life of crime in their young years. They are called the "Captains of the Sands" because the waterfront is their headquarters. And as a commander they have an urchin of 14 who is the worst of the lot, not only a thief but the perpetrator of an attack that resulted in serious injury yesterday

4   JORGE AMADO

afternoon. Unfortunately the identity of this leader is unknown.

What has become necessary is immediate action by the police and the juvenile court so that this gang may be eliminated and the police can pick up these precocious criminals who have not let the city sleep in peace or have the rest it so well deserves, and put them into reform school or prison. Let us go on now to the story of yesterday's attack, the victim of which was a respected businessman of our town whose residence was robbed of more than a thousand and his servant wounded by the heartless leader of that gang of young bandits.

AT THE RESIDENCE OF COMMANDER JOSÉ FERREIRA

On the Corredor da Vitória, in the heart of the most fashionable district of the city, stands the beautiful dwelling of Commander José Ferreira, one of the wealthiest and most distinguished businessmen of this city, with a dry goods establishment on the Rua Portugal. It is a pleasure to see the commander's small palace, surrounded by gardens, with its colonial architecture. Only yesterday this cove of peace and honest toil suffered an hour of indescribable agitation and fright with the invasion it underwent by the "Captains of the Sands."

The clocks were striking three in the afternoon and the city was smothering with heat when the gardener noticed some children dressed in rags loitering about the commander's residence. The gardener tried to drive those unwelcome visitors away. And since they went on their way down the street, Ramiro, the gardener, went about his business in the garden at the rear of the villa. Minutes later, however, came the

ATTACK

Five minutes had not gone by when Ramiro the gardener heard frightened screams coming from inside the residence. They were the cries of people who were truly terrified. Arming himself with a sickle, the gardener went into the house and barely had time to see several urchins who, like a pack of demons (in Ramiro's curious expression), fled, leaping out the windows, loaded down with valuable objects from the dining room. The maid who had screamed was taking care of the commander's wife, who suffered a slight swoon because of the shock she had been through. The gardener hurried out to the garden where he got into the

FIGHT

It so happened that in the garden the charming child named Raul Ferreira, 11 years old, grandson of the commander, who was visiting his grandparents, was talking to the leader of the "Captains of the Sands," who can be recognized by a scar he has on his face. In his innocence, Raul was laughing with the thug, who doubtless intended to rob him. The gardener then threw himself onto the thief. He did not expect, however, the reaction of the urchin, who showed himself to be a master of fights of that nature. The result was that when he thought he had a good grip on the head of the gang, the gardener received a stab in the shoulder and immediately thereafter another on the arm, obliging him to free the criminal, who fled.

The police have investigated the event, but up till the writing of this report no trace of the "Captains of the Sands" has been found. Commander José Ferreira, interviewed by our reporters, estimates his loss at more than a thousand *reis*, since a small watch belonging to his wife was worth 900 alone and it was stolen.

MEASURES URGED

The inhabitants of the aristocratic neighborhood are alarmed and fearful that the attacks will be repeated, for this was not the first one carried out by the "Captains of the Sands." They urge measures to bring proper punishment to such scoundrels and calm to our most distinguished families. We hope that his honor the Chief of Police and the no less honorable Juvenile Judge will take the proper measures against these criminals who are so young and so daring.

THE OPINION OF INNOCENCE

Our reporters also heard from little Raul, who, as we said, is 11 years old and is already one of the brightest students at the Antônio Vieira School. Raul showed great courage and told us about his conversation with the terrible chief of the "Captains of the Sands."

"He said that I was a fool and didn't know what playing was. I answered that I had a bicycle and lots of playthings. He laughed and said he had the street and the waterfront. I liked him because he was like one of those movie children who run away from home to have adventures."

Then we began to think about that other delicate problem of childhood, the movies, which give children so many erroneous ideas of life. Another problem deserving of the attention of the Juvenile Judge. We shall return to it.

(Account published in the *Jornal da Tarde*, on the "Police News" page along with a picture of the commander's house and one of him at the time he received a decoration.)

LETTER FROM THE SECRETARY OF THE CHIEF OF POLICE TO THE EDITOR OF THE *JORNAL DA TARDE*

Editor of the *Jornal da Tarde*

DEAR SIR:

The account published yesterday in the second edition of your paper about the activities of the "Captains of the Sands," a gang of delinquent children, and the attack carried out against the residence of Commander José Ferreira having come to the attention of the Chief of Police, he hastens to write to the editor of the paper that the solution of the problem lies more in the hands of the juvenile judge than in those of the police. The police in this case must act in obedience to a request from the juvenile judge. It will take serious steps, however, so that similar attacks will not be repeated and so that the perpetrators of the one on the day before yesterday will be arrested and punished as they deserve.

From what has been said, it has been clearly shown that the police do not deserve any criticism concerning their attitude regarding this problem. They did not act with greater effect because they were not asked to by the juvenile judge.

Sincerely,
Secretary of the Chief of Police

(Published on page 1 of the *Jornal da Tarde*, with a picture of the Chief of Police and a long and praiseful commentary.)

LETTER FROM THE JUVENILE JUDGE TO THE EDITOR OF THE *JORNAL DA TARDE*

Editor of the *Jornal da Tarde*
City of Salvador
State

MY DEAR SIR:

In one of the rare moments of leisure left me by the multiple and various worries of my thorny position as I thumbed through your excellent evening paper I came across a letter from the tireless Chief of Police of the State in which he spoke about the reasons for the Police's being unable up till now to intensify their meritorious campaign against the juvenile delinquents who infest our city. The Chief of Police justifies himself by declaring that he had no orders from the juvenile judge for actions against juvenile delinquency. Not wishing in any way to blame the brilliant and tireless Chief of Police, I am obliged, in the name of truth (the same truth that I hold high as the beacon that lights the path of my life with its pure beam), to declare that the excuse does not hold. It does not hold, sir, because it is not up to the juvenile judge to pursue and apprehend juvenile delinquents, but rather to name the place where they must undergo punishment, appoint a guardian to follow whatever changes are brought against them, etc. . . . It is not the role of the juvenile judge to apprehend juvenile delinquents. It is his role to watch over their subsequent fate. And the Chief of Police will always find me where duty calls me, because never in 50 years of unsullied life have I neglected to fulfill it.

Only most recently have I sent several minors, delinquent or abandoned, to the Reformatory for Minors. I am not to blame, however, if they run away, if they are not impressed with the example of work they find in that educational establishment, and if, through escape, they abandon an environment where they breathe an atmosphere of peace and work and where they are treated with the greatest affection. They run away and they become even more perverse, as if the example they had received was evil and harmful. Why? That is a problem to be solved by psychologists and not by me, a simple amateur in philosophy.

What I want to make crystal clear, sir, is that the Chief of Police can count on the best help from this magistracy of minors to intensify the campaign against juvenile delinquents.

Yours most sincerely,

Juvenile Judge

(Published in the *Jornal da Tarde* with a picture of the juvenile judge in a column along with a small commentary of praise.)

LETTER FROM A MOTHER,
A SEAMSTRESS, TO THE EDITOR OF
THE *JORNAL DA TARDE*

DEAR SIR:

Pleaze excuse the mistakes becauze I am not acustomed to this bizness of writing and if I write to you today its to dot a couple of eyes. I saw an article in the paper about the "Captains of the Sands" and then the police come and say they was going to chase them and then the children's doctors talking about it being too bad they didnt straiten out in the reform school where he sent the poor things. Its to talk about the reformatory that Im writing these poor lines. I wanted your paper to send omebody to take a look at that reformatory and see how they treat poor peoples children who have the bad luck to fall into the hands of those heartless guards. My son Alonso had six months there and if I hadnt been able to get him out of that hellhole I dont know if the poor boy would have lived six months. The least that happens to peoples kids is that they beat them two or three times a day. The director is dead drunk all the time and likes to hear the whip sing a song on the backs of poor peoples kids. I saw that a lot of times becauze they dont stop for people and said it was to make an example. That was why I got my son out of there. If your paper could send somebody there secret theyd see what food they eat, the slave labor they have to do, that not even a strong man can take, and the beatings they get. But it has to be secret becauze if they find out everything will be fine. Drop by all of a sudden and youll see Im right. Thats why there are "Captains of the Sands." Id rather see my son among them than in the reformatory. If you want to see something to break your heart go there. You also might want to talk to Father José Pedro who was chaplain there and saw all of it. He could tell it and with better words I havent got.

Maria Ricardina, seamstress

(Published on the fifth page of the *Jornal da Tarde*, among advertisements, with no pictures or commentary.)

LETTER FROM FATHER JOSÉ PEDRO TO THE EDITOR OF THE *JORNAL DA TARDE*

Editor of the *Jornal da Tarde*

GREETINGS IN CHRIST:

Having read in your excellent newspaper the letter by Maria Ricardina, who called on me as a person who could clarify what life is like for children kept in the Children's Reformatory, I am obliged to come out of the obscurity in which I live to come to tell you that unfortunately Maria Ricardina is right. The children in the aforementioned reformatory are treated like animals, that is the truth. They have forgotten the lesson of the gentle Master, sir, and instead of winning over the children with good treatment, they make them even more rebellious with continuous beatings and truly inhuman physical punishment. I have gone there to bring the children the consolation of religion and found them little disposed to accept it, due, naturally, to the hatred they are storing up in those hearts so worthy of charity. What I have seen, sir, would fill a volume.

Thank you for your attention.

Your servant in Christ,

Father José Pedro

(Letter published on the third page of the *Jornal da Tarde*, under the heading: "Can It Be True?" and with no commentary.)

LETTER FROM THE DIRECTOR OF THE REFORMATORY TO THE EDITOR OF THE *JORNAL DA TARDE*

DEAR SIR:

I have been following with great interest the campaign that your excellent Bahian newspaper, which you edit with such clear intelligence, has been conducting against the fearsome crimes of the "Captains of the Sands," a gang of delinquents who terrorize the city and stop it from living in peace.

That was how I came to read two letters of accusation
against the establishment I direct and which modesty (and only
modesty, sir) prevents me from calling model.

As for the letter from a little woman of the people, I shall not
bother with it, it doesn't merit a reply from me. She is doubtless
one of the many who come here and want to stop the Reformatory from fulfilling its sacred mission of educating their sons.
They rear them in the street, always on a spree, and since here
they are submitted to an exemplary life, they are the first to
complain when they should be kissing the hands of those who
are turning their sons into good men. First they come to ask for
a place for their children. Then they miss them, miss the products of the thefts they bring home, and then they come and
complain against the Reformatory. But as I have already said,
sir, that letter doesn't bother me. A woman of the people isn't
going to understand the work I am doing as head of this establishment.

What saddened me, sir, was the letter from Father José
Pedro. This priest, forgetting the functions of his calling, threw
out grave accusations at the establishment. This priest (whom I
shall call a priest of the devil, if you will permit me a little sar-
casm, sir) abused his function by coming into our educational
establishment at hours prohibited by the rules and I must raise
a serious complaint against him: he has incited the minors put
under my charge by the State to revolt, to disobey. Ever since
he crossed the threshold of this establishment, the cases of
rebellion and rule-breaking have increased. This priest is nothing but an instigator of the general bad character of the minors
under my care. And that is why I am going to close the doors of
this house of education to him.

Nevertheless, sir, picking up the words of the seamstress who
wrote to your paper, I am the one who invites you to send a
reporter to the Reformatory. I make a point of this. In that way
we and the public too will know for certain and in truth the
way in which minors are treated as they are regenerated by the
Bahian Reformatory for Juvenile Delinquents and Abandoned
Boys. I expect your reporter next Monday. And if I don't say
that he can come whenever he likes, it is because visits must be

made on the days authorized by the rules, and it is my custom always to obey the rules. This is the only reason I invite your reporter for Monday. I will be most gratified if you print this. In this way the false vicar of Christ will be confounded.

Your thankful admirer,
Director of the Bahian Reformatory for Juvenile Delinquents and Abandoned Boys

(Published on the third page of the *Jornal da Tarde* with a photograph of the Reformatory and an item advising that on Monday next a reporter of the *Jornal da Tarde* will visit the Reformatory.)

A MODEL ESTABLISHMENT WHERE PEACE AND WORK REIGN— A DIRECTOR WHO IS A FRIEND—EXCELLENT FOOD— CHILDREN WHO WORK AND PLAY—CHILD THIEVES ON THE ROAD TO REGENERATION—UNFOUNDED ACCUSATIONS—ONLY AN INCORRIGIBLE WILL COMPLAIN—THE "BAHIAN REFORMATORY" IS ONE BIG FAMILY—WHERE THE "CAPTAINS OF THE SANDS" OUGHT TO BE.

(Titles in article published in the second Tuesday edition of the *Jornal da Tarde*, taking up the whole front page, on the Bahian Reformatory, with several pictures of the building and one of the Director.)

IN THE MOONLIGHT IN AN OLD ABANDONED WAREHOUSE

THE WAREHOUSE

In the moonlight, in an old abandoned warehouse, the children are sleeping.

In olden days this had been the sea. On the large, black rocks near the warehouse the waves sometimes broke fiercely, sometimes lapped softly. The water used to pass beneath the dock under which many children are resting now, lighted by a yellow moonbeam. From this dock innumerable fully-laden sailing ships used to leave, some were enormous and painted strange colors, for the adventure of an ocean crossing. They came here to fill their holds and tie up at this dock, whose planks are worm-eaten now. Formerly the mystery of the ocean sea spread out before the warehouse, nights before it were dark green, almost black, that mysterious color that is the color of the sea at night.

Today the night is clear before the warehouse. Before it the sands of the waterfront now extend. Under the dock there is no sound other than the waves. The sands have invaded everything, have made the sea retreat many yards. In a short time, slowly, the sands went conquering before the warehouse. The sailing ships that used to leave fully laden can no longer tie up at its dock. The muscular black men who had come out of slavery no longer worked there. A nostalgic sailor no longer sang on the old dock. The sands, very white, extended out before the warehouse. And the immense building was never again filled with bales, sacks, cases, abandoned in the middle of the sands, a black spot on the whiteness of the shore.

For years it had been inhabited exclusively by rats, who ran through it playfully, gnawed the wood of the monumental doors, lived there as exclusive masters. For a certain time a stray dog sought it out as a refuge from the wind and the rain. On the first night he didn't sleep, busy tearing rats that passed in front of him apart. Later he slept a few nights, barking at the moon in the early hours of the morning, for a large part of the roof was in ruins and the moonbeams penetrated freely, lighting up the thick plank floor. But he was a dog with no set place and he soon left in search of another dwelling, the darkness of a doorway, underneath a dock, the warm body of a bitch. And other rats returned to rule until the Captains of the Sands cast their eyes on the abandoned building.

At that time the door had fallen off to one side and one of the group, on a certain day when he was strolling along the extension of their domains (because all the sandy area of the waterfront, as all the city of Bahia too, belongs to the Captains of the Sands), went into the warehouse.

It would be a much better sleeping place than just the sands, than the docks of other warehouses where the water rose so high sometimes that it threatened to carry them off. And from that night on a large number of the Captains of the Sands slept in the old abandoned warehouse in the company of the rats, under the yellow moon. Before the vastness of the sands, a whiteness without end. In the distance the sea breaking on the beach. Through the door they saw the lights of ships entering and leaving. Through the ceiling they saw the sky with its stars, the moon that lighted them up.

Then, later, they transferred the collection of objects that their day's work brought them to the warehouse. Strange things then entered the warehouse. No stranger, however, than those children, urchins of all colors and of the most varied ages, from nine to sixteen, who at night lay down on the floor and under the dock and slept, indifferent to the wind that howled about the building, indifferent to the rain that often bathed them, but with their eyes fastened on the lights of the ships, their ears fixed on the songs that came from the smaller vessels . . .

Here too is the dwelling of the chief of the Captains of the Sands: Pedro Bala, the Bullet. He has been called that since early times, since he was five years old. Today he is fifteen. For ten of those years he has wandered about the streets of Bahia. He never knew anything about his mother, his father died of a bullet wound. He was left alone and he spent years learning about the city. Today he knows all its streets and all its alleys. There isn't a shop, store, establishment that he doesn't know. When he joined the Captains of the Sands (the newly-constructed waterfront attracted all the abandoned children of the city to its sands) the chief was Raimundo the Halfbreed, a strong and copper-colored mulatto.

Raimundo the Halfbreed didn't last long in the leadership. Pedro Bala was much more active, he knew how to plan jobs, he knew how to deal with the others, he had the authority of a leader in his eyes and his voice. One day they fought. Raimundo's misfortune was to pull out a razor and cut Pedro's face, a scar that he had for the rest of his life. The others intervened and, since Pedro was unarmed, took his side and waited for the revenge that wasn't long in coming. One night when Raimundo tried to beat up Outrigger, Pedro took over for the little black boy and they rolled around in the most sensational fight the sands of the waterfront had ever seen. Raimundo was taller and older. Pedro Bala, however, his blond hair flying, the red scar on his face, had a frightening agility and from that day on Raimundo not only gave up the leadership of the Captains of the Sands but the sands themselves. A while later he signed on board a ship.

Everybody recognized Pedro Bala's right to the leadership and it was during that time that the city began to hear about the Captains of the Sands, abandoned children who lived by stealing. No one ever knew the exact number of children who lived that way. There were at least a hundred, and more than forty of them slept in the ruins of the old warehouse.

Dressed in rags, dirty, half-starved, aggressive, cursing, and smoking cigarette butts, they were, in truth, the masters of the city, the ones who knew it completely, the ones who loved it completely, its posts.

NIGHT WITH THE
"CAPTAINS OF THE SANDS"

The great night of peace in Bahia comes from the waterfront, envelops the sloops, the fort, the breakwater, extends out over the hillsides and the towers of the churches. The bells no longer toll Hail Marys because six o'clock has come and gone a long time ago. And if the moon hasn't come up the sky is full of stars on this clear night. The warehouse stands out against the sands that preserve the footprints of the Captains of the Sands who have already retired for the night. In the distance the weak light from the lamp at the Gate of the Sea, a sailors' bar, seems to be dying. A cold wind that raises the sands is blowing and it makes walking difficult for black Big João, who is going in for the night. He walks along curved by the wind like the sail of a ship. He's tall, the tallest of the gang and the strongest too, a black boy with short kinky hair and taut muscles, even though he's only thirteen years old, four of which have been spent in the most absolute freedom, running through the streets of Bahia with the Captains of the Sands. Ever since that afternoon when his father, a gigantic carter, was hit by a truck as he tried to pull his horse to the side of the street. Big João didn't go back to the little house on the hill. Before him was the mysterious city, and he went out to conquer it. The city of Bahia, black and religious, is almost as mysterious as the green sea. That's why Big João never went back. At the age of nine he joined up with the Captains of the Sands, when the Halfbreed was still leader and the gang wasn't too well known because the Halfbreed didn't like taking chances. Big João soon became one of the leaders and he was always invited to the meetings of the older ones to plan their robberies. Not that he was a good organizer of attacks or had a lively intelligence. On the contrary, he got headaches if he had to think. He would stand with his eyes burning, as he also did when he saw someone mistreating small children. Then his muscles would tense and he was ready for any fight. But his enormous physical strength made him feared. Legless would say of him:

"This black boy here is dumb, but he's a bone-crusher . . ."

And the little ones, those small boys who came to the gang all full of fear, had a most determined protector in him. Pedro, the leader, liked to listen to him too. And Big João knew quite well that it wasn't because of his strength that he had the Bullet's friendship. Pedro found the black boy good and never tired of saying:

"You're a good man, Big Boy. You're better than just people. I like you," and he would pat the leg of the black boy, who became flustered.

Big João is coming to the warehouse. The wind is trying to hold back his steps and he's bent way over, resisting the wind that's raising the sand. He went to the Gate of the Sea to have a drink of cane liquor with God's-Love, who'd arrived today from a fishing trip in the southern seas. God's-Love is the most famous *capoeira* foot fighter in the city. Who is there who doesn't respect him in Bahia? In the play of Angolan *capoeira* no one can stand up to God's-Love, not even Zé Moleque, who was famous in Rio de Janeiro. God's-Love gave him the latest news and told him that the next day he would come to the warehouse to continue the *capoeira* lessons that Pedro Bala, Big João, and Cat are taking. Big João smokes a cigarette and heads for the warehouse. The prints of his big feet are left on the sands but the wind soon erases them. The black man is thinking that the seaways are dangerous on a windy night like this.

Big João goes under the dock—his feet sink into the sand—trying not to touch the bodies of his comrades who are already asleep. He goes into the warehouse. He peeps in for a moment, undecided until he spots the light of the Professor's candle. There he is, at the far corner of the big shed, reading by candlelight. Big João thinks that the light there is even smaller and flickers more than the lamp at the Gate of the Sea and that the Professor is eating his eyes out with so much reading of those books with small print. Big João goes over to where the Professor is, although he always sleeps by the warehouse door, like a mastiff, his knife near his hand to avoid any surprise.

He walks among the groups chatting, among the children sleeping, and comes over by the Professor. He squats down beside him and stays there watching the other's attentive reading.

João José, the Professor ever since the day he'd stolen a story book from a bookcase in a house in Barra, had become an expert in such thefts. He never sold the books, however, piling them up in a corner of the warehouse, covered with bricks so the rats wouldn't chew them. He read them all with an anxiety that was almost a fever. He liked to know things and he was the one who on many nights told the others stories about adventurers, men of the sea, historical and legendary figures, stories that made those lively eyes extend out to sea or up to the mysterious hillsides of the city in an urge for adventure and heroism. João José was the only one among them who did any reading and yet he'd only spent a year and a half in school. But his daily practice in reading had awakened his imagination completely and he may have been the only one who had a certain awareness of the heroic side of their lives. That knowledge, that vocation for telling stories, made him respected among the Captains of the Sands, even though he was frail, thin, and sad, his dark hair hanging over squinting myopic eyes. They'd nicknamed him Professor because in one stolen book he'd learned to do magic tricks with handkerchiefs and coins and also because when he told the stories he'd read and many he'd invented, he would weave a great and mysterious magic spell that transported them to many different worlds and he made the eyes of the Captains of the Sands shine as only the stars in the Bahia night could shine. Pedro Bala never made a decision without consulting him and several times it was the Professor's imagination that created the best plans for a robbery. No one knew, however, that one day, years later, he would be the one to tell with descriptions that would amaze the nation the story of these lives and many other stories of men who struggled and suffered. Perhaps the only one who knew it was Don'Aninha, priestess of the temple of the Cross of Oxó of Afoxê, because Don'Aninha knows everything that Iá tells her by means of a game with seeds on a stormy night.

Big João spent a long time watching the reading. Those letters didn't say anything to the black boy. His look went from the book to the flickering light of the candle and from that to the Professor's uncombed hair. He finally got tired and asked in a full, warm voice:

"Nice, Professor?"

The Professor took his eyes off the book, laid his slim hand on the shoulder of the black boy, his most ardent admirer:

"A crazy story, Big Boy." His eyes were shining.

"About sailors?"

"It's about a black man like you. A real he-man black."

"Will you tell it to me?"

"I'll tell it to you as soon as I finish reading it. You'll see that only a black man . . ."

And he turned his eyes back to the pages of the book. Big João lighted a cheap cigarette, silently offered another to the Professor, and squatted smoking as if standing guard over the other's reading. Throughout the warehouse there was a sound of laughter, conversation, shouts. Big João could easily make out Legless's voice, shrill and nasal. Legless talked loud, laughed a lot. He was the spy of the group, the one who knew how to worm his way into the house of a family for a week, passing himself off as a good boy who'd lost his parents to the aggressive immensity of the city. Lame, his physical defect had given him the nickname. But it also gave him the sympathy of any mother who saw him at her door, humble and woe-begotten, asking for a little something to eat and a place to spend the night. Now, in the middle of the warehouse, Legless was making fun of Cat, who'd wasted a whole day stealing a wine-colored ring of no real value, a fake stone, with fake beauty too.

It had been a week before that Cat had told half the world:

"I've seen a ring, you guys, that even a bishop doesn't wear. A nice big ring, fine for my finger. Real fine. You'll see when I bring it back . . ."

"Where's the showcase?"

"On a sucker's finger. A fat guy who gets on the Brotas street-car at the Baixa dos Sapateiros every day."

And Cat didn't rest until he got it in the crush of a streetcar at seven o'clock in the evening, pulling the ring off the man's finger, sneaking away in the confusion because the owner had noticed it right away. He proudly displayed the ring on his middle finger. Legless laughed:

"Risking jail for a piece of junk! An ugly thing . . ."

"What's it to you? I like it and that's that."

"You're a real jackass. The pawnbroker won't give you a penny for it."

"But it looks nice on my finger. I'm fixing to gobble up something nice with it."

They were naturally talking about women in spite of the fact that the oldest was only sixteen. They'd learned the mysteries of sex at an early age.

Pedro Bala, who was coming in, broke up the start of a fight. Big João left the Professor reading to go over to the leader. Legless was laughing to himself, muttering about the ring. Pedro called him and went with him and Big João to the corner where the Professor was.

"Come here, Professor."

The four sat down. Legless lighted the butt of an expensive cigar, savoring it. Big João was peering at the piece of sea that could be seen through the door, beyond the sand. Pedro spoke:

"González at the '14' spoke to me today . . ."

"Does he want more gold chains? The last time . . ." Legless cut in.

"No. He wants hats. But only felt. Straw's no good, he says there's no market for it. And also . . ."

"What else?" Legless interrupted again.

"If it's been worn a lot it's no good."

"He wants a lot. If he paid something it would be worth it . . ."

"You know, Legless, he keeps his mouth shut. Maybe he doesn't pay good, but he's tight-lipped. You can't get anything out of him, not even with a hook."

"He pays rotten too. And it's in his own interest not to say anything. If he was to open his mouth to everybody there's no kind of influence would keep him out of the pokey . . ."

"O.K., Legless, if you don't want a piece of the action, beat it, but let us get our things straight."

"I'm not saying I'm not in. I'm just saying that working for a thieving foreigner is a bad deal. But if you want to . . ."

"He says he'll pay better this time. Something to make it worthwhile. But only felt hats, in good shape and new. You, Legless, can take some guys and get it done. Tomorrow night González is sending over a clerk from the '14' to bring the dough and take the bonnets."

"The movies are a good place," the Professor said, turning to Legless.

"The Vitória's a good spot . . ." and Legless made a disdainful gesture. "Just go into the lobby and a hat is guaranteed . . . All fat cats there."

"They've also got guards all over the place."

"Are you worried about guards? Now if it was a cop . . . Guards are only for playing hide-and-seek. Will you come with me, Professor?"

"I'll come. I even need a hat myself."

Pedro Bala spoke:

"Pick whoever you want, Legless. This is your show. Except for João and the Cat. I've got something for them to do tomorrow . . ." He turned to Big João. "Something with God's-Love."

"He already told me. And he say's he's coming over at night for some *capoeira*."

Pedro turned to Legless, who was already leaving to go arrange with Lollipop for the formation of the group going after hats the following day:

"Hey, Legless, tell them that if anyone is spotted to run off somewhere else. Not to come back here."

He asked for a cigarette. Big João gave him one. Legless was already off looking for Lollipop. Pedro went in search of the Cat, he had something to talk to him about. He came back later, stretched out near the Professor. The latter returned to his book, over which he hunched until the candle burned out and the darkness of the warehouse enveloped him. Big João walked slowly to the door, where he lay down, the knife in his belt.

Lollipop was thin and very tall, a tight face, half-yellowish, eyes sunken and deep, his mouth twisted and not given to smiles. Legless teased him first, asking if he was "saying his prayers," then he got onto the subject of the hat-stealing and they decided they'd take a certain number of boys whom they chose carefully, marked out the zones of operation, and separated. Lollipop then went to his usual corner. He slept there invariably, where the warehouse walls form an angle. He'd arranged his things with loving care: an old blanket, a pillow he'd taken from a hotel once when he'd gone in carrying a traveler's bag, a pair of pants he wore on Sundays along with a shirt of indefinite color but more or less clean. And fastened to the wall with small tacks two pictures of saints: a Saint Anthony carrying a Christ Child (Lollipop's name was Antônio and he'd heard that Saint Anthony was Brazilian), and an Our Lady of the Seven Sorrows, who had her breast run through with arrows and who had a withered flower beneath her picture. Lollipop picked up the flower, smelled it, saw it had lost its scent. Then he fastened it alongside the scapular he carried on his chest and from the pocket of the old jacket he wore he took a red carnation that he'd picked in a park, right under the nose of the guard, at that imprecise hour of dusk. And he put the carnation under the picture while he gazed at the saint with a fervent look. Then he knelt. The others had started up with a lot of raillery at first when they saw him on his knees praying. They got used to it, however, and nobody paid any more attention. He began to pray and his ascetic look became even more pronounced, his child's face became paler and more somber, he lifted his long, thin hands to the picture. His whole face had a kind of glow and his voice took on tonalities and vibrations that his companions didn't recognize. It was as if he were out of the world, not in the old, rundown warehouse, but in some other land along with Our Lady of the Seven Sorrows. His prayer, however, was simple and hadn't even been learned from a catechism. He asked Our Lady to help him someday so he could enter that school in Sodré out of which men came transformed into priests.

Legless came over to work out a detail of the hat business and since he'd seen him praying had a wisecrack all ready, a wisecrack that made him laugh just thinking about it and which would upset Lollipop completely, but when he got close and saw Lollipop praying, his hands uplifted, his eyes fixed nobody knew where, his face open in ecstasy (it was as if he were clothed in happiness), he stopped, the mocking laugh disappeared from his lips, and he stood looking at him half with fear, possessed by a feeling that had a touch of envy and a touch of despair in it.

Legless was stock still, looking. Lollipop didn't move. Only his lips showed a slow movement. Legless was in the habit of making fun of him, as of all the others in the group, even Professor, whom he liked, even Pedro Bala, whom he respected. As soon as anyone joined the Captains of the Sands he formed a bad opinion of Legless. Because he would immediately give him a nickname, laugh at some gesture of the newcomer, some phrase. He ridiculed everything, he was one of those who brawled the most. He even had a reputation for being mean. Once he did some terribly cruel things to a cat that had come into the warehouse. And one day he'd cut a waiter in a restaurant with a switchblade just to steal a roast chicken. One day, when he had an abscess on his leg, he coldly scraped it with a knife and in view of everybody squeezed it, laughing. Many in the gang didn't like him but those who looked the other way and became his friends said he was "a good egg." Deep down in his heart he was sorry for the bad luck they all had. And laughing and ridiculing was the way he ran away from his own bad luck. He was like a remedy. He stood still, watching

Lollipop as he concentrated on his prayers. On the face of the praying boy an exaltation could be seen, something that Legless thought was joy or happiness at first. But he looked closely at the other's face and saw that it was an expression he couldn't define. And he thought, contracting his little face, that maybe that's why he'd never thought about praying, turning toward the heaven that Father José Pedro spoke about so much when he came to see them. What he wanted was happiness, joy, fleeing from all the misery that surrounded and smothered them. There was, it's true, the wide freedom of the streets. But there was also the loss of all love, the lack of any kind words. Lollipop was seeking that in heaven, in the pictures of saints, in the withered flowers he brought for Our Lady of the Seven Sorrows the way a romantic lover in chic neighborhoods brings a proposal of marriage to the one he loves. But Legless didn't see how that could be enough. He wanted something immediate, something that would make his face smiling and gay, that would free him from the need to laugh at everybody and everything. That would also free him from the anguish, that urge to weep that came over him on winter nights. He didn't want what Lollipop had: a face full of exaltation. He wanted joy, a hand that would caress him lovingly, someone, who with a lot of love, could make him forget his physical defect and the many years (maybe they'd only been months or weeks, but for him they would always be long years) he had lived alone on the streets of the city, antagonized by the men who passed, shoved by guards, beaten up by older urchins. He'd never had a family. He'd lived in the house of a baker whom he called "my godfather" and who beat him. He ran away as soon as he was able to understand that running away would set him free. He went hungry, one day he was arrested. He wants loving, a hand that will pass over his eyes and make him be able to forget that night in jail when drunken policemen made him run around a holding room on his lame leg. In each corner there was one with a long piece of rubber hose. The marks left on his back had disappeared. But inside him the pain of that hour had never gone. He'd run around the room like an animal pursued by other stronger ones. His lame leg refused to help him.

And the rubber hose slapped on his back when fatigue made him stop. At first he wept a lot, then, he doesn't know why, the tears dried up. After a time he couldn't take any more, fell to the floor. He was bleeding and even today he can still hear the policemen laughing and how that fat man in a gray vest and smoking a cigar laughed. Then he found the Captains of the Sands (it was the Professor who brought him, they'd made friends on a park bench) and he stayed with them. It didn't take him long to make his mark because he, better than anyone, knew how to put on great pain and in that way trick ladies whose houses would be visited later by the gang, who already knew all the places where there were objects of value and all the habits of the house. And Legless had great satisfaction when he thought about how those ladies who had taken him for a poor orphan were cursing him. That was how he got his revenge, because his heart was full of hate. In a confused way he wanted to have a bomb (like one of those in a certain story the Professor told) that would wipe out the whole city and blow everybody into the air. In that way he would be happy. Maybe he would be too if he saw someone, possibly a woman with gray hair and soft hands, who would hug him against her breast, would stroke his face and make him sleep a good sleep, a sleep that wouldn't be full of dreams of that night in jail. He would be happy that way, there wouldn't be any more hate in his heart. And he wouldn't have any more disdain, envy, or hatred for Lollipop, who with his hands raised and his eyes staring, flees his world of suffering for a world he learned about talking to Father José Pedro.

A sound of conversation draws closer. A group of four is coming into the silence that now reigns in the warehouse night. Legless shakes himself, laughs behind the back of Lollipop who goes on praying. He shrugs his shoulders, decides to leave the working out of details of the theft of the hats for tomorrow morning. And since he's afraid of sleep, he goes over to greet the group coming in, asking for a cigarette, joking about the adventures with women the four are telling about:

"A bunch of squirts like you? Who's going to believe that

you're capable of mounting a woman? It must have been some faggot dressed up as a girl."

The others are annoyed:

"You like to mess around too. If you want to, all you've got to do is come with us tomorrow. That way you can get to know the broad, she's stacked."

Legless laughs sardonically:

"I don't like fairies."

And he goes off walking through the warehouse.

Cat still hasn't gone to sleep. He always goes out after eleven o'clock. He's the dandy of the group. When he arrived, pale and pink, Good-Life tried to get him. But way back then Cat already had an unbelievable agility and hadn't come as Good-Life had thought from a family home. He came from the midst of the Street Indians, children who live under the bridges in Aracaju. He'd made the trip on the tail-end of a train. He was quite familiar with the life of abandoned children. And he was over thirteen already. So he knew right off the motives of Good-Life, a stocky, ugly mulatto, why he treated him so nicely. He offered him cigarettes and gave him part of his dinner and ran through the city with him. After they'd snatched a pair of new shoes displayed by the door of a shop on the Baixa dos Sapateiros together, Good-Life had said:

"Let me have them, I know where we can sell them."

Cat looked at his own dusty shoes:

"I was thinking of using them myself. I need a pair . . ."

"You with such a good pair on you . . . ?" Good-Life was surprised. He rarely wore shoes and was barefoot at the time.

"I'll pay you your share. How much do you think it is?"

Good-Life looked at him. Cat was wearing a necktie, a patched jacket, and amazingly was wearing socks:

"You really are a dude, aren't you?" He smiled.

"I wasn't born for this life. I was born for the big world," Cat said, repeating a phrase he'd heard from a traveling salesman once in a bar in Aracaju.

Good-Life found him decidedly handsome. Cat had a petulant air and yet there wasn't any effeminate beauty, he was pleasing to Good-Life, who, besides everything else, hadn't had much luck with women, because he looked much younger than the thirteen years he was, short and squat. Cat was tall and on his fourteen-year-old lips the fuzz of a mustache he was cultivating was beginning to appear. Good-Life loved him at the start, because he said with certainty:

"You keep them . . . I'll give you my share."

"O.K. I owe you."

Good-Life tried to take advantage of the other's thanks in order to begin his conquest. And he ran his hand down Cat's back, who slipped away with just a body movement. Cat laughed to himself and didn't say anything. Good-Life thought he shouldn't insist because he might scare the boy. He knew nothing about Cat and couldn't imagine that the latter was on to his game. They walked together for part of the night, looking at the city lights (Cat was amazed), and around eleven o'clock they went to the warehouse. Good-Life showed Cat to Pedro and then took him to the place where he slept:

"I've got a sheet here. It's big enough for two."

Cat lay down. Good-Life stretched out next to him. When he thought the other one was asleep he embraced him with his hand and with the other began to pull down his pants slowly. In a minute Cat was on his feet:

"You're fooling yourself, mulatto. I'm a man."

But Good-Life no longer saw anything, he only saw his desire, the urge he had for Cat's white body, of rolling his head in Cat's dark hair, of feeling the firm flesh of Cat's thighs. And he leaped onto him with the intention of knocking him down and raping him. But Cat moved his body out of the way, stuck out his leg, Good-Life fell on his face. A group had already formed around them. Cat said:

"He thought I was queer. Do your dirty things to yourself."

He took off with Good-Life's sheet for another corner and went to sleep. They were enemies for a long time but finally became friends again and now when Cat is tired of a little chippy he gives her to Good-Life.

One night Cat was going through the red-light district, his hair all shiny with cheap grease, a necktie on, whistling as if

he were one of those city hoodlums. The women looked at him
and laughed:

"Look at that spring chicken . . . I wonder what he wants
around here?"

Cat answered with smiles and kept on his way. He was waiting for one of them to call him and make love to him. But he
didn't want to pay for it, not just because the coins he had
wouldn't add up to fifteen hundred *milreis*, but because the
Captains of the Sands didn't like to pay women. They had little black girls of sixteen to fall down with on the sand.

The women were doubtless looking at his boyish figure.
They found him handsome in his vice-ridden boyhood and
would have liked to have made love to him. But they didn't call
to him because it was time for waiting for the men who paid
and they had to think about their rent and their next day's
meal. They contented themselves with laughing and making
jokes. They knew that out of that would come one of those
swindlers who take over a woman's life, take her money, beat
her, but give her a lot of loving too. A lot of them would have
liked to be the first woman for such a young hoodlum. But it
was ten o'clock, time for the paying customers. And Cat went
uselessly back and forth. That was when he saw Dalva, who
was coming down the street wrapped up in a fur coat in spite
of the summer night. She went by him almost without looking.
She was a woman of some thirty-five years, strong body, a face
full of sensuality. Cat wanted her at once. He was after her. He
watched when she went into a house and didn't come out. He
stayed on the corner waiting. Minutes later she would appear
at the window. Cat went up and down the street but she didn't
even look at him. Then an old man went by, heard her call,
went in. Cat kept waiting, but even after the old man had
come out in a great hurry, trying not to be seen, she didn't
come back to the window.

Night after night Cat went back to the same corner, just to
watch her. Everything he got in the way of money now went to
buying used clothes and to looking elegant. He had a touch of
low-life elegance that was more in his way of walking, of wearing his hat, and making a casual knot in his tie rather than in

the clothing itself. Cat had a desire for Dalva in the same way that he desired food when he was hungry, that he desired sleep when he was sleepy. He no longer paid any attention to the calls of the other women when after midnight they'd already taken care of the next day's expenses and wanted some juvenile love from the little hoodlum. Once he went with one of them only to find out about Dalva's life. That was how he found out that she had a lover, a flute player in a café who took the money she made and always had wild drinking bouts in her place, upsetting the lives of all the whores in the building.

Cat came back every night. Dalva never even looked at him. That made him love her all the more. He would remain painfully waiting until a half hour after midnight when the flutist would arrive and, after kissing her through the window, would go in through the dimly-lighted door. Then Cat would go to the warehouse, his head full of thoughts: If the flutist didn't come one day . . . If the flutist should die . . . He was weak, maybe he couldn't even stand up to the weight of Cat's fourteen years. And he squeezed the switchblade he carried in his shirt.

And one night the flutist didn't come. On that night Dalva had walked through the streets like a madwoman, she'd come home late, she hadn't taken any man in and now she was there, posted at her window in spite of the fact that twelve o'clock had struck a long time ago. After a while the street was becoming deserted. The only ones left were Cat on the corner and Dalva, who was still waiting at her window. Cat knew that this was his night and he was happy. Dalva was desperate. Cat began to stroll from one side of the street to the other until the woman noticed him and made a signal. He came right over, smiling.

"Aren't you the kid who hangs out on the corner all night?"

"I'm the one who hangs out on the corner. As for the kid business . . ."

She smiled sadly:

"Will you do me a favor? I'll give you something," but then she thought and made a gesture. "No. You must be waiting for your little nibble and you haven't got any time to waste."

"I can, sure. The one I'm waiting for isn't coming now."

"Then what I want, boy, is for you to go to the Rua Rui Barbosa. Number thirty-five. Look for Gastão. He's on the second floor. Tell him I'm waiting."

Cat left in humiliation. First he thought about not going and never coming back to see Dalva. But then he decided to go so he could get a close look at the flute player, who'd had the nerve to abandon such a pretty woman. He reached the building (a dark tenement with many floors), he went up the stairs, on the second floor he asked a boy sleeping in the hallway which was Mr. Gastão's room. The boy pointed to the last apartment. Cat knocked on the door. The flutist came to open it, he was in his shorts and Cat saw a woman in the bed. They were both drunk:

"Dalva sent me."

"Tell that bag to stop bothering me. I've had it up to here with her . . ." and he put his open hand onto his throat.

From inside the room the woman spoke:

"Who's that little pimp?"

"Keep out of this," the flutist said, but then he added, "It's a message from that bag Dalva. She's in a tizzy because I haven't come back."

The woman gave off a sottish drunken laugh:

"But you only love your little Bebé now, don't you? Come give me a kiss, you angel without wings."

The flutist also laughed:

"See, squirt? Tell that to Dalva."

"I see an old whore stretched out there, yes, sir. What undertaker fixed you up with her, eh, buddy?"

The flutist looked at him very seriously:

"Don't talk about my girlfriend," and then, "Do you want a drink? It's first-class stuff."

Cat went in. The woman on the bed covered herself. The flutist laughed:

"It's just a kid. Don't be afraid."

"That old whore doesn't tempt me," Cat said. "Not even to jerk me off."

He drank the cane liquor. The flutist had already gone back

to the bed and was kissing the woman. They didn't see that Cat was leaving and was taking the prostitute's purse, which had been left on the chair on top of her clothes. On the street Cat counted sixty-eight *milreis*. He threw the purse under the stairs and put the money into his pocket. And he whistled on his way to Dalva's street.

Dalva was waiting for him by the window. Cat looked straight at her:

"I'm coming in . . ." and he went in without waiting for an answer.

Dalva, still in the hallway, asked him:

"What did he say?"

Cat replied:

"Sit here," and he pointed to the bed.

"This kid . . ." she murmured.

"Look, sweety, he's tied up with another woman, see? I told them both off too. Then I skinned the old whore," he put his hand into his pocket, took out the money. "Let's split it."

"So he's with someone else, eh? But my Lord of Bonfim will cripple them both. The Lord of Bonfim is my patron saint."

She went over to where she had the religious picture. She made her vow and came back.

"Keep your money. You earned it fair and square."

Cat repeated:

"Sit down, here."

This time she sat down, he grabbed her and put her down on the bed. Then she moaned with love and from the little slaps he gave her, and murmured:

"This kid is like a man . . ." He got up, smoothed his pants, went over to where the picture of Gastão the flutist was, and tore it up.

"I'm going to get a picture taken for you to put up there."

The woman laughed and said:

"Come here, my little devil. What a hoodlum you're going to be. I'll teach you lots of things, my little puppy."

She closed the door of the room. Cat took his clothes off.

That's why Cat leaves every midnight and doesn't sleep in

the warehouse. He only returns in the morning to go out with the others for the day's adventures.

Legless went over and teased him:

"Now you'll show me the ring, eh?"

"What do you care about that?" Cat was smoking a cigarette. "You just wanted to come to see if you could run across a woman who'd love you, crippled the way you are, right?"

"I don't go to whorehouses. I know where things worth the trouble are."

But Cat wasn't in a mood for chatting and Legless continued his wandering about the warehouse.

Legless leaned up against a wall and let time pass. He watched Cat leave around eleven-thirty. He smiled because he'd washed his face, put grease on his hair, and was walking with that sway that hoodlums and sailors have. Then Legless spent a long time looking at the sleeping children. There were fifty of them, more or less, with no father, no mother, no master. All they had for themselves was the freedom to run in the streets. They didn't always lead an easy life, getting what they needed to eat and wear by carrying baggage, stealing wallets and hats, holding up people, sometimes begging. And the gang was made up of more than a hundred children, because a lot of others didn't sleep in the warehouse. They spread out in the doorways of the tall buildings, on the docks, in overturned boats on the sands of the Pôrto da Lenha, where the firewood came in. None of them complained. Sometimes one of them would die from an illness they couldn't treat. When Father José Pedro dropped by at the right time, or the *mãe-de-santo* priestess Don'Aninha, or God's-Love too, the patient had some relief. Never what a child would have at home, however, Legless was thinking. And he found that the joy of that freedom was slight when compared to the misfortune of that life.

He turned around because he heard some movement. Someone was getting up in the middle of the building. Legless recognized the little black boy Outrigger, who was stealthily going to the sands outside the warehouse. Legless thought he was going to hide something he'd stolen and didn't want to show his comrades. And that was a crime against the laws of the gang. Legless followed Outrigger, crossing over the sleepers. The black boy had already gone through the warehouse door and was turning around the left side of the building. The starry sky was above. Outrigger was walking fast now. Legless noticed that he was going to the other end of the warehouse, where the sand was even finer. He went around the other side then and got there in time to see Outrigger meeting a shape. Then he recognized him: it was Almiro, a gang member, twelve years old, fat, and lazy. They lay down together, the black boy caressing Almiro. Legless managed to hear some words: "my little boy, my little boy." Legless drew back and his anguish grew. All of them were looking for affection, anything out of that life: the Professor in those books he read all night long, Cat in the bed of a prostitute who gave him money, Lollipop in the prayers that transfigured him, Outrigger and Almiro with love on the sands of the waterfront. Legless felt the anguish coming over him and it was impossible to sleep. If he slept he would see those bad dreams of jail. He wanted someone to appear whom he could torture with wisecracks. He was looking for a fight. He thought of scratching a match on the leg of someone sleeping. But when he looked at the warehouse door he only felt sorrow and a crazy urge to flee. And he ran along the sand, running aimlessly, fleeing from his anguish.

Pedro Bala awoke because of a noise nearby. He was sleeping on his stomach and he peeked under his arms. He saw a boy getting up and cautiously approaching Lollipop's corner. Pedro Bala, half asleep as he was, thought it was a matter of pederasty at first. And he remained alert so as to expel the passive member from the gang, because one of the rules of the gang was that they would not admit passive pederasts. But he woke up completely and then he remembered that Lollipop wasn't anything like that. It must have been a case of theft. In fact, the boy was already opening Lollipop's trunk. Pedro Bala leaped on top of him. The struggle was quick. Lollipop woke up but the others kept on sleeping.

"Were you stealing from a comrade?"

The other boy remained silent, rubbing his wounded jaw. Pedro Bala went on:

"You leave tomorrow . . . I don't want you with our people anymore. You can go with Ezequiel's people, who live by stealing from one another."

"I only wanted to see . . ."

"What did you come to see with your hands?"

"I swear, it was only to take a look at the medal he has."

"Let's have the straight story or I'll give you a licking."

Lollipop intervened:

"Leave him alone, Pedro. He just may have come to take a look at the medal. It's a medal Father José gave me."

"That's the one," the boy said, "I just wanted to take a look. I swear," but he was trembling with fear. He knew that life for someone expelled from the Captains of the Sands was hard. Either he joined Ezequiel's gang, who spend all day in jail, or he ended up in the Reformatory.

Lollipop intervened again and Pedro Bala went back beside the Professor. Then the boy said with a still trembling voice:

"I'm going to tell it so you'll know. It was a girl I saw today. She was in the Cidade de Palha. I'd gone into a store with the idea of lifting a jacket, when she came over and asked me what I wanted. Then we started to talk. I told her I'd bring her a present tomorrow. Because she was good, real good to me, see?" and now he was shouting and seemed enraged.

Lollipop took the medal the priest had given him, looking at it. Suddenly he held it out to the boy:

"Take it. Give it to her. But don't tell Pedro Bala."

Dry Gulch came into the warehouse during the wee small hours. The backlands mulatto's hair was disheveled. He was wearing canvas shoes, the same as when he'd come out of the underbrush. His gloomy face came into the building. He passed over the body of Big João. He spat in front of himself, rubbed his foot over it. He was carrying a newspaper under his arm. He looked all over, searching for someone. He grasped the newspaper with his large callused hands, then he saw where the Professor was. And without any thought about the lateness of the hour he went over to him and started calling him:

"Professor . . . Professor . . ."

"What is it?" the Professor was half asleep.

"I want something."

The Professor sat up. Dry Gulch's gloomy face was half invisible in the darkness.

"Oh, it's you, Dry Gulch. What do you want?"

"I want you to read this so I can hear the news about Lampião that's in the *Diário*. They've got his picture."

"Let me read it to you tomorrow."

"Read it today or tomorrow I'll teach you the best way to imitate a canary."

The Professor looked for a candle, lighted it, began to read the news in the paper. Lampião had gone into a village in the State of Bahia, had killed eight soldiers, deflowered virgins, sacked the coffers of the Town Hall. Dry Gulch's gloomy face lighted up. His tight mouth relaxed into a smile. And, happy now, he left the Professor, who put out the candle, and went back to his corner. He was carrying the newspaper so he could cut out the picture of Lampião's gang. Inside he had the joy of springtime.

THE PITANGUEIRAS STOP

They waited for the policeman to leave. He took his time, looking at the sky, observing the deserted street. The streetcar disappeared around the bend. It was the last streetcar on the Brotas line that night. The policeman lighted a cigarette. With the wind that was blowing it took three matches. Then he raised the collar of his coat because it was a damp chill that the wind was bringing in from the farmlands where mango trees and sapodillas swayed. The three boys were waiting for the policeman to go away so they could cross the street and enter the unpaved alley. God's-Love had been unable to come. He'd spent the whole afternoon at the Gate of the Sea waiting for the man who didn't come. If he'd come it would have been easier because he wouldn't argue with God's-Love because he owed the *capoeira* fighter a lot. But he hadn't come, the information was wrong, and God's-Love already had a trip set up for that night. He was going to Itaparica. During the afternoon they'd practiced *capoeira*. Cat showed the promise of being a fighter in time, capable of mixing with God's-Love himself. Pedro Bala had a lot of skill too. The least agile of the three was black Big João, very good in a fight where he could use his enormous physical strength. Even so, he learned enough to free himself from someone stronger than he. When they got tired they went into the main room. They ordered four drinks and Cat took a deck of cards out of his pants pocket. An old greasy deck with thick cards. God's-Love was sure the man would come, the fellow who'd given him the information was a guy to be trusted. It was a deal that would bring in a lot and God's-Love preferred calling on the Captains of the Sands, his friends, rather than on some waterfront lowlife. He knew that the Captains of the Sands were worth more than a lot of men and they kept their mouths shut. The Gate of the Sea was almost deserted at that hour. Only two sailors from a bay ship were drinking beer in the rear and talking. Cat put the deck on the table and proposed:

"Who's ready for a round?"

God's-Love looked at the cards:

"They're more than just marked, Mr. Cat. A pretty old deck . . ."

"If you've got another one it's all the same to me."

"No. Let's go along with these here."

They began the game. Cat laid two cards down face up on the table, the others bet on one, the dealer stayed with the other. At first Pedro Bala and God's-Love won. Big João wasn't playing (he was only too familiar with Cat's deck), he only looked on, laughing with his white teeth when God's-Love said he was lucky that day because it was the feast of Xangô, his saint. He knew that luck would only last for the start and that when Cat began to win he'd never stop. At a certain moment Cat began to win. When he won the first time he said with a half-sad voice:

"It's about time. I've had a mother run of bad luck!"

Big João smiled even wider. Cat won again. Pedro Bala stood up, gathered in the coins he'd won. Cat looked at him with mistrust:

"You're not going to play anymore?"

"Not this time, I've got to piss . . ." and he went to the rear of the bar.

God's-Love kept on losing. Big João was laughing and the *capoeira* fighter was going under. Pedro Bala had come back but he didn't play. He was laughing with Big João. God's-Love lost everything he'd won. Big João muttered:

"He's got to go to his pocket . . ."

"I'm still behind," Cat said.

He noticed that Pedro had come back:

"Aren't you going to play anymore? Aren't you going to bet on the queen?"

"I'm tired of playing . . ." and Pedro Bala winked at Cat as if saying that he should content himself with God's-Love.

God's-Love bet five *milreis* from his pocket. He'd only won twice during the last rounds and he was quite mistrustful. Cat opened the deck on the table. He drew a king and a seven.

"Who's in?" he asked.

No one moved. Not even God's-Love, who was looking at the deck suspiciously. Cat asked:

"Do you think they're marked? You can take a look. I play a clean game . . ."

Big João let out one of those loud ringing laughs of his. Pedro Bala and God's-Love laughed too. Cat looked at Big João with rage:

"This black boy is dumb as a donkey in a door. You haven't seen anything . . ."

But he didn't finish the sentence because the two sailors from the bay ship, who'd been watching the game for some time already, came over. One of them, the shorter, who was drunk, spoke to God's-Love:

"Can anybody join the fun?"

God's-Love pointed to Cat:

"This boy is the dealer."

The sailors looked at the boy suspiciously. But the short one nudged the other with his elbow and whispered something in his ear. Cat was laughing inside because he knew he was saying it would be easy to get the money away from the kid. They both anteed up and God's-Love found it strange that Pedro Bala anteed too. Big João, however, not only didn't find it strange but anteed up himself too. He knew it was necessary to cover up for the sailors and the people in the gang had to lose too. The sailors, just as had happened with God's-Love, started winning. But the wind of luck didn't blow for long and soon only Cat was winning out of the four of them. Pedro Bala kept making remarks:

"When this guy Cat is lucky he's got it all . . ."

"When he loses too, he loses all night long," Big João answered and that reply of his gave a lot of confidence to the sailors about the honesty of the game and the possibility of their luck's changing. And they kept on betting and losing. The short one said:

"Our luck has got to change . . ."

The other one, who had a small mustache, was playing in silence and betting more every time. Pedro Bala was also raising the amount of his bets. At a certain moment the one with the mustache turned to Cat:

"Can the house cover five?"

Cat scratched his head full of cheap Vaseline, putting on a look of indecision that his friends knew he didn't have:

"O.K. I'll cover it. Just so you can make up your damage."

The one with the mustache bet five *milreis*. The short one put up three. They both bet on an ace against a jack for the dealer. Pedro Bala and Big João bet on the ace too. Cat began to deal the cards. The first one was a nine. The short man was drumming with his fingers, the other one was tugging at his mustache. A deuce came next and the short one said:

"Now it's the ace. A two, then a one . . ." and he drummed with his fingers.

But a seven turned up and then a ten and after that a jack. Cat cleared the table while Pedro Bala put on a face of great annoyance and said:

"Tomorrow, when bad luck hits you, you'll see me clean you out."

The short one confessed that he was cleaned out. The one with the little mustache put his hands in his pockets:

"All I've got is some small change to pay for the beers. The kid's good."

They got up, nodded to the group, paid for the beer they'd drunk at the other table. Cat invited them to come back another day. The short one answered that their ship was leaving that night for Caravelas. Only when they got back. And they left arm in arm, talking about their bad luck.

Cat counted his winnings. Not counting the money Pedro Bala had lost, there was a pot of thirty-eight *milreis*. Cat gave Pedro Bala back his money, then Big João, and sat thinking for a moment. He put his hand into his pocket and took out the five *milreis* God's-Love had lost before:

"Take it, nice guy. It was a trick, I don't want to pocket your dough . . ."

God's-Love kissed the bill with satisfaction, patted Cat on the back:

"You'll go a long way, kid. You can get rich with those tricks."

But the sun was already going down and the man wasn't coming. They ordered another drink. With nightfall the wind coming off the sea grew stronger. God's-Love began to get impatient. He was smoking cigarette after cigarette. Pedro Bala was looking at the door. Cat was dividing the thirty-eight *milreis* into threes. Big João asked:

"I wonder how Legless made out snatching hats?"

No one answered. They were waiting for the man and now they had the feeling he wasn't coming. The information had been wrong. They didn't even hear the song coming in off the sea. The Gate of the Sea was deserted and Mr. Filipe was almost asleep behind the bar. It wouldn't be long, however, before it would be full and then any deal with the man would be impossible. He wouldn't want to talk there with the whole place full. They might know him and he didn't want that. The Captains of the Sands didn't want it either. Cat really didn't know what it was all about. And Pedro Bala and Big João didn't know much more. They knew as much as God's-Love, to whom the deal had been proposed and who had accepted it for Pedro Bala and the Captains of the Sands. He himself, however, only had vague information and they would learn everything from the man who'd set up a meeting at the Gate of the Sea in the afternoon. But he hadn't arrived by six o'clock. Instead of him the one who'd spoken to God's-Love came. He got there just as the group was about to leave. He explained that the man couldn't come. But that he was waiting for God's-Love that night on the street where he lived. He should go around one o'clock in the morning. God's-Love declared that he couldn't go but that he was leaving the matter with the Captains of the Sands. The intermediary looked mistrustfully at the boys. God's-Love asked:

"Haven't you ever heard of the Captains of the Sands?"

"Yes, maybe. But . . ."

"In any case, they're the ones who are going to take care of the business. That's how it is . . ."

The intermediary seemed to accept it. They set up a date for one in the morning and went their way. God's-Love went to his ship, the Captains of the Sands to the warehouse, the intermediary disappeared on the docks.

Legless still hadn't returned. There was nobody in the warehouse. They must have all been scattered out on the streets of the city, scrounging for their dinner. The three went out again and went to eat in a cheap restaurant in the market. Coming out of the warehouse, Cat, who was very happy with the outcome of the game, tried to trip Pedro Bala up. But the latter avoided it and threw Cat down:

"I've been practicing that, dummy."

They went into the restaurant, making a lot of noise. An old man who was the waiter came over mistrustfully. He knew that the Captains of the Sands didn't like to pay and that the one with the scar on his face was the one to be most feared of all of them. In spite of there being quite a few people in the restaurant, the old man said:

"We've run out. We haven't got any more grub."

Pedro Bala replied:

"Don't spin me a yarn, old man. We want to eat."

Big João pounded on the table:

"If not we'll turn this grease pot upside down."

The old man looked at him indecisively. Then Cat dumped the money on the table:

"Today we're going to spend."

It was a convincing argument. The waiter began to bring the dishes: a plate of chitterlings and then black-bean stew. Cat was the one who paid. Then Pedro Bala suggested that they be on their way to Brotas; since they were walking they had a lot of ground to cover.

"It isn't worth taking the trolley," Pedro Bala said. "It's better if nobody knows we're going there."

Then Cat said he'd meet them there later. He had something to do first. He was going to tell Dalva not to expect him that night.

And there they were now at the Pitangueiras stop, waiting for the policeman to go away. Hidden in a doorway, they didn't speak. They heard the flight of the bats as they attacked the ripe sapodillas at their feet. Finally the policeman left and they stood looking until his form disappeared around the bend in the street. Then they crossed and went into the drive with the villas and hid in a doorway again. The man wasn't long in coming. He got out of a cab on the corner, paid the driver, and came up the walk. The only thing that could be heard was his steps and the sound of the leaves that the wind was rustling in the trees. When the man drew close Pedro Bala came out of the doorway. The others came behind him and the way they stood they looked like two bodyguards. The man moved closer to the wall he was walking along. Pedro went over to him. When he was in front of him he stopped.

"Have you got a light, sir?" He held a snuffed-out cigarette in his hand.

The man didn't say anything. He took out a box of matches, handed it to the boy. Pedro struck one and while he was lighting the cigarette he looked at the man. Then he gave back the box and asked:

"Is your name Joel?"

"Why?" the man wanted to know.

"God's-Love sent us."

Big João and Cat had come over. The man looked at the three of them with surprise:

"But you're just kids. This isn't any business for kids."

"Just say what it is; we know how to do things right," Pedro Bala shot back as the other two approached.

"But it's something that maybe not even men . . ." and the

man put his hand to his mouth as if he'd said more than he should have.

"We know how to keep a secret as good as under lock and key. And the Captains of the Sands always, always do a good job . . ."

"The Captains of the Sands? That gang the newspapers are talking about? Abandoned kids? That's who you are?"

"It sure is. And people who get things done."

The man seemed to be thinking. Then he finally decided:

"I'd rather turn this business over to men. But since it's got to be tonight . . . The way things are . . ."

"You'll see how we work. Don't be afraid."

"Come with me. But let me go ahead. You stay a few steps behind me."

The boys obeyed. At one doorway the man stopped, opened, and waited on the inside. From inside came a big dog who licked his hands. The man had the three of them come in; they crossed a drive with trees; the man opened the door to the house. They went into a small parlor, the man put his hat and coat on a chair and sat down. The three remained standing. The man signaled for them to sit down and at first they looked suspiciously at the broad and comfortable easy chairs. Pedro Bala and João sat down, with Big João sitting only on the edge of the chair, as if afraid he would dirty it. The man looked as though he were going to laugh. Suddenly he got up and spoke, looking at Pedro, whom he recognized as the leader:

"What you people are going to do is hard and at the same time easy. What you have to know now is that it's something nobody must know about."

"It won't go beyond these four walls," Pedro Bala said.

The man took out his pocket watch:

"It's a quarter after one. He won't be back until two-thirty . . ." He was still looking at the Captains of the Sands with indecision.

"Then there's not much time," Pedro spoke. "If you want us to go you'd better spit it out right away . . ."

The man decided:

"Two streets up from here. It's the next to the last villa on the right. You'll have to watch out for a dog that must be loose already. He's ugly."

Big João interrupted:

"Have you got a piece of meat?"

"What for?"

"For the dog. One piece should be enough."

"I'll take a look later." He was looking at the boys. He seemed to be wondering if he could trust them. "You'll go in the back way. Next to the kitchen, on the outside of the house, there's a room over the garage. It belongs to the servant, who must be in the house now waiting for his master. You'll go in through his room. You've got to look for a package like this one, exactly like this . . ." He went to the pocket in his coat and brought out a package tied with a pink ribbon. "Just like this. I don't know if it's still in his room. It might be that the servant has it in his pocket. If that's how it is nothing more can be done about it." And a sudden despair seemed to come over him. "If I'd only been able to have gone this afternoon . . . It certainly must have been in the room then. But now, who knows?" and he covered his face with his hands.

"Even if the servant's got it, we can bring it back . . ." Pedro said.

"No. It's essential that no one know how that package was stolen. What you're going to do is exchange packages, if the other one is in the room."

"What if the servant's got it?"

"Then . . ." and the man's expression became upset again. Big João thought he heard a name that sounded like Elisa. But maybe it was an illusion on the part of Big João, who sometimes heard things nobody else did. The black boy was a big liar.

"Then we'll swap the packages just the same. You can rest easy. You don't know the Captains of the Sands."

In spite of his despair the man smiled at Pedro Bala's boldness:

"Then you can go. Afterwards, it has to be before two o'clock, come back here. But only if the street's deserted. I'll wait for you. Then we'll settle our accounts. But I want to tell you something in all frankness. If you're caught and arrested don't get me involved in the case. I won't do anything for you because my name can't be mixed up in this at all. Try to get rid of this package and don't call me for any reason. It's a case of win or lose . . ."

"In that case," Pedro Bala answered, "we'll have to fix a price first. How much are you going to pay us?"

"I'll pay a hundred *milreis*. Thirty for each one and ten extra for you," he pointed at Pedro.

Cat moved in his chair. Pedro signaled him to be silent.

"You can give us fifty apiece and then we can do business. That's 150 clams for the three of us. If not, you won't get your package."

The man didn't hesitate long. He looked at the hands on his watch:

"O.K."

Then Cat spoke up:

"It's not that we don't trust you. But the whole thing might go wrong and you said yourself that it wouldn't matter what happened to us."

"So?"

"It's only right for you to give us something up front."

Big João backed up Cat with a nod. Pedro Bala repeated the other one's last words:

"Only right, yes. In case we don't get to you afterwards . . ."

"Only right," the man repeated too. He took his wallet out. He removed a 100 *milreis* note. He gave it to Pedro:

"It's time to get going. It's getting late."

They went out. Pedro Bala said:

"Rest easy. An hour from now we'll be back with the package."

In front of the house (the street was completely deserted, in a window of the house a light was on and they saw the shadow of a woman who was walking back and forth) Big João slapped his head:

"I forgot the meat for the dog."

Pedro Bala was looking at the window with the light on, he turned:

"Don't worry. This whole thing smells like a love affair to me. That guy laid the missy from here and now the servant has got the letters that the two wrote each other and wants to blow the whistle. That package is full of perfume. It's what the other one has we've got to get."

He made a sign for the two of them to wait on the other side of the street, went over to the main gate of the house. As soon as he was there a huge dog came up barking. Pedro Bala tied a rope around the lock in the gate while the dog ran back and forth barking softly. Then he called the other two:

"You," he pointed to Cat, "stay here on the street to give the alarm if anyone comes. You, João, come in with me."

They climbed up the bars of the fence. Pedro Bala pulled on the bolt with the rope and the gate opened. Cat had gone to the corner. The dog, when he saw the gate open, rushed into the street and rummaged in a garbage can. Pedro Bala and Big João jumped over the wall, closed the gate so the dog couldn't get in, went on in through the trees. In the lighted window of the house the shape of the woman continued pacing. Big João said in a low voice:

"I feel sorry for her."

"Who told her to go to bed with other men . . . ?"

The black boy remained near the house to pass on a signal from Cat if someone was coming. They had special whistles for such cases. Pedro Bala went around the house, reached the kitchen. The door was open, the same as the one to the room over the garage. Before going up the stairs that led to the room, however, Pedro peeked into the kitchen door. There was a light in the pantry and a man playing solitaire. "It must be that servant," Pedro thought and quickly withdrew to the garage stairway. He went up two steps at a time and entered the man's room. There wasn't any light. Pedro closed the door, lighted a match. There was only a bed, a trunk, and a coa-track against the wall. The match went out but Pedro was already on top of the bed, which he went over with his hands. Then he looked under the mattress. There wasn't anything there either. He got off the bed then and without making any sound went over to the trunk. He lifted the lid, lighted a match that he held in his teeth. He went through the clothes care-fully, there wasn't anything. He spat out the match (then he thought that maybe the man didn't smoke and put it in his pocket) and went over to the coatrack. Nothing in the pockets of the clothes hanging there. Pedro Bala lighted another match, looked all over the room.

"The man must have them. They've got to be there."

He opened the door of the room, went down the stairs. He reached the kitchen door, the man was still sitting there. Then Pedro Bala noticed that he was sitting on top of the package. A tip was showing under the man's leg. Pedro thought that everything was lost. How was he going to get the package from under the man's leg? He went out the kitchen door to where Big João was. Only if he and João attacked the man. But there'd be a lot of hollering and everybody would know about the robbery. And the man who'd hired them didn't want to hear about anything like that. Suddenly he got an idea. He went over close to where he'd left João, whispered softly. Big João came right away. Pedro spoke very softly:

"Look, Big Boy, that servant there is sitting on top of the package. You go to the street door, ring the bell, and then disappear. It's so the man will get up and I'll snatch the package. But scram out right away so the man doesn't see you, he'll think he was dreaming. Give me enough time to get to the kitchen."

He went quickly back to the kitchen door. A minute later the bell rang. The servant got up hurriedly, buttoned his jacket, and went to the front of the house through the hall, where he turned on a light. Pedro Bala went into the pantry, switched the packages, and ran off to the edge of the estate. He leaped over the fence, whistled for Cat and Big João. Cat came right away. But Big João didn't appear. They went back and forth looking but the black boy didn't appear. Pedro began to get nervous, thinking that the servant might have surprised Big João and was struggling with him now. But when he'd passed by that place he hadn't heard any noise . . . He said:

"If he takes too long they'll be coming."

They whistled again, there was no answer. Pedro Bala decided:

"Let's go back in . . ."

But they heard Big João's whistle and soon he was beside them. Pedro asked:

"Where were you?"

Cat had taken the dog by the collar and pushed him inside the gate. They took the rope off the latch and disappeared along the other side of the street. There João explained:

"When I stuck my finger in the bell the lady up there got all scared. She threw open the window, it looked like she was going to jump right there. She was looking out like to scare you. She was even crying. Then I felt sorry and climbed up the drain pipe to tell her not to cry anymore because there was no reason to. That we'd swiped the papers. And since I had to explain everything to her it held me up . . ."

Cat asked with great curiosity:

"She was good, eh?"

"She was pretty, yes. She ran her hand over my head, then she said thank you very much, God protect you."

"Don't be a booby, boy. I was asking if she was good for bed. If you got a look at her hips . . ."

The black boy didn't reply. A car was coming down the street. Pedro Bala patted the black boy on the shoulder and Big João knew that the leader was approving of what he'd done. Then his face opened up in satisfaction and he murmured:

"I'd like to see the Spaniard's face when his boss opens the package and doesn't find what he expected."

And on another street now, the three of them gave off that broad, free, and noisy laugh of the Captains of the Sands, which was like a hymn of the people of Bahia.

THE LIGHTS OF
THE CARROUSEL

The "Great Japanese Carrousel" was nothing but a small native merry-go-round that arrived after a sad pilgrimage through inland towns during those winter months when the rains are long and Christmas is still far off. So faded was the paint, paint that had once been blue and red, that the blue was a dirty white now and the red was almost pink, and so many pieces were missing on certain horses and benches that Nhôzinho França decided not to set it up in any of the main squares of the city but in Itapagipe. The families there aren't so rich, there are a lot of streets where only workers live, and poor children would appreciate the faded old carrousel. The canvas also had a lot of holes along with an enormous gash that left the carrousel at the mercy of the rain. It had been beautiful once, it had even been the pride and joy of the children of Maceió in other days. At that time it stood alongside a Ferris wheel and a sideshow, always on the same square, and on Sundays and holidays rich children dressed in sailor suits or like little English lords, the girls in Dutch costumes or fine silk dresses, came to claim their favorite horses, the little ones sitting on the benches with their nannies. The fathers would go on the Ferris wheel, others preferred the sideshow, where they could push up against women, often touching their thighs and buttocks. Nhôzinho França's carnival was the joy of the city in those days. And, above all, the carrousel brought in money, tirelessly turning with its lights of all colors. Nhôzinho found life good, the women pretty, the men friendly to him, but he found that drink was good too, it made the men more friendly and the women prettier. And in that way he drank away first the sideshow and then the Ferris wheel. Then, since he didn't wish to be separated from the carrousel, for which he had a special affection, he took it down one night with the help of some friends and began to wander through the towns in Alagoas and Sergipe. During this time his creditors cursed him with every ugly name they knew. Nhôzinho did a lot of traveling with his carrousel. After covering all the small towns in the two states, getting drunk in all their bars, he went over into the State of Bahia and even gave a performance for Lampião's gang. He was in a poor town in the backlands and he didn't just lack money for the transportation of his carrousel. He didn't have any for the miserable hotel where he stayed and which was the only one in town or for a shot of cane liquor or beer that wasn't cooled but which he liked all the same. The carrousel, set up on the grass on the square by the church, had been still for a week. Nhôzinho França was waiting for Saturday night and Sunday afternoon in order to see if he could pick up a few pennies to enable him to get to a better place. But on Friday Lampião entered the town with twenty-two men and then the carrousel had to work. Like children, the big bandits, men who had twenty or thirty deaths to their credit, found the carrousel nice, found that looking at its spinning lights, listening to the very old music of its player piano, and getting on those beat-up wooden horses was the highest form of happiness. So Nhôzinho França's carrousel saved the small town from being sacked, the girls from being deflowered, the men from being killed. Only two members of the Bahian state police who were shining their boots in front of the police station were shot by the bandits, before they saw the carrousel set up on the square by the church. Because maybe even the Bahian state policemen might have been spared by

Lampião on that night of supreme happiness for the bandit gang. Then they were like children, enjoying the happiness they had never enjoyed in their childhood as peasant children: mounting and riding a wooden horse on a carrousel, where there was music from a Pianola and where the lights were of all colors: blue, green, yellow, purple, and red, like the blood that poured out of the bodies of murder victims.

That was what Nhôzinho told Dry Gulch (who was all excited by it) and Legless on that afternoon when he found them in the Gate of the Sea and invited them to help him run the carrousel during the time it was set up in Bahia, in Itapa-gipe. He couldn't promise any set wages, but there might be enough for each one to get five *milreis* a night. And when Dry Gulch showed his skills at imitating all kinds of animals, Nhôzinho França got all enthusiastic, ordering another bottle of beer and declaring that Dry Gulch would stand by the entrance calling people in while Legless would help him with the machinery and be in charge of the Pianola. He himself would sell tickets when the carrousel was stopped. When it was turning, Dry Gulch would. "And every so often," he said, winking, "one of us can take off for a shot of something while the other does double duty."

Dry Gulch and Legless had never picked up on an idea with such enthusiasm. They had seen carrousels many times but almost always from a distance, surrounded by mystery, their swift horses ridden by rich and whiney children. Legless had even once (on a certain day when he went into an amusement park set up on the Passeio Público) got to buy a ticket for one, but a policeman kicked him out of the place because he was dressed in rags. Then the ticket-taker refused to give him back his ticket, which led Legless to stick his hand into the change drawer that was open and he had to disappear from the Pas-seio Público in rapid fashion while all up and down the street cries of "Stop thief!" could be heard. There was tremendous confusion while Legless very calmly went down Gamboa de Cima, carrying in his pockets at least five times what he had paid for the ticket. But Legless doubtless would have preferred riding on the carrousel, up on that fantastic mount with a dragon's head that was without a doubt the strangest of all on the marvel that the carrousel was in his eyes. His hatred for policemen and love for distant carrousels grew even greater. And now, all of a sudden, a man had shown up who was paying for beer and performing the miracle of calling him to live alongside a real carrousel for a few days, moving with it, riding its horses, watching the lights of all colors going around from close by. And for Legless, Nhôzinho França wasn't the drunkard across the poor table from him at the Gate of the Sea. In his eyes he was an extraordinary being, something like the God Lollipop prayed to, something like Xangô, who was the saint of Big João and God's-Love. Because not Father José Pedro and not even the priestess Don'Aninha would be capable of bringing off that miracle. In the Bahian nights, on a square in Itapagipe, the lights of the carrousel would spin madly, moved by Legless. It was like a dream, a quite different dream from the ones Legless was used to having on his nights of anguish. And for the first time his eyes felt moist with tears that hadn't been brought on by pain or rage. And his damp eyes looked on Nhôzinho França as on an idol. For him Legless would even open the throat of a man with the knife he carries between his pants and the old black vest that serves him as a jacket.

"It's a beauty," Pedro Bala said, looking at the old carrousel when it was set up. And Big João opened his eyes in order to see better. Hanging around it were the blue, green, yellow, and red bulbs.

It's old and faded, Nhôzinho França's carrousel is. But it has its beauty. Maybe it's in the bulbs, or in the Pianola music (old waltzes out of a time long lost) or maybe in the wooden mounts. Among them there's a duck for the smaller children to sit inside. It has its beauty, yes, because in the unanimous opinion of the Captains of the Sands it's something marvelous. Who cares if it's old, broken, and faded if it pleases children?

It was an almost unbelievable surprise when Legless arrived at the warehouse that night saying that he and Dry Gulch were

going to work on the carrousel for a few days. A lot of them
didn't believe it, they thought it was just another trick on the
part of Legless. Then they went to ask Dry Gulch, who, as
always, was stuck in his corner examining a revolver he'd stolen from a weapons shop. Dry Gulch nodded yes and said a
couple of times:

"Lampião rode on it. Lampião's my godfather . . ."

Legless invited everybody to come see the carrousel the next
night when they would finish setting it up. And he went out to
meet Nhôzinho França. At that moment all the little hearts
that were beating in the warehouse envied Legless's supreme
happiness. Even Lollipop, who had pictures of saints on his
wall, even Big João, who that night would go with God's-Love
to Procópio's *candomblé* rites in Matatu, even the Professor,
who read books, and, who knows, maybe Pedro Bala too, who
never envied anyone because he was the leader of them all.
They all envied him, yes. The way they envied Dry Gulch, who
in his corner, his straight halfbreed hair hanging down, his
eyes squinting, and his mouth twisted in that rictus of rage,
pointed the revolver, now at one of the boys, now at a rat who
was passing, now at the stars, of which there were many in
the sky.

The next night they all went with Legless and Dry Gulch
(the latter had spent the day off helping Nhôzinho set up the
carrousel) to see the assembled merry-go-round. And they
stood before it in ecstasy over its beauty, their mouths open
with admiration. Legless showed them everything. Dry Gulch
took them one by one to show them the horse that had been
ridden by his godfather Virgulino Ferreira Lampião. There
were almost a hundred children looking at the old carrousel of
Nhôzinho França, who at that time was in the throes of a tremendous binge at the Gate of the Sea.

Legless showed them the engine (a small motor that missed
a lot) with the pride of an owner. Dry Gulch didn't get off the
horse that Lampião had gone around on. Legless was very
careful with the carrousel and wouldn't let them touch it, handle anything.

It was when the Professor asked:

"Do you know how to work the machinery yet?"

"Tomorrow I'm going to learn . . ." Legless said with a certain displeasure. "Tomorrow Mr. Nhôzinho is going to teach me."

"Then tomorrow, when the show is over, you can start it turning with just us. You get the thing started and we'll get on board."

Pedro Bala supported the idea enthusiastically. The others anxiously awaited Legless's answer. Legless said yes and then some of them clapped, others cheered. It was when Dry Gulch left the horse Lampião had ridden and came over to them:

"Do you want to see something nice?"

They all wanted to. The boy from the backlands got up onto the carrousel, wound up the Pianola, and the music of an old waltz started up. Dry Gulch's somber face opened up in a smile. He was watching the Pianola, watching the boys wrapped in joy. They were listening religiously to that music coming from the bowels of the carrousel in the magic of the night of the city of Bahia only for the adventurous and poor ears of the Captains of the Sands. They were all silent. A worker who was coming along the street, seeing the group of boys on the square came over to them. And he stood there too, listening to the old music. Then the light of the moon spread out over them all, the stars shone even brighter in the sky, the sea grew completely calm (perhaps Iemanjá had also come to listen to the music) and the city was like a giant carrousel on which the Captains of the Sands were spinning on invisible horses. In that musical moment they felt themselves masters of the city. And they drew close to each other, they felt like brothers because all of them were without love or comfort and now they had the love and comfort of the music. Dry Gulch certainly wasn't thinking about Lampião at that moment. Pedro Bala wasn't thinking of someday being leader of the city's whole underworld. Legless about jumping into the sea where dreams are all beautiful. Because the music was coming out of the belly of the old carrousel just for them and for the workman

who had stopped. And it was an old sad waltz, long forgotten
by all the men in the city.

People are pouring out of all the streets. It's Saturday night,
tomorrow men won't have to go to work. They can hang
around the street tonight. A lot of them prefer going to bars,
the Gate of the Sea is full, but the ones with children had taken
them to the poorly lighted square. In compensation, the lights
of the carrousel are spinning there. The children look at them
and clap their hands. In front of the ticket office Dry Gulch is
doing animal imitations and calling for customers. He's wearing a cartridge belt, as if he were in the backlands. Nhôzinho
França thought that would attract people's attention and Dry
Gulch looks just like a *cangaceiro* with his leather hat and
crossed cartridge belts. And he imitates animals until men,
women, and children gather in front of him. Then he offers
tickets that the children buy. A joy spreads out over the whole
square. The lights of the carrousel make everyone happy. In
the center, squatting down, Legless helps Nhôzinho França get
the motor started. And the carrousel spins, loaded with children, the Pianola plays its old waltzes. Dry Gulch sells tickets.

Couples in love stroll about the square. Mothers buy popsi-
cles and sherbets, a poet sitting facing the sea composes a
poem about the lights of the carrousel and the children's joy.
The carrousel lights up all the square and all the hearts. At
every moment people come out of streets and alleys. Dry
Gulch, dressed as a bandit, imitates animals. When the carrousel stops spinning, the children invade it, waving their tickets of admission and it's hard to count them. When one of
them can't find a place his face grows sad with disappointment
and he impatiently awaits his turn. And when the carrousel
stops those on it don't want to get off and Legless has to come
and say:

"Everybody off! Everybody! Or buy another ticket."

Only then do they leave the old horses who never grow tired
in their endless run. Others get on the mounts and the race
begins again, the lights spinning, all the colors making one
single strange tone, the Pianola playing its ancient music.

Loving couples are also going around on the benches and while the carrousel spins they whisper words of love. There are even those who exchange a kiss when the motor fails and the lights go out. Then Nhôzinho França and Legless lean over the engine and look for what's wrong until the spinning begins again, drowning out the protests of the children. Legless has already learned all the mysteries of the motor.

At a certain moment Nhôzinho França sends Legless to take Dry Gulch's place selling tickets. And he has Dry Gulch ride the carrousel. And the boy takes the horse that was used by Lampião. And while the ride lasts he goes along pulling on the reins as if he were riding a real horse. And he makes motions with his arms as if shooting at those in front of him and in his imagination he sees them dropping, bathed in blood, under the shots of his repeater. And the horse runs and runs faster and faster and he kills them all because they're all soldiers or rich ranchers. Then he possesses all the women on the benches, sacks villages, towns, trains, riding his horse, armed with his rifle.

Then it's Legless's turn. He goes along silently, a strange commotion overcomes him. He goes along like a believer to mass, a lover to the breast of his beloved, a suicide to death. He goes pale and limping. He mounts a blue horse that has stars painted on its wooden rump. His lips are tight, his ears don't hear the music of the Pianola. He only sees the spinning lights, and he comes to the realization that he's on a carrousel, spinning on a horse like all those children who have fathers and mothers, a home and someone to kiss them and love them. He thinks that he's one of them and he closes his eyes to hold the certainty better. He no longer sees the policemen beating him, the man with the vest who's laughing. Dry Gulch killed them on his ride. Legless is tense on his horse. It's as if he were running over the sea toward the stars in the most wonderful trip in the world. A trip such as one the Professor had never read about or made up. His heart is beating so hard that he holds his hand tight against it.

That night the Captains of the Sands didn't come. Not only did the carrousel ride on the square end very late (at two o'clock in the morning men were still spinning around), but many of them, including Pedro Bala, Good-Life, Outrigger, and the Professor were busy on different matters. They made a date for the next day, between three and four in the morning. Pedro Bala asked Legless if he knew how to run the engine all right now:

"It's no good causing any damage for your boss," he explained.

"I know it backwards and forwards. It's a snap."

The Professor, who was playing checkers with Big João, asked:

"Wouldn't it be good if we stopped by the square in the afternoon? It might just be worth something."

"I'll go," Pedro Bala said. "But I don't think a lot of us should go. The crowd might get suspicious seeing so many together."

Cat said he couldn't go in the afternoon. He had something to do since he'd be busy on the carrousel that night. Legless teased him:

"A day can't go by without your mixing it up with that bag, right? You're going to end up a dish of mush . . ."

Cat didn't answer. Big João wasn't going in the afternoon either. He had to meet God's-Love to go have some black-bean stew at the house of Don'Aninha, the *mãe-de-santo*. Finally it was decided that a small group would work the square that afternoon. The others would go wherever they wanted to. Only at night they'd all get together to ride on the carrousel. Legless warned them:

"You've got to bring some gasoline, for the motor."

The Professor (he'd already beaten Big João in three games) took up a collection to buy half a gallon of gasoline:

"I'll bring it."

But Sunday afternoon brought the arrival of Father José Pedro, who was one of the very few people who knew where the most permanent abode of the Captains of the Sands was. Father José Pedro had become their friend a long time ago. The friendship had come about through Good-Life. The latter had gone one day, after mass, into the sacristy of a church where Father José Pedro served. He had gone in out of curiosity more than anything else. Good-Life wasn't one of those who worked to stay alive. He liked to let life run on without worrying too much. He was more of a parasite on the group. One day, when he felt like it, he would go into a house and bring out something of value or lift a man's watch. He almost never put them into the hands of a fence himself. He would bring them back and give them to Pedro Bala, as a contribution to the gang. He had a lot of friends among the stevedores on the docks, in several poor houses in the Cidade de Palha, in a lot of places in Bahia. He would eat in one person's house, then in that of another. In general he didn't dislike anybody. He was content with Cat's leftover women and he knew the city better than anyone, its streets, its strange places, a party where you could eat and dance. When it had been some time that he hadn't contributed to the economy of the gang with some object of value, he would make an effort, arrange something that would bring in money, and give it to Pedro Bala. But he really didn't like any kind of work, honest or dishonest. What he liked was to lie on the sands of the waterfront hours on end watching the ships, squatting by the doors of the harbor warehouse listening to stories of brave deeds. He dressed in rags, because only providence could give him something to wear when his clothes started falling apart. He liked to stroll at his leisure along the streets of the city, going into parks to smoke a cigarette sitting on a bench, entering churches to look at the beauty of the old gold, sauntering along the streets paved with large black stones.

On that morning when he saw the people coming out of mass, he went into the church indifferently and moved about up to the sacristy. He was looking at everything, the altars, the saints, he laughed at the black Saint Benedict. There was nobody in the sacristy and he saw a gold object that must have been worth a lot of money. He looked around again, he didn't see anyone. He was reaching out his hand when someone touched him on the shoulder. Father José Pedro had just come in:

"Why are you doing that, my son?" he asked with a smile as he took the golden reliquary out of Good-Life's hand.

"I was only taking a look, Reverend. It's great," Good-Life replied with a certain apprehension. "It's real great. But I wasn't thinking of taking it. I was just about to put it down. I come from a good family."

Father José Pedro looked at Good-Life's clothes and laughed. Good-Life also looked at his rags:

"It's just that my father died, you know. But I was even in a good school . . . I'm telling the truth. Why should I rob something like that?" he pointed to the reliquary. "In a church besides. I'm not a pagan."

Father José Pedro smiled again. He knew perfectly well that Good-Life was lying. For a long time he'd been waiting for an opportunity to establish relations with the abandoned children of the city. He thought that was the mission he was meant to have. He'd already made so many visits to the Reformatory for Minors but there he raised all kinds of difficulties because he didn't espouse the ideas of the director that it's necessary to whip a child in order to correct errors. And the director even had his own ideas about errors. Father José Pedro had heard people talk about the Captains of the Sands for some time and he had a dream of getting in contact with them, to be able to bring all those hearts to God. He had an enormous will to work with those children and help them be good. That's why he tried the best he could with Good-Life. Who knows, maybe through him he could get in touch with the Captains of the Sands? And so it was.

Father José Pedro was not considered a great mind among the clergy. He was, indeed, one of the most humble among that legion of priests in Bahia. In truth, he'd spent five years as a factory worker before entering the seminary. The manager of the factory, on a day when the bishop visited it, decided to make a show of generosity and said that "since Your Grace was complaining about the lack of priestly vocations," he was prepared to pay the costs of studies for a seminarian or someone who wanted to study for the priesthood. José Pedro, who was at his loom, went over and said he wanted to be a priest. The boss and the bishop were both startled. José Pedro wasn't young and he hadn't had much education. But the boss didn't want to back down in front of the bishop. And José Pedro went to the seminary. The other seminarians made fun of him. He never managed to be a good student. Good behavior, that was about it. Also among the most devout, those closest to the church. He didn't agree with many of the things that went on in the seminary and that was why the boys persecuted him. He couldn't manage to penetrate the mysteries of philosophy, theology, or Latin. But he was pious and wanted to catechize children or Indians. He suffered a great deal, mainly after two years, when the factory owner stopped paying his expenses and he had to work as beadle in the seminary to be able to continue. But he succeeded in being ordained and was assigned as an aide in a church in the state capital while waiting for a parish. But his great desire was to catechize the abandoned children of the city, the boys who, without father or mother, lived by theft in the midst of all vices. Father José Pedro wanted to bring all those hearts to God. So he began to visit the Reformatory for Minors, where the director received him with great courtesy at first. But when he declared himself against corporal punishment, against letting the children go without food for days on end, things changed. One day he felt the need to write a letter about the situation to the editor of a newspaper. Then he was barred from entering the Reformatory and a complaint against him was lodged with the Archdiocese. That's why he never had a parish after that. But his greatest wish was to meet the Captains of the Sands. The problem of abandoned and delinquent children that worried almost no one in the whole city was Father José Pedro's greatest worry. He wanted to get close to those children, not just to bring them to God, but also to see if there wasn't some way to better their situation. Father José Pedro didn't have much influence. He didn't have any influence at all, nor did he know either how to go about gaining the confidence of those little thieves. But he did know that their life consisted of a lack of

comfort and all love, a life of hunger and abandonment. And
if Father José Pedro didn't have beds, food, and clothing to
bring them, at least he had words of love, a lot of it, certainly,
in his heart for them. Father José Pedro was mistaken about
one thing in the beginning: offering them the possibility of a
more comfortable life in exchange for the free abandonment
they enjoyed loose on the streets. Father José Pedro knew very
well that he couldn't get the attention of those children with
the Reformatory. He knew the laws of the Reformatory too
well, those written and those practiced. And he knew that
there was no possibility there for a child to become good and
hard-working. But Father José Pedro trusted in some friends
he had, saintly and religious old women. They could take
charge of several of the Captains of the Sands, educating them,
feeding them. But that would mean giving up completely the
great things life had for them: the adventure of freedom in the
streets of the most mysterious and beautiful city in the world,
in the streets of Bahia de Todos os Santos, the bay of all saints.
And as soon as Father José Pedro established relations with
the Captains of the Sands through Good-Life, he saw that if
he put forth that proposition to them he would lose all the
trust they had now placed in him and they would move from
the warehouse and he would never see them again. Nor did he
have absolute confidence in those aged old maids who lived in
the church and who took advantage of the breaks between
masses to gossip about other people's lives. He remembered
that in the beginning they had been annoyed with him because
when he finished celebrating mass for the first time in that
place a group of church biddies came up to him with the evi-
dent aim of helping him change vestments for the office of the
mass. And all around he heard gushing exclamations:

"Good little Father . . . Angel Gabriel . . ."

A skinny old woman clasped her hands in adoration:

"My sweet little Jesus Christ . . ."

They seemed to be adoring him and Father José Pedro
revolted. He knew that in reality the great majority of priests
didn't revolt and got fine presents of chickens, turkeys, embroidered handkerchiefs, and sometimes even old gold watches

that had come down through generations in the same family. But Father José Pedro had a different idea of his mission, he thought the others were in error and it was with a sacred furor that he said:

"Haven't you ladies anything to do? Don't you have homes to take care of? I'm not your sweet little Jesus Christ or your Angel Gabriel . . . Go home and do some work, get lunch ready, sew."

The church biddies looked at him startled. It was as if he were the anti-Christ himself. The priest finished:

"Working at home you will serve God better than staying here sniffing at priests' cassocks . . . Go on, go on . . ."

And while they went off frightened he repeated more with dismay than rage:

"My sweet little Jesus Christ . . . The name of the Lord in vain."

The church biddies went straight to Father Clóvis, who was fat, bald, and very good-humored, the favorite confessor of all of them. Amidst exclamations of surprise they told him what had just happened. Father Clóvis looked at the biddies tenderly and consoled them:

"It'll go away . . . This is the beginning. Later on he'll see that you ladies are saints, true daughters of the Lord. This will go away. Don't be upset. Go say an Our Father and don't forget that there's benediction today."

He laughed when they'd gone. And he murmured to himself:

"These newly-ordained priests will spoil everything . . ."

Later on the church biddies approached Father José Pedro after a while. The truth is that they never came to have a perfect intimacy with him. His serious air, his goodness that was held back for when it was needed, and his horror at intrigues in the sacristy made them respect him more than love him. Some, however, generally those who were widows or the wives of bad husbands, became more or less friends with him. Something else removed him from the church biddies: he was everything a preacher shouldn't be. He had never succeeded in describing hell with the conviction of Father Clóvis, for example. His rhetoric was poor and wanting. But he had faith, he was a believer. And it would have been hard to say that Father Clóvis even believed in hell.

At first Father José Pedro had thought of bringing the Captains of the Sands to the biddies. He thought that in that way he would not only save the children from a miserable life but that he would also save the church biddies from pernicious uselessness. He would manage to have them dedicate themselves to the boys with the same fervent devotion they showed the church, its fat priests. Father José Pedro guessed (more than he knew) that if they spent their days in useless chatter in church or embroidering handkerchiefs for Father Clóvis, it was because they hadn't had, in their unfortunate existence as virgins, a son, a husband to whom they could dedicate their time and love. Now he would bring them sons. Father José Pedro pondered that project for a long time . . . He even went so far as to bring a boy who had run away from the Reformatory to the house of one of them. That was a long time before he met the Captains of the Sands, when he'd only heard talk about them. The experiment turned out poorly: the boy ran away from the lady's house carrying off several silver objects, preferring the freedom of the streets, even dressed in rags and with no assurance of meals, to the good clothes and steady meals with the obligation of reciting the tierce aloud and attending several masses and benedictions every day. Then Father José Pedro understood that his experiment had failed more through the fault of the old maid than that of the boy. Because obviously—Father José Pedro thought—it's impossible to change an abandoned and thieving child into a sexton. But it's quite possible to change him into a working man . . . And when he met the Captains of the Sands he hoped to enter into an agreement with some of them and with the biddies to try a new experiment, well-directed this time. But soon after Good-Life introduced him to the gang, of whom he soon gained the confidence of most, he saw that it was completely useless to think about that project. He saw that it was absurd because freedom was the deepest feeling in the hearts of the Captains of the Sands and that he had to try other means.

In the early days the boys looked at him with mistrust. They had heard on the street many times that priests were a drag, that the priest business was for women. But Father José Pedro had been a worker and he knew how to treat the boys. He treated them as men, as friends. And so he gained their confidence, became the friend of all of them, even of those who, like Pedro Bala and the Professor, didn't like to pray. He only had great difficulty with Legless. While the Professor, Pedro Bala, and Cat were indifferent to the priest's words (the Professor, however, liked him because he brought him books), Lollipop, Dry Gulch, and Big João, mainly the first, paid close attention to what he said, Legless put up a resistance that had been very tenacious at first. But Father José Pedro ended up winning them all over. And at least in Lollipop he discovered a priestly vocation.

But that afternoon it was with little satisfaction that they saw him arrive. Lollipop went over and kissed the priest's hand. Dry Gulch too. The rest bowed. Father José Pedro explained:

"Today I've come with an invitation for all of you."

Their ears were attentive. Legless muttered:

"He's going to call us to benediction. I just want to see who's for it . . ."

But he fell silent because Pedro Bala looked at him angrily. The priest gave him a kind smile. He sat down on a crate. Big João saw that his cassock was old and dirty. It was darned with black thread and was too big for the priest's thinness. He nudged Pedro Bala, who noticed too. Then the Bullet said:

"People, Father José Pedro, who's our friend, has got something for us. Hurray for Father José Pedro!"

Big João knew that it was all because of the torn cassock, too big for the priest's thinness. The others answered with a "hurray," the priest smiled, waving his hand. Big João couldn't take his eyes off the cassock. He thought that Pedro Bala was a real leader, he knew everything, knew how to do everything. For Pedro Bala Big João would let himself be cut with a knife like that black man in Ilhéus when he did it for Barbosa, the big boss of the scrublands. Father José Pedro put his hand into the pocket of his cassock, took out his black breviary. He opened it and from it drew several ten *milreis* notes:

"This is for you all to ride the carrousel today . . . I invite you all to take a ride today on the carrousel on the square in Itapagipe."

He had hoped that the faces would be more animated. That an extraordinary joy would reign in the whole place. Because then he would be even more convinced that he was serving God when from those five hundred *milreis* that Dona Guilhermina Silva had given him for candles for the altar of the Virgin he had taken fifty *milreis* in order to take the Captains of the Sands to the carrousel. And since the faces didn't suddenly become happy, he was puzzled, the notes in his hand, looking at the crowd of boys. Pedro Bala stroked his hair (which fell over his ears), he tried to speak, he couldn't. Then he looked at the Professor and it was the latter who explained:

"Father, you're a good man." He felt like saying that the priest was a good man like Big João, but he thought perhaps the priest might be offended if he compared him to the black boy. "As a matter of fact Legless and Dry Gulch are both working on the carrousel. And we've been invited," he paused briefly, "by the owner, who's their friend, to ride free at night. We won't forget your invitation . . ." The Professor was speaking slowly, choosing his words, thinking that it was a delicate moment, making up a lot of things and Pedro Bala backed him up with nods. "Another time. But you won't be mad at us for not accepting, will you? It didn't work out," and he was looking at the priest, whose face was happy again.

"No. Another time." He looked at the boys, smiling. "It's even better this way. Because the money I had . . ." and he suddenly fell silent at the deed he was about to recount. And he thought that maybe it had been a lesson from God, a warning that he had done something bad. His look was so strange that the boys stepped closer.

They were looking at the priest without understanding. Pedro Bala scratched his head as when he had a problem to solve, the Professor tried to speak. But Big João understood everything, in spite of his being the slowest wit of all:

"Did it belong to the church, Father?" and he covered his mouth, angry at himself.

The others understood. Lollipop thought that it would have been a great sin but felt that the priest's goodness was greater than the sin. Then Legless came over limping more than usual as if fighting with himself and almost shouted first, then lowering his voice:

"We can stick it back where it was . . . It's duck soup for us. Don't be sad . . ." and he smiled.

And Legless's smile and the friendship that the priest read in the eyes of all of them (could those have been tears in João's eyes?) restored his calm, serenity, and confidence in his act and in his God. He said in a natural voice:

"An old widow gave five hundred *milreis* for candles. I took out fifty so you people could ride on the carrousel. God will judge whether or not I did the right thing. Now I'll just buy candles."

Pedro Bala felt that he had a debt to pay the priest. He wanted the priest to know that they understood. And since there was nothing else at hand he was ready to skip the work they could have done that afternoon and invited the priest:

"We're going to the carrousel to see Dry Gulch and Legless this afternoon. Do you want to come with us, Father?"

Father José Pedro said he did because he knew that was another step forward in his intimacy with the Captains of the Sands. And a group went to the square with the priest. Several didn't go, including Cat, who went to see Dalva. But those who went looked like a group of good little boys coming from catechism. If they'd been better dressed and cleaned up they could have passed for schoolboys, they were going along in such an orderly fashion. On the square they went around everything with the priest. With pride they showed Dry Gulch imitating animals, dressed like a *cangaceiro*, Legless making the carrousel run all by himself because Nhôzinho França had gone off to have a beer in a bar. It was a shame that in the afternoon the lights of the carrousel weren't turned on. It wasn't as pretty as at night, the lights spinning in all colors. But they were proud of Dry Gulch imitating animals, of Legless running the carrousel, having the children get on, having the children get off. The Professor, with a pencil stub and a box cover, sketched Dry Gulch dressed as a bandit. He had a special skill for drawing and sometimes he picked up money sketching on the sidewalk men who were passing, young ladies with their boyfriends. These would stop for a minute, laugh at the still imprecise drawing, the girls would say:

"It's a good likeness . . ."

He would pick up some coins and then he would set about fixing up the sketch done in chalk, broadening it, putting in men from the waterfront and women of the demi-monde, until a policeman chased him off the sidewalk. Sometimes he already had a large group watching and someone would say:

"That boy's got promise. It's a shame the government doesn't take note of these vocations . . ." and he recalled cases of street urchins who, aided by families, were great poets, singers, and painters.

The Professor finished the sketch (in which he put the carrousel and Nhôzinho França falling down drunk) and gave it to the priest. They were all in a tight group looking at the drawing that the priest was praising when they heard:

"Why, it's Father José Pedro . . ."

And the skinny old woman's lorgnette fell upon the group like a weapon of war. Father José Pedro was half-despondent, the boys looked with curiosity at the bones and the neck and the breast of the old woman where a very expensive barrette sparkled in the sunlight. There was a moment in which they all remained silent until Father José Pedro got up his courage and said:

"Good afternoon, Dona Margarida."

But the widow Margarida Santos raised her gold lorgnette again.

"Aren't you ashamed to be seen in this company, Father? A priest of the Lord? A man of responsibility in the midst of this rabble . . ."

"They're children, ma'am."

The old woman gave a haughty look and had a sneer of disdain on her mouth. The priest went on:

"Christ said: suffer the little children to come unto me . . ."

"Little children . . . Little children . . ." the old woman spat out.

"Woe unto him who does harm unto a child, the Lord said," and Father José Pedro raised his voice above the disdain of the old woman.

"These aren't children, they're thieves. Rascals and thieves. These aren't children. They might even be the Captains of the Sands . . . Thieves," she repeated with disgust.

The boys were looking at her with curiosity. Only Legless, who had come from the carrousel since Nhôzinho França had now returned, was looking at her with rage. Pedro Bala took a step forward, tried to explain:

"Father was only trying to be . . ."

But the old woman gave him a shove and stepped back:

"Don't come close to me, don't come close to me, you filth. If it weren't for Father I'd call a policeman."

Pedro Bala gave a scandalous laugh there, thinking that if it weren't for Father the old woman would no longer have her barrette or her lorgnette either. The old woman withdrew with an air of great superiority, not without first saying to Father José Pedro:

"You won't go far that way, Father. You have to be more careful about whom you associate with."

Pedro Bala was laughing even harder and the priest laughed too, if he did feel sorry for the old woman, for the old woman's lack of understanding. But the carrousel was spinning with well-dressed children and in a short time the eyes of the Captains of the Sands turned toward it and they were full of the desire to ride the horses, spin with the lights. "They were children, yes," the priest thought.

At nightfall there was a downpour. The black clouds then disappeared from the sky and the stars shone, the full moon was also shining. In the small hours of the morning the Captains of the Sands arrived. Legless started up the engine. And they forgot that they weren't like other children, they forgot that they had no home, no father or mother, that they lived by stealing, like men, that they were feared in the city as thieves. They forgot the words of the old woman with the lorgnette. They forgot everything and they were equal to all children, riding the mounts on the carrousel, spinning with the lights. The stars were shining, the full moon shone. But more than anything in the Bahia night the blue, green, yellow, and red lights of the Great Japanese Carrousel were shining.

DOCKS

Pedro Bala bounced his four-hundred *reis* coin off the wall of the Customhouse, it fell in front of Good-Life's. Then Lollipop threw his, the coin landed between Good-Life's and Pedro Bala's. Good-Life was squatting, watching closely. He took the cigarette out of his mouth:

"That's the way it goes. If you start off bad . . ."

And they continued the game, but Good-Life and Lollipop lost their four-hundred pieces, which Pedro Bala put in his pocket:

"I'm luck itself."

Opposite them the sloops were anchored. Men and women were coming out of the market. That afternoon they were waiting for God's-Love's sloop. The *capoeira* fighter was out fishing, as he was a fisherman by profession. They continued their penny-pitching until Pedro Bala cleaned the other two out. The scar on his face was gleaming. He liked to win like that, in a clean game, especially when his fellow-players were as good as Lollipop (who'd been the champion of the gang for a long time) and Good-Life. When they were finished Good-Life turned his pockets inside-out.

"You've got to lend me something, even if it's only one coin. I'm wiped out."

Then he looked at the sea, the sloops at anchor:

"God's-Love is late. Do you want to go to the docks?"

Lollipop said he'd stay and wait for God's-Love, but Pedro Bala went to the docks with Good-Life. They went through the waterfront streets, their feet sinking into the sand. A ship was casting off from Warehouse 5, there was the movement of people coming and going. Pedro Bala asked Good-Life:

"Did you ever want to be a sailor?"

"You can see . . . I like it here. I've got no urge to ship out."

"Well, I have. It's nice climbing up a mast. And how about a storm? Do you remember that story that the Professor read us? The one where there was a storm? Wild . . ."

"Terrific, yeah."

Pedro Bala remembered the story. Good-Life thought it would be foolish to leave Bahia when he grew up, it would be so nice to live the easy life of a drifter, a switchblade in his pocket, a guitar under his arm, a dark girl to fall onto the sand with. It was the life he wanted when he became a full-fledged man.

They reached the doorway to Warehouse 7. João de Adão, a husky black stevedore, an old striker, feared and loved all up and down the waterfront, was sitting on a crate. He was smoking a pipe and his muscles showed under his shirt. When he saw the boys he greeted them:

"Look at my friend Good-Life. And Captain Pedro."

He always called Pedro "Captain Pedro" and he liked to chat with them. He offered Pedro Bala an edge of the crate. Good-Life squatted in front of them. In a corner an old black woman was selling oranges and coconut candy, wearing a chintz skirt and a blouse that let her breasts show, still firm in spite of her age. Good-Life kept looking at the woman's breasts while he peeled an orange he'd picked from her stand.

"You still got a pretty good pair, eh, aunty?"

The black woman smiled:

"These kids today have no respect for their elders, friend João de Adão. Where'd you ever hear tell of a fresh kid like this talking about breasts with a worn-out old woman like me?"

"Come off it, aunty. You can still make it . . ."

The black woman laughed good-humoredly:

"I've shut the gates, Good-Life. I'm beyond the age. Ask this one . . ." She pointed to João de Adão. "I saw when almost a boy like you he led the first strike here on the docks. In those days nobody knew what the devil a strike was. Do you remember, old friend?"

João de Adão nodded yes, closed his eyes remembering the faraway times of the first strike he'd led on the docks. He was one of the oldest dockhands, even though nobody thought he was as old as he was.

Pedro Bala spoke:

"Black skin, white hair, three times thirty-three."

The woman showed her completely white tuft of hair. She'd taken off the kerchief that covered her head and Good-Life joshed:

"That's why you go around with that bandana, black woman full of proudfoot bull . . ."

João de Adão asked:

"Do you remember Raimundo, friend Luísa?"

"The 'Blond,' the one who died in the strike? How couldn't I remember. He was somebody who'd pass by every afternoon to have a few words with me. He liked to fool around . . ."

"They killed him right here that day when the cavalry charged the people." He looked at Pedro Bala. "Did you ever hear tell of him, Captain?"

"No."

"You were four years old. After that you went from one person's house to another for a year until you ran away. Then people only got to hear about you when you became the leader of the Captains of the Sands. But people knew that you'd take care of yourself. How old are you now?"

Pedro was trying to figure and João de Adão interrupted him himself:

"You're round about fifteen. Isn't that so, friend?"

The woman nodded. João de Adão went on:

"Any time you want you've got a place here on the docks. We've kept a place for you."

"Why?" Good-Life asked, since Pedro Bala was only looking with surprise.

"Because his father was Raimundo and he died right here

fighting for the people, for the people's rights. He was quite a man. He was worth ten of the kind you find around here."

"My father?" Pedro Bala asked. He'd only heard vague rumors about those stories.

"He was your father. People called him the Blond. When the strike happened he talked to the people, he didn't look like a stevedore. He was caught by a bullet. But there's a place for you on the docks."

Pedro Bala was scratching the asphalt with a stick. He looked at João de Adão:

"Why didn't you ever tell me this?"

"You were too small to understand. Now you're getting to be a man," and he laughed with satisfaction.

Pedro Bala laughed too. He was happy to know the story of his father because he'd been a brave man. But he asked slowly:

"And did you know my mother?"

João de Adão thought for a moment:

"I don't know anything. When I met the Blond he didn't have a woman. But you were living with him."

"I knew her." It was the black woman speaking. "A slip of a woman. There was a story going around that your father had stolen her away from home, that she came from a rich family up there above," and she pointed to the upper city. "She died when you weren't even six months old. In those days Raimundo was working in the cigarette factory in Itapagipe. He came to the waterfront later on."

João de Adão repeated:

"Any time you want . . ."

Pedro Bala nodded. Then he asked:

"It was a wild thing, the strike, wasn't it?"

And they stayed there listening to João de Adão tell about the strike. When he finished Pedro Bala said:

"I'd like to make a strike. It must be great."

A ship was coming in. João de Adão got up:

"Now we've got to load that Dutchman."

The ship was whistling in its docking maneuvers. Stevedores were heading for the big warehouse from all sides. Pedro Bala looked at them with warmth. His father had been one of them, had died defending them. The men going there were white, mulatto, black, a lot of blacks. They were going to fill the hold of a ship with backs of cacao, bales of tobacco, sugar, all the products of the State that were going to faraway lands where other men like those, tall and blond perhaps, would unload the ship, leave its hold empty. His father had been one of them. He'd only just found out. And he'd made speeches to them up on a crate, had fought, had caught a bullet the day the cavalry faced the strikers. Maybe his father's blood had fallen right there where he was sitting. Pedro Bala looked at the surface, which was paved now. Under that asphalt the blood that had poured out of his father's body was there. That's why any day he wanted he'd have a place on the docks, among those men, the place that had been his father's. And he would also have to carry loads . . . A hard life that, with hundred-pound bales on your back. But he'd also be able to lead a strike, just like his father and João de Adão, fight the police, die for their rights. In that way he'd avenge his father, help those men fight for their rights (Pedro Bala vaguely knew what that was). He imagined himself in a strike, fighting. And his eyes smiled, the same as his lips.

Good-Life, who was sucking on his third orange, interrupted his dream:

"Are you wool-gathering, buddy?"

The old black woman looked at Pedro Bala with affection:

"He's got his father's face. But he's got his mother's wavy hair. If it wasn't for that cut on his face you wouldn't have to try hard to see Raimundo. A good-looking man . . ."

Good-Life chuckled. He asked how much he owed, paid her two hundred *reis*. Then he looked at the black woman's breasts again, asked:

"Have you got a daughter, aunty?"

"What do you want to know for, you devil?"

Good-Life laughed:

"I could get friendly with her . . ."

The woman threw her slipper at him. Good-Life dodged:

"If I had a daughter she wouldn't be for your sweet talk, you bum."

Then she remembered:

"Aren't you going to Gantóis today? There's going to be drumming like you never heard. A first-class fandango. It's Omolu's feast day."

"Lots of grub? And rice drinks?"

"If they've got any . . ." She looked at Pedro Bala. "Why don't you go, white boy? Omolu isn't just a black folks' saint. She's a saint for all poor people."

Good-Life extended his hand as a salute when she spoke of Omolu, goddess of smallpox. Night was falling. A man bought some coconut candy. The lights suddenly went on. The black woman got up. Good-Life helped her lift her stand onto her head. In the distance Lollipop appeared with God's-Love. Pedro Bala looked at the men on the docks who were carrying bundles onto the Dutch ship once more. Drops of sweat were gleaming on the broad black and mulatto backs. The muscular necks were bent under the loads. And the cranes squeaked noisily. To lead a strike someday, like his father . . . Fight for rights . . . One day a man like João de Adão could tell his story to other boys by the entrance to the docks the way they told his father's. His eyes had an intense glow in the newly-fallen night.

They helped God's-Love unload the good catch. Iemanjá had helped him. A man who had a fish-stand in the market bought his whole load. Then they went to eat at a restaurant in the market. Lollipop went to see Father José Pedro, who was teaching him to read and write. He stopped by the warehouse first to pick up a box of pens he'd lifted from a stationery store that morning. Pedro Bala, Good-Life, and God's-Love went to the *candomblé* in Gantóis (Love was an *ogan*, an acolyte), where Omolu appeared in her red vestments and advised her poor children in the most beautiful canticle ever heard that their misery would soon be over, that she would take the smallpox to the houses of the rich and that the poor would be well-fed and happy. The drums throbbed in Omolu's night. And she foretold the day of vengeance for the poor. Black

women danced, the men were happy. The day of vengeance
was coming.

Pedro Bala went along the streets of the city alone because
Good-Life had gone with God's-Love to dance in a dive. He
went down the slopes that led to the lower city. He walked
slowly, as if he were carrying a weight inside himself, he
walked as if bent over inside. He was thinking about that
afternoon's talk with João de Adão, a talk that had made him
happy because he'd ended up discovering that his father
had been a brave man on the docks, a man who'd left a story
behind. But João de Adão had also spoken about the rights of
the dock workers. Pedro Bala had never heard talk about that
and yet it had been for those rights that his father had died.
And later on at the Gantóis *macumba*, Omolu, bedecked in
red, had said that the day of vengeance for the poor would not
be long in coming. And all that pressed down on Pedro Bala's
heart, just as those hundred-pound bales press down on the
back of the stevedores' heads.

When he finished his descent he headed for the sands, feeling like going to a warehouse to see if he could sleep. A dog
barked as he passed, thinking he was going to claim the bone
he was gnawing on. At the end of the street Pedro Bala saw a
shape. It looked like a woman walking in a hurry. He shook
his boy's body the way a young animal shakes his when he
sees a female and with quick steps he caught up with the
woman who was going onto the sands now. The sand squeaked
underfoot and the woman noticed that she was being followed. Pedro Bala was able to get a good look at her when she
passed under the lampposts: she was a rather young black girl,
she may have been only fifteen, like him. But her breasts stood
up in a point and her buttocks rolled under her dress, because
black people, even when they're walking normally, seem to be
dancing. And desire grew in Pedro Bala, it was a desire that
grew out of the wish to stifle the anguish that was pressing
down on him. By thinking about the bouncing buttocks of the
black girl he no longer thought about the death of his father

defending the rights of the strikers, about Omolu asking for
vengeance on the night of the *macumba*. He was thinking
about pulling the black girl down onto the firm sand, caressing her firm breasts (maybe virgin breasts, a girl's breasts in
any case), possessing her warm black woman's body.

He quickened his steps because the black girl had left the
street that cut through the sands and had gone onto them, getting away from the lampposts. But when she noticed that
Pedro Bala was getting closer and closer she went straight
ahead almost at a run. Pedro understood that she was heading
for one of those streets that lay beyond the warehouses, hidden between the hillside and the sea and that she was crossing
the sands to take a shortcut and get away from him more easily. There was a silence over the whole waterfront, only the
squeaking of the sand under their steps made the girl's heart
quiver with fear and Pedro Bala's with impatience. He was
walking much faster than the girl and he would catch up with
her in ten more steps. And she still had a long way to go across
the sands before getting to the warehouses and the streets that
are on the other side of the warehouses. Pedro was smiling, a
smile with clenched teeth, just like a wild animal on the desert
hunting another animal for his lunch.

Just as he was lifting his hand to touch her shoulder and
make her turn her head, the black girl began to run. Pedro Bala
ran after her and soon caught up. But he was going so fast that
he ran into her and they both rolled on the sand. Pedro leaped
up laughing and went over to her as she was trying to stand up:

"You don't have to, beautiful. Right here is fine."

The black girl's face showed terror. But when she saw that
her pursuer was a boy of fifteen or sixteen she felt a little better and asked angrily:

"What do you want?"

"Don't be stuck-up, girl. Let's have a little talk . . ."

And he grabbed her by the arm and pulled her back down
onto the sand. Fear came over her again, mad terror. She was
coming from her grandmother's and was going home where
her mother and sisters were waiting for her. Why had she come
by night, why had she taken a chance on the sands of the

waterfront? Didn't she know that the sands of the waterfront are the love beds of all the tramps, all the thieves, all the sailors, all the Captains of the Sands, all those who can't pay for a woman and are thirsting for a body in the sacred city of Bahia? She didn't know that, she'd only just turned fifteen, there hadn't been much time since she'd become a woman. Pedro Bala was only fifteen too, but for a long time he'd known not only the sands and their secrets but also the secrets of the love of women. Because if men know these secrets long before women, the Captains of the Sands know them long before any man. Pedro Bala wanted her because he'd been feeling the desires of a man for a long time and he knew the caresses of love. She didn't want him because she'd just turned into a woman and she wanted to keep her body for a mulatto who would know how to make her feel passion. She didn't want to give it to the first one who found her on the sands. And her eyes were wide with fear.

Pedro Bala ran his hand over the black girl's curly hair:

"You're a mouthful, dark girl. We're going to have beautiful children . . ."

She fought to get away from him:

"Leave me alone. Leave me alone, you bastard."

And she looked around to see if she could spy someone to shout to, someone she could ask for help, someone who would help her preserve her virginity, which she'd been taught was a precious thing. But in the night on the sands of the waterfront of Bahia nothing could be seen but shadows and nothing could be heard but the moans of love, the tumbling of bodies rolling together in the sand.

Pedro Bala stroked her breasts and she, in the depths of her terror, began to feel a thread of desire, like a trickle of water that flows between mountains and soon grows until it's transformed into a great river. And that made her terror greater. If she didn't resist desire and let him possess her she'd be lost, she'd leave a bloodstain on the sand that the stevedores would laugh at the next morning. The certainty of her weakness gave her new courage and strength. She lowered her head and bit Pedro's hand as he held her breast. Pedro gave a cry, pulled his hand away, she got up and ran. But he caught her and now his desire was mingled with rage.

"Let's stop playing around," and he tried to pull her down.

"Let me go, you bastard. Do you want to ruin me, you son of a bitch? Let me go, I've got nothing for you."

Pedro didn't answer. He'd known others who played coy. Usually because they had a lover waiting for them. He didn't think for a moment that the black girl could be a virgin. But she resisted and cursed him, and bit, beat her small fists against Pedro Bala's chest.

"What's with you, girl? Do you think I'm going to let you go before you give in? Cut the pride. Your man won't find out, nobody's going to know. And you'll see what a good man is like . . ."

And now he was trying to caress her, he wanted to overcome her anger, make her feel desire. His hands went down along her body, laid her down forcefully. Now she was repeating a refrain:

"Leave me alone, you bastard . . . Leave me alone, you bastard . . ."

He raised her cheap cotton skirt, the black girl's firm thighs appeared. But one was on top of the other and Pedro Bala tried to separate them. The girl reacted again, but as the boy was stroking her she felt the sudden arrival of desire and didn't curse anymore, but asked with anguish:

"Leave me alone, I'm a virgin. Be good, you don't want me. You'll find someone else later. I'm a virgin, you're going to hurt me."

He looked at her, she was weeping with fear and also because her will was weakening, her breasts were swollen.

"Are you really a virgin?"

"I swear by Almighty God, by the Virgin," and she kissed her crossed fingers.

Pedro Bala hesitated. The girl's swollen breasts under his fingers. The firm thighs, the curly hair of her sex.

"Are you telling the truth?" and he kept on stroking her.

"I am, I swear. Let me go, my mother's waiting for me."

She was crying and Pedro Bala felt sorry but desire was loose in him. Then he proposed in the girl's ear (and tickled her with his tongue):

"I'll only do it in the rear."

"No. No."

"You'll still be a virgin. It's nothing."

"No. It'll hurt."

But he was caressing her, a shiver ran up her body. She began to understand that if she didn't satisfy him the way he wanted her virginity would be left behind there. And when he promised (his tongue excited her in the ear again):

"If it hurts I'll withdraw . . ." she consented.

"You swear you won't do it in front?"

"I swear."

But after, when he'd satisfied himself for the first time (and she'd cried out and bitten her hands), seeing that he still had desire, he tried to deflower her. But she felt it and leaped up like a madwoman:

"Aren't you satisfied with what you did to me, you bastard? Do you want to ruin me?"

And she was sobbing loudly, waving her arms like a crazy woman, her whole defense was her shouts, her tears, her curses against the leader of the Captains of the Sands. But for Pedro Bala the black girl's best defense was her terror-filled eyes, the eyes of a weaker animal who doesn't have the strength to defend itself. And since his greatest desire had already been satisfied and since that anguish from earlier in the evening was coming back over him, he said:

"If I let you go, will you come back tomorrow?"

"Yes, I'll come back."

"I'll only do what I did today. I'll let you stay a virgin . . ."

She nodded yes. Her eyes were like those of a crazy person and at that moment she only felt pain and fear, the urge to flee. Now that Pedro's hands, lips, sex were no longer touching her flesh, her desire had disappeared and she was only thinking about defending her virginity. She breathed deeply when he said:

"Then you can go. But if you don't come back tomorrow . . . When I catch you you'll find out how many boards it takes to make a bed . . ."

She began to walk without answering anything. But the boy went along with her:

"I'll take you so some hoodlum doesn't grab you."

The two of them went along and she was weeping. He tried to put his hand on her, she wouldn't let him and moved away. He tried again, again she put his hand away. Then he said:

"What the devil is that about?"

And they walked holding hands. She was weeping and the crying bothered Pedro Bala, it was bringing back his upset from earlier in the evening, the vision of his father dying in the struggle, the vision of Omolu announcing vengeance. He began to curse to himself about meeting the girl and he picked up the pace in order to get to the start of the street as soon as possible. She was weeping and he spoke angrily:

"What's the matter with you? Nothing happened to you . . ."

She only looked into his eyes. In spite of still going along with him and in spite of being terrified they were full of hatred and contempt. Pedro lowered his head, he didn't know what to say, he had no more desire or rage, only sadness in his heart. They heard the music of a samba that a man was singing on the street. She sobbed louder, he was kicking the sand. Now he felt weaker than she, the girl's hand was heavy as lead in his. He let go of her hand, she moved away from him, Pedro didn't protest. He wanted not to have met her, not to have met João de Adão either or to have gone to Gantóis. They reached the street, he said:

"Now you can go, nobody will hurt you."

She looked at him again with hate and started to run. But at the next corner she stopped, turned toward him (as he kept looking at her) and rained curses on him in a voice that filled him with fear:

"I hope plague and hunger and war fall down on you, you bastard. God will punish you, you bastard. Son of a bitch, bastard, bastard," her solitary voice crossed the street, struck Pedro Bala.

Before she disappeared around the corner she spat on the ground with supreme contempt and kept repeating:

"Bastard . . . Bastard . . ."

First he stood there, then he started running across the sands as if the wind were lashing him, as if he were fleeing from the black girl's curses. And he felt like leaping into the sea to wash away all that upset, the urge to avenge himself on the men who'd killed his father, the hatred he felt for the rich city that stretched out across the water, Barra, Vitória, Graça, the despair of his life of an abandoned and persecuted child, the sorrow he felt for the poor little black girl, a child too.

"A child too," he heard in the voice of the wind, in the samba they were singing, a voice saying it inside him.

THE OGUN ADVENTURE

Another night, a dark winter night in which the sloops didn't venture out to sea, a night of the wrath of Iemanjá and Xangô where the flashes of lightning were the only light in a sky loaded with dark and heavy clouds, Pedro Bala, Legless, and Big João were taking the *mãe-de-santo* priestess Don'Aninha to her distant house. She had come to the warehouse in the afternoon, she needed a favor from them, and while she was explaining night fell, fearsome and terrible.

"Ogun is angry . . ." the priestess Don'Aninha explained.

That was the business that had brought her there. In a raid on a *candomblé* (which even though it wasn't hers, no policeman would dare raid Aninha's *candomblé*, was under her protection) the police had carried off Ogun, who had been resting on the altar. Don'Aninha had used all her power with a policeman to get the return of the saint. She'd even gone to the house of a professor from the Faculty of Medicine, her friend, who came to study black religion at her *candomblé*, to ask him to have the God returned. The professor was really thinking that the police ought to give him back the idol. But to add to his collection of black idols and not to put back on its altar in the distant *candomblé*. That's why, because Ogun was in a police detention room, Xangô was unleashing his lightning that night.

Finally Don'Aninha had come to the Captains of the Sands,

her friends for a long time, because all blacks and all poor people in Bahia are friends of the great *mãe-de-santo*. She had a friendly and maternal word for each one of them. She cured illnesses, brought lovers together, her fetishes killed evil men. She explained to Pedro Bala what had happened. The leader of the Captains of the Sands didn't get to *candomblés* very often, just as he didn't listen to Father José Pedro's lessons very much. But he was a friend of the priest as well as of the priestess and among the Captains of the Sands when one is a friend he acts like a friend.

Now they were taking Aninha home. The night all around was stormy and angry. The rain made them huddle under the *mãe-de-santo*'s big white umbrella. There was drumming in the *candomblés* to ease the anger of Ogun and perhaps in one or in many of them Omolu was announcing the poor people's vengeance. Don'Aninha said to the boys in a bitter voice: "They won't let poor people live in peace . . . They don't even leave the poor people's God alone. Poor people can't dance, can't sing to their God, can't ask a favor of their God." Her voice was bitter, a voice that didn't seem to be that of the priestess Don'Aninha. "They're not content with killing poor people with hunger . . . Now they take away poor people's saints . . ." and she raised her fists.

Pedro Bala felt a wave inside himself. Poor people had nothing. Father José Pedro said that the poor would go to heaven one day, where God would be the same for everybody. But Pedro Bala's young reasoning didn't see justice in that. In the kingdom of heaven they would be equal. But they were unequal on earth now, the scale always tilted to one side.

The imprecations of the *mãe-de-santo* filled the night more than the sound of the different drums that were soothing Ogun. Don'Aninha was tall and thin, an aristocratic type of black woman and, like no other black woman in the city, she knew how to wear her traditional Bahian dress. She had a pleasant face, but just a look from her was enough to bring on absolute respect. In that she was like Father José Pedro. But now she was in a terrible mood and her curses against the rich and the police were filling the Bahia night and Pedro Bala's heart.

When they left her, surrounded by her *filha-de-santo* sister-hood who were kissing her hand, Pedro Bala promised:

"Don't worry, Mother Aninha, I'll bring you Ogun tomorrow."

She patted his blond head, smiled. Big João and Legless kissed the black woman's hand, they went down the slope. The *agogô* bells and the *atabaque* drums resounded, soothing Ogun.

Legless didn't believe in anything, but he owed Don'Aninha favors. He asked:

"What are we going to do? The police have got the dingus . . ."

Big João spat, he was a bit fearful:

"Don't call Ogun a dingus, Legless. He'll punish you . . ."

"He's in jail, he can't do anything," Legless laughed.

Big João shut up because he knew that Ogun was ever so great, even in jail he could punish Legless. Pedro Bala scratched his head, asked for a cigarette:

"Let me think about it. Remember, we promised Aninha. Now we've got to come through."

They went down to the warehouse. The rain was coming in through the holes in the roof, most of the boys were huddled together in corners where there were still tiles. The Professor had tried to light his candle but the wind seemed to be playing a game with him, blowing it out from one minute to the next. Finally he gave up reading for the night and was kibitzing a game of blackjack that Cat was running in a corner assisted by Good-Life. Coins on the floor, but no sound made Lollipop deviate from his prayers before the Virgin and Saint Anthony.

On rainy nights like that they couldn't sleep. From time to time a flash of lightning would light up the warehouse and then the thin and dirty faces of the Captains of the Sands could be seen. Many of them were children who were still afraid of dragons and legendary monsters. They would get closer to the older ones, who only felt cold and sleepy. Others, the black ones, heard the voice of Xangô in the thunder. Rainy nights like that were terrible for all of them. Even for Cat, who had a woman in whose breast he could hide his young head, stormy nights were bad nights. Because on nights like that men who didn't have a place to lay their fearful heads down in the city,

who didn't even have a bachelor's cot, and want to hide their
fear by a woman's breast, pay to sleep with Dalva and pay
well. So Cat would stay at the warehouse, running games with
his marked deck, aided in his larceny by Good-Life. They were
all together, restless, all the more alone, feeling that they
lacked something, not just a warm bed with a roof over it but
also the tender words of a mother or sister that made the fear
go away. They were all huddled together and some were shivering with cold under their tattered shirts and pants. Others
had jackets, stolen or picked out of trash barrels, jackets they
used as overcoats. The Professor even had an overcoat, so long
that it dragged on the ground.

Once upon a time, and it was summer, a man wearing a
thick overcoat had stopped to have a drink at one of the stands
in the city. He looked like a foreigner. It was in the middle of
the afternoon and the heat ate away at a person's skin. But the
man didn't seem to feel it, wearing his new overcoat. The Professor thought he was funny and had the face of someone with
money and he began to make a sketch of him (with the enormous overcoat, larger than the man, the overcoat was the man
himself) in chalk on the pavement. And he was laughing with
satisfaction because the man would probably give him a two
milreis silver piece. The man turned in his chair and looked at
the almost finished picture. The Professor laughed, he found the
sketch good, the overcoat dominating the man, it was more than
the man. But the man didn't like it at all, he let himself be taken
by a great rage, got up from his seat and gave the Professor a
couple of kicks. One caught the boy in the kidneys and he
rolled on the sidewalk moaning. The man then put his foot on
his face, choking him, and he said before going away:

"Take that and mind your own business, that'll teach you
not to make fun of a man."

And he went off, tossing some coins in his hand, after half
rubbing out the picture with his foot. The waitress came over
and helped the Professor get up. She looked with pity at the
boy, who was feeling the place where his kidneys hurt, looked
at the sketch, and said:

"What a brute! The picture even looked like him . . . Stupid!"

She put her hand in her pocket where she kept her tips, took out a one *milreis* silver piece, tried to give it to the Professor. But he refused with his hand, he knew she was going to need it. He looked at the half-obliterated design, went on his way still holding his kidneys. He was going along almost without thinking, with a lump in his throat. He'd wanted to please the man, earn a silver piece from him. He'd got three kicks and some brutal words. He didn't understand. Why were they hated like that in the city? They were poor children with no father or mother. Why did those well-dressed men hate them so much? He went along with his pain. But it so happened that on the way to the warehouse, on the deserted sands beneath the sun, he again met the man in the overcoat minutes later. It looked as though he was heading toward one of the two ships moored at the docks and now he was carrying the overcoat on his arm because the sun was scorching. Professor took out his switchblade (he didn't use it very much) and went over to the man. The heat had driven all the people off the sands and the man with the overcoat was taking a shortcut to the docks across them. The Professor followed silently behind the man, when he caught up to him he confronted him with the knife in his hand. The sight of the man had transformed the confusion of his feelings into one single feeling: revenge. The man looked at him in terror. The Professor loomed up in front of him with the knife open. He muttered:

"Get away, you guttersnipe."

The Professor advanced with the knife, the man turned white.

"What's this? What's this?" and he looked all around in hopes of seeing somebody. But only far away on the docks could the shape of men be seen. Then the man with the overcoat started running when the Professor leaped on him and cut his hand with the knife. The overcoat was abandoned on the ground and blood from the man's hand dripped onto the sand. The Professor went in the opposite direction, stopped for an instant not knowing what to do. A policeman wouldn't be long in coming, then a lot of them, coming in pursuit along with the man. If the man's ship were leaving right away everything would be all right, the chase wouldn't last long. But if it took its time in sailing the man would surely go after him until he caught him and put him behind bars. Then the Professor remembered the waitress. He walked over to the lunch stand that was across the way and signaled to the waitress. She came and immediately understood when she saw him with the over-coat. The Professor told her:

"He's got a cut on the hand."

She laughed:

"You got your revenge, eh?"

She took the overcoat into the lunch stand, hid it. The Professor disappeared until the ship was beyond the breakwater. But from where he was he saw two policemen searching across the sands and on the neighboring streets. That was how the Professor got that overcoat that he never wanted to sell. He'd acquired an overcoat and a lot of hate. And a long time later, when the whole nation admired his murals (the themes were the lives of abandoned children, old beggars, workers and dock-hands breaking their chains), they noted that the fat burghers always appeared wearing enormous overcoats, which had more personality than they themselves.

Pedro Bala, Big João, and Legless went into the warehouse. They went over to the group playing cards around Cat. When they arrived, the game halted for a moment. Cat looked at the three:

"Want to play some blackjack?"

"Do I look like a fool?" Legless answered.

Big João sat down to watch, Pedro Bala went off in a corner with the Professor. He wanted to set up a way to steal the image of Ogun from the police. They discussed it for part of the night and it was already eleven o'clock when Pedro Bala, before going out, spoke to all the Captains of the Sands:

"People, I'm about to go through a rough time. If I don't show up by tomorrow you'll know that the police have got me and I won't be long in going to the Reformatory, until I can escape. Or until you people get me out of there . . ."

And he left. Big João went to the door with him. The Professor came back over to Cat. The younger ones viewed the leader's departure with a certain worry. They had great trust in

Pedro Bala and without him a lot of them wouldn't know how
to get by.

Lollipop came out of his corner, leaving a prayer half-said:
"What's up?"

"Pedro went out to do something hard. If he's not back by
tomorrow he'll be locked up . . ."

"We'll bust him out," Lollipop answered naturally, and it
didn't seem that minutes before he'd been praying before a picture of the Virgin for the salvation of his petty thief's soul.
And he went back to his saints to pray for Pedro Bala.

The game started up again. Rain and lightning, thunder and
clouds in the sky. An intense cold in the warehouse. Drops of
water fell onto the boys playing cards. But the game had lost
their attention now. Cat himself was forgetting to win, there
was a kind of confusion in the whole warehouse. It lasted until
Professor said:

"I'm going out to see how things are going . . ."

Big João and Cat went with him. That night it was Lollipop
who lay by the door of the warehouse with the knife under his
head. And near him Dry Gulch scanned the night with his
somber face. And he thought about where Lampião's gang
might be in the immensity of the scrublands in that stormy
night. Maybe they were fighting with the police that night, the
way Pedro Bala was going to now. And Dry Gulch thought
that when Pedro Bala was as big as a man he'd be as brave as
Lampião. Lampião was the lord of the backlands, of the endless scrub. Pedro Bala would be master of the city, the tenements, the streets, the waterfront. And Dry Gulch, who was
from the backlands, would be able to travel in scrub and in cit-
ies. Because Lampião was his godfather and Pedro Bala was
his friend. He imitated the crowing of a cock and that indi-
cated that Dry Gulch was happy.

Pedro Bala, while he went up the Montanha slope, went over
his plan mentally. It had been put together with the help of the
Professor and it was the riskiest thing he'd undertaken till
then. But Don'Aninha was well worth running a risk for.
When someone was sick she would bring her cures made of

leaves, take care of him, often cure him. And when a Captain of the Sands appeared at her temple she would treat him like a man, like an *ogan* acolyte, give him the best to eat, the best to drink. The plan was risky, he might not be able to bring it off. Pedro Bala might do some time in jail and end up being sent to the Reformatory where life was worse than a dog's. But there was the chance to bring it off, and Pedro Bala would gamble everything on that possibility. He reached the Largo do Teatro. The rain was falling, the policemen were huddled under their capes. He began to go slowly up the São Bento slope. He turned down São Pedro, crossed the Largo da Piedade, went up Rosário, now he was on Mercés, in front of Police Headquarters, looking at the windows, the movement of the policemen and plainclothesmen as they came and went. From time to time a streetcar passed, rumbling on its tracks, lighting up the now illuminated street even more. Don'Aninha's policeman friend had said that Ogun was in the holding cell, thrown on top of a cabinet among a lot of other objects picked up in raids on thieves' homes. That was where they kept all the people who'd been arrested during the night, before they could have a hearing by the police chief or the deputies on duty and they would then be sent to jail or turned out onto the street. In a corner there, first in a cabinet that soon became full, then beside it or on top, they placed worthless objects taken in police raids. Pedro Bala's plan was to spend the night or part of it in the holding pen and when he left (if he managed to leave) to carry off Ogun's image with him. He had a big advantage: he wasn't known to the police. Only a very few policemen knew him as a street urchin, although all policemen and even a few detectives were hot to capture the leader of the Captains of the Sands. All they knew about him was that he had a scar on his face—and Pedro Bala touched the cut. But they thought he was bigger than he really was and they also had the notion that Pedro Bala must be a mulatto and older. If they found out that he was the leader of the Captains of the Sands they might not even send him to the Reformatory. More probably he would go directly to the Penitentiary. Because you can escape from the Reformatory, but it's not easy from the

Penitentiary. So . . . and Pedro Bala walked on to Campo
Grande. But he was no longer going along with that unconcerned walk of a city street urchin. Now he was swaying like a
sailor's son, wearing a cap because of the rain, the collar of the
black jacket (it must have belonged to a very large man before)
turned up.

The policeman was under a tree because of the rain. But Pedro
came up to him like someone who was afraid. And when he
spoke to the policeman his voice was that of a child who was
afraid of the stormy night in the city.
    "Mr. Policeman . . ."
    The policeman looked at him:
    "What is it, urchin?"
    "I don't come from here. I'm from Mar Grande, I came with
my father today."
    The policeman wouldn't let him go on:
    "So what?"
    "I haven't got any place to sleep. I wondered if you'd let me
sleep at the police station . . ."
    "The police station isn't a hotel, you bum. Beat it, beat it,"
and he made a sign for Pedro to go away.
    Pedro tried to start up a conversation again, but the police-
man threatened him with his stick:
    "Go sleep in the park . . . Get out of here . . ."
    Pedro went off with a teary face. The policeman stood watch-
ing the boy. Pedro halted at the streetcar stop, waited. Nobody
got off the first car. But a couple got off the second one. Pedro
jumped on the woman, the man saw that he was trying to
snatch her purse and held Pedro by the arm. It was so poorly
done that if one of the Captains of the Sands had passed by he
doubtless wouldn't have recognized his leader. The policeman,
who had witnessed the scene, was beside them:
    "So that's the way you've come from out of town, is it? A
thieving punk."
    He went off leading Pedro by the arm. The boy went along
with a face somewhere between fear and a smile:
    "I only did it so you'd grab me . . ."

"What?"

"Everything I said is true. My father's a sailor, he's got a sloop in Mar Grande. He left me here today, he didn't come back because of the storm. I don't know where to sleep, I asked to sleep at the police station. You wouldn't let me so I made like I was going to rob the woman just so's you'd grab me . . . Now I've got a place to sleep."

"And for a long time to come," was the policeman's only reply.

They went into Headquarters. The policeman went down a corridor, left Pedro Bala in the detention room. There were five or six men there. The policeman jeered:

"Now you can sleep, you son of a bitch. And after the deputy gets here we'll see how long you're going to sleep here . . ."

Pedro was silent. The other prisoners didn't pay any attention to him, they were interested in teasing a pederast who'd been arrested and said his name was "Mariazinha." In a corner Pedro saw the cabinet. The image of Ogun was to one side next to a basket filled with wastepaper. Pedro went over, took off his jacket, laid it over the image. And while the others were talking he rolled Ogun up (he wasn't big, there were other images that were much larger) in his jacket and lay down on the floor. He laid his head on the bundle and pretended to be asleep.

The prisoners for that night continued joking with the pederast, except for an old man who was trembling in a corner. Pedro didn't know whether from the cold or from fear. But he heard the voice of a young black man asking "Mariazinha":

"Who busted your cherry?"

"Come on, leave me alone . . ." the pederast answered laughing.

"No. Tell us. Tell us," the others said.

"Oh, it was Leopoldo . . . Oh!"

The old man was still trembling. A hoodlum with a face sucked dry by TB spotted the old man in the corner:

"Why don't you go sniff the tail of that little old man?" he asked Mariazinha, who pouted.

"Can't you see right off that I don't go for old men? Come on, I don't want to talk anymore . . ."

Now a policeman was enjoying things by the door and the one with the sucked-in face turned to the old man who was all curled up:

"But I'd bet you'd like it if he gave you some today, eh, uncle?"

"I'm an old man . . . I didn't do anything," the old man mumbled more than spoke. "I didn't do anything, my daughter's waiting for me . . ."

Pedro, who had his eyes closed, guessed that the old man was crying. But he went on pretending that he was asleep. Ogun was hurting his head bones. The prisoners continued teasing the pederast and the old man until another policeman arrived and spoke to the old man:

"You, old man. Let's go . . ."

"I didn't do anything . . ." the old man said once more. "My daughter's waiting for me . . ." He spoke to everyone, policemen and prisoners. And he was shaking so much that they all felt sorry for him and even the hoodlum with the sucked-in face lowered his head. Only the pederast was smiling.

The old man didn't come back. Then it was the pederast. He took a long time. The one with the sucked-in face explained that Mariazinha came from a good family. They were calling his house, naturally, asking them to come get him so they wouldn't have to pick him up again that night. Every so often when he'd taken too much cocaine he'd raise a row on the street and be brought in by a policeman. When Mariazinha came back it was only to pick up his hat. Then he saw Pedro Bala lying there and said:

"This one's so young. But he's lovely . . ."

Pedro spat with his eyes closed:

"Beat it, fag, before I bust your face . . ."

The others laughed and only then did they notice Pedro:

"What are you in for, churchmouse?"

"None of your business, monkey-face . . ." Pedro Bala answered the one with the sucked-in face.

Even the policeman laughed and explained Pedro's story to the others. But the young black man was called and the others fell silent. They knew he'd knifed a man in a dive that night.

When the black man came back his hands were swollen from blows. He explained:

"He said I'm going to be tried for minor assault . . . And he gave me a couple dozen . . ."

He didn't say any more, he looked for a corner, made himself comfortable. The others remained silent too. And one by one they went to the deputy's office. Some were set free, others were sent to jail, others came back beaten. The storm had stopped and dawn was coming up. Pedro was the last to be called. He left his jacket where he had Ogun rolled up.

The deputy was a young lawyer who flashed a ruby on his finger and had a cigar in his jaw. When Pedro came in with the policeman the deputy asked for coffee in a loud voice. Pedro stood before the desk. The policeman said:

"This is the boy from the robbery in Campo Grande."

The deputy made a gesture:

"Go see if that coffee is coming or not . . ."

The policeman withdrew. The deputy read the report of the policeman who had arrested Pedro Bala, looked at the boy:

"What have you got to say? And don't you dare lie to me . . ."

Pedro told a long story in a frightened voice. That his father was a sloopman from Mar Grande and that day he'd come with his sloop and brought him along. But he'd gone right back to pick up another cargo and left him wandering around the city, because the sloop would be coming back to Bahia later in the afternoon and then he could go back with his father. But with the storm his father couldn't make it back and he didn't know anybody and was caught in the rain with no place to sleep. He asked a man on the street where he could sleep, the man answered at the police station. Then he asked the policeman to take him to sleep at the police station, but the policeman wouldn't, then he acted as if he were going to rob the woman just to be taken, to be able to sleep under a roof.

"And I didn't steal anything or run away . . ." he ended.

The deputy, who was sipping his coffee, said to himself:

"A child that age couldn't have invented that story . . ." Then, since he had literary interests, he murmured: "You've got quite a tale there . . ." and he smiled good-humoredly.

"What's your father's name?" he asked Pedro.

"Augusto Santos," the boy answered, giving the name of a sloopman from Mar Grande.

"If you're telling the truth I'm going to let you go. But if you're trying to fool me with that story, you'll find out . . ."

He pushed a button to call the policeman. Pedro's nerves were all tense. The policeman came in, the deputy asked him if Headquarters had a registry of sloopmen from Mar Grande who anchored by the Market docks.

"We do, yes, sir."

"Go see if a certain Augusto Santos is listed and come back and tell me. And hurry up, my time's almost up."

Pedro Bala looked at the clock: it said five-thirty in the morning. The policeman took a few minutes, the deputy paid no more attention to Pedro, who was standing in front of his desk. Only when the policeman returned and said:

"There is one, yes, sir . . . He was at the dock today but he left right away . . ." did the deputy make a gesture with his hand and speak to the policeman:

"Let this kid go."

Pedro asked permission to get his jacket. He tucked it under his arm and it didn't look as if the image was wrapped up in it. They went back along the corridor and the policeman left him at the door. Pedro headed toward the Largo dos Alitos, went around the old barracks, turned down Gamboa de Cima. Now he was running, but he heard steps behind him. It seemed that he was being followed. He looked. Professor, Big João, and Cat were coming behind him. He waited until they caught up and he asked with curiosity:

"What are you doing in these parts?"

The Professor scratched his head:

"Can't you see we got up early today. And we were walking here with nothing to do, that was when we ran into you running along . . ."

Pedro opened his jacket, showed them the image of Ogun. Big João laughed with satisfaction:

"How'd you put it over on them?"

They were going down the slope, slippery with the night's rain. And Pedro Bala recounted his night's adventure. Cat asked:

"Weren't you just a little bit scared?"

At first Pedro Bala thought of saying no, then he confessed:

"To tell the truth, I was shit afraid . . ."

And he laughed at Big João's pleased face. The sky was blue now, without clouds, the sun was shining and from the hillside they could see the sloops leaving from the Market docks.

GOD GRINS LIKE
A LITTLE BLACK BOY

The Christ Child was too big a temptation.

It didn't feel like a midday in winter. The sun was dropping a clean light down onto the streets. It didn't burn but the warmth of it was more like the caress of a woman's hand. In the nearby park flowers were bursting out with colors. Daisies and sunflowers, roses and carnations, dahlias and violets. There seemed to be a delicate perfume on the street, very thin, but one that Lollipop felt entering his nostrils as if to intoxicate him. At the door of some rich Portuguese's house he'd eaten the leftovers from a lunch that had almost been a banquet. The maid who'd brought him the full plate had said, looking at the streets, the winter sun, the men passing without their coats:

"We're getting a beautiful day."

Those words went along with Lollipop down the street. A beautiful day, and the boy went along unconcerned, whistling a samba that God's-Love had taught him, remembering that Father José Pedro had promised to do everything to get him a place in the seminary. Father José Pedro had told him that all the beauty that fell and wrapped the earth and men was a gift from God and that it was necessary to thank God. Lollipop looked at the blue sky where God must be and thanked him with a smile and he thought that God really was good. And

thinking about God he also thought about the Captains of the
Sands. They stole, they fought in the streets, they cursed, they
laid black girls on the sand, sometimes they wounded men or
police with switchblades or knives. But they were good all the
same, they were friends of one another. If they did all that it
was because they had no home, no father or mother, their life
had no regular meals and they slept in a building that almost
had no roof. If they didn't do all that they would have died of
hunger because rare were the houses where they were given
food for one, clothing for another. Not even the whole city
gave enough for everyone. Lollipop thought they were all condemned to hell. Pedro Bala didn't believe in hell, Professor
either, they laughed at him. Big João believed in Xangô, in
Omolu, in the gods of the blacks, who'd come from Africa.
God's-Love, who was a brave fisherman and a *capoeira* fighter
without equal, also believed in them, mixing them in with the
saints of the whites, who'd come from Europe. Father José
Pedro said it was superstition, error, but it wasn't their fault.
Lollipop grew sad at the beauty of the day. Would they all be
condemned to hell? Hell was a place of eternal fire, it was a
place where the condemned burned during a life that never
ended. And in hell there were unknown martyrs, the same as
at the police station, the same as in the Reformatory for
Minors. A few days before, Lollipop had heard a German
monk describing hell in a sermon at Mercy Church. In the
pews men and women received the fiery words of the monk
like whiplashes on their backs. The monk was ruddy-faced
and sweat stood out on his face. His language was mixed up
and hell came out of it even more terrible, the flames licking
bodies that had been beautiful on earth and had been given
over to love, hands that had been agile and given over to theft,
to handling knives and switchblades. In the monk's sermon
God was righteous and punishing, he wasn't Father José
Pedro's God of beautiful days. Afterwards it was explained to
Lollipop that God was the supreme goodness and supreme justice. And Lollipop wrapped his love of God in a covering of
fear of God and now he was living between the two feelings.
His life was the unfortunate life of an abandoned child and

that's why it had to be a life of sin, of almost daily thefts, of lies at the doors of rich houses. That's why in the beauty of the day Lollipop looks at the sky with eyes large with fear and asks the pardon of God, so good (but also so just . . .), for his sins and those of the Captains of the Sands. Because they weren't to blame. Life was to blame.

Father José Pedro said that life was to blame and did everything to improve their life, because he knew it was the only way of getting them to have a clean existence. One afternoon, however, when the priest was present and João de Adão was present, the dockworker said that the badly-organized society was to blame, the rich were to blame . . . That as long as nothing was changed the boys couldn't be men of goodness. And he said that Father José Pedro would never be able to do anything for them because the rich wouldn't let him. Father José Pedro had been very sad that day and when Lollipop went to console him by explaining that he didn't agree with what João de Adão was saying, the priest answered, shaking his head:

"There are times when I get to thinking that he's right, that this is all wrong. But God is good and he'll know how to fix it . . ."

Father José Pedro thought that God would pardon them and he wanted to help them. And since he couldn't find the means, but found a barrier before him (everybody wanted to treat the Captains of the Sands either as criminals or as children just like those reared with home and family), he was a bit in despair, sometimes he was perplexed. But he hoped that God would inspire him one day and until then he went along with the boys, managing sometimes to keep them away from evil acts. He was even one of those most active in wiping out pederasty in the group. And that was one of his great experiences in learning how to act in dealing with the Captains of the Sands. As long as he told them they had to put an end to it because it was a sin, something immoral and ugly, the boys laughed behind his back and continued sleeping with the youngest and the prettiest. But the day the priest, this time aided by God's-Love, asserted that it was something unworthy of a man, that it made a man the same as a woman, worse than a woman, Pedro Bala took extreme measures, he expelled the passive ones from the group. And no matter what the priest said, he didn't want them there anymore.

"If they come back, filth comes back, Father."

In a manner of speaking Pedro Bala excised pederasty from among the Captains of the Sands the way a doctor cuts out a sick appendix from the body of a man. The difficult part for Father José Pedro was reconciling things. But he went about trying and sometimes he would smile with satisfaction at the results. Except when João de Adão laughed at him and said that only revolution could obtain all that. High up there in the upper city the rich men and women wanted the Captains of the Sands in jail or in the Reformatory, which was worse than jail. Down below there on the docks, João de Adão wanted to put an end to the rich, make everything equal, give the children schools. The priest wanted to give houses, schools, love, and comfort to the children without revolution, without putting an end to the rich. But there was a barrier all around. He felt lost and asked God for inspiration. And with a certain terror he saw without wanting to that when he thought about the problem under consideration that the dockworker João de Adão was right. Then he was taken by fear, because that wasn't what they'd taught him, and he would pray for hours on end for God to give him illumination.

Lollipop had been Father José Pedro's great conquest among the Captains of the Sands. He had the reputation of being one of the evilest of the gang, they said that once he'd put a knife to the throat of a boy who didn't want to loan him money and stuck it in slowly, without trembling, until blood began to flow and the other one gave him everything he wanted. But they also said that he took his switchblade and cut Chico Lardass when the mulatto was torturing a cat that had ventured into the warehouse in search of rats. On the day that Father José Pedro began to talk about God, heaven, Christ, kindness, and mercy, Lollipop began to change. God was calling him and he heard his powerful voice in the warehouse. He saw God in his dreams and he heard the call of God that Father José Pedro spoke about. And he turned completely around for God, heard God's voice, prayed to pictures that Father José Pedro had given him. The first day they began to make fun of him in the warehouse. He smacked one of the younger ones and the rest fell silent. The next day the priest told him that he'd done a bad thing, that you had to suffer for God, and then Lollipop gave his switchblade, which was almost new, to the boy he had hit. And he didn't hit anyone anymore, avoided fights, and if he didn't avoid stealing it was because that was the means of life they had, they had no other way at all. Lollipop heard the call of God, which was intense, and he wanted to suffer for God. He would kneel for hours on end in the warehouse, sleep on the bare floor, pray even when sleep was trying to make him keel over, flee the black girls who offered him love on the hot waterfront sands. But then he was in love with God-pure-goodness and he suffered in order to pay for the suffering God had gone through on earth. Then came that revelation of the God of justice (God became vengeance for Lollipop) and the fear of God entered his heart and mingled with his love of God. His prayers were longer, the terrors of hell mingled with the beauty of God. He would fast all day long and his face became thin like a hermit's. He had the eyes of a mystic and he thought he saw God in his dreams at night. For that reason he kept his eyes away from the buttocks and breasts of the black girls who walked along as though dancing before everybody's eyes on the poor streets of the city. His hope was to be a priest of his God someday, to live only for his contemplation, to live only for him. The goodness of God made him hope to attain it. The fear of God's taking vengeance for Lollipop's sins made him despair.

And it's that love and that fear that make Lollipop hesitate in front of the display that noon hour, full of beauty. The sun is soft and clear, the flowers are open in the park, there is peace and calm all around. But more beautiful than every-thing is the image of the Virgin of the Immaculate Conception and Child in the showcase of that shop with a single door. In the window are pictures of saints, prayer books with deluxe bindings, gold rosaries, silver reliquaries. But inside, right at the end of the display of silver that reaches the door, the image of the Virgin of the Immaculate Conception holds the Child out to Lollipop. Lollipop thinks that the Virgin is handing him God, God a child and naked, poor like Lollipop. The sculptor had made the Child thin and the Virgin sad over the thinness of her Child, showing him to men who were fat and rich. That's why the image is there and not sold. The Child in images is always fat, the look of a rich child, a Rich God. There he's a Poor God, a poor child, just like Lollipop, even more like the youngest member of the gang, exactly like a babe in arms a few months old who'd been abandoned on the street when his mother died of an attack while she was carrying him in her arms and Big João brought him to the warehouse where he stayed until nightfall (the children returned and peeped in and laughed at the Professor and the Big Fellow bustling about getting milk and water for the baby), when the *mãe-de-santo* Don'Aninha came and took him with her, nestling him on her breast. Except that he was a black child and the Child is white. In everything else the likeness is exact. The Child, thin and poor, even has a weepy face in the arms of the Virgin. And she's offering him to Lollipop, to Lollipop's caresses, to Lollipop's love. Outside the day is beautiful and the sun is soft, the flowers are in bloom. Only the Child is hungry and cold on that day. Lollipop will take him to the warehouse of the Captains of the Sands. He will pray for him, take care of him, feed him with his love. Can't they see that unlike all the other images he isn't held in the Virgin's arms, he's loose in her hands, that she's offering him to Lollipop's love? He takes a step. Inside the store there's only a young woman, waiting for customers and painting her lips with a new brand of lipstick. It would be quite easy to lift the Child. Lollipop takes another step, but the fear of God assaults him. And he stands still, thinking.

He'd sworn to God, in his fear, that he'd only steal to eat or when it was something commanded by the laws of the gang, a robbery where he'd been appointed by Pedro Bala. Because he thought that breaking the laws (they'd never been written down but they existed in the conscience of each one) of the Captains of the Sands was also a sin. And now he was going to steal only to have the Child with him, to feed it with his love. It was a sin, it wasn't in order to eat, nor was it to fulfill the laws of the gang. He was going to steal in order to have the Child with him, to feed it with his love. It was a sin, it wasn't in order to eat or to drive off the cold. God was just and he would punish him, he would give him the fire of hell. His flesh would burn, his hands, which had carried off the Child, would burn for a lifetime that never ended. The Child belonged to the owner of the store. But the owner of the store had so many and all fat and rosy, he wouldn't miss just one, a skinny cold one! The others had their bellies wrapped in expensive diapers, always blue but made of rich material. This one was completely naked, his belly was cold, he was thin, not even the sculptor had had pity on him. And the Virgin was offering him to Lollipop, the Child was loose in her arms . . . The owner of the store had so many . . . How could he miss this one? Maybe he wouldn't care, maybe he would even laugh when he found out that Child had been stolen, the one he'd never been able to sell, who was loose in the Virgin's arms, before whom the church biddies who had come to buy things would say with horror:

"Not that one . . . It's so ugly, God forgive me . . . And, besides, it's not being held in the arms of Our Lady. If it falls to the floor that's that. Not that one . . ."

And the Child remained there. The Virgin was offering him to the love of passersby, but no one wanted him. The church biddies didn't want to take him to their altars where the Christ Childs wear golden sandals, with gold crowns on their heads. Only Lollipop saw that the Child was hungry and thirsty, he was cold too and he wanted to take him. But Lollipop had no money, nor was he in the habit of paying for things. Lollipop could take him with him, could give the Child something to eat, to drink, to wear, everything lifted because of his love of God. But if he did it God would punish him, hell's fire would consume him, for a lifetime that never ended, his hands, which had taken the Child, his head, which had thought of taking the Child. Then Lollipop remembered that just thinking about it was a sin. That he was sinning by just thinking about committing the sin. The German monk had said that many times a person sinned with his thought. Lollipop was sinning, he felt that he was sinning, he was afraid of God and he started running so as not to go on sinning. But he didn't run very far, he stopped on the corner, he couldn't stay too far away from the image. He looked into other windows, in that way he wasn't sinning. He put his hands into his pockets (he held his hands . . .), he turned his thoughts away. But now men returning to work after lunch were passing in front of him and a thought seized him: in a little while the other employees of the store would return and it would be impossible to take the Child. It would be impossible . . . And Lollipop went back to the store with religious objects.

There was the Child, and the Virgin was offering him to Lollipop. A clock struck one in the afternoon. The other employees wouldn't be long in returning. How many of them were there? Even if only one, the shop was so small that it would be impossible to take the Child. The Virgin seems to be telling him that. It's the Virgin who's telling him that if he doesn't take the Child now he won't be able to take it again, she seems to be saying just that. And it must have been she, yes, it was she, who made the young woman go behind the curtain in the back of the store and leave it empty. Yes, it was the Virgin who is now holding the Child out to Lollipop as far as her arms can reach and calling to him in her sweet voice:

"Take him and take care of him . . . Take good care of him . . ."

Lollipop comes forward. He sees hell and God's punishment, his hands and his head burn in a life that never ends. But he shakes his body as if tossing the vision far away from him, receives the Child that the Virgin hands him, holds it against his breast and disappears down the street.

He doesn't look at the Child. But he feels that now, held tightly against his chest, the Child is smiling, he's not hungry anymore, or thirsty, or cold. The Child is smiling the way the little black baby who was only a few months old smiled when he found himself in the warehouse and saw that Big João was giving him spoonfuls of milk with his enormous hands, while the Professor held him tight against the warmth of his chest.

That's how the Child was smiling.

FAMILY

It was Good-Life who told Pedro Bala that in the house there in Graça they had enough gold things to scare you. The owner of the house, from the looks of it, was a collector, Good-Life had heard a drifter say that there was a room in the house filled to the brim with gold and silver objects that would fetch a fortune in a pawnshop. That afternoon Pedro Bala went to take a look at the house with Good-Life. It was a modern, elegant building with a garden in front and a garage in back, the spacious residence of rich people. Good-Life spat between his teeth, making a flower on the sidewalk with his spit, and he said:

"And they say only two old-timers live in all this, how about that?"

"A wild setup . . ." Pedro Bala commented.

A maid opened the front door and went out into the garden. In the hallway, which was in their sight, they spotted pictures on the wall, statuettes on tables. Pedro Bala laughed:

"If Professor could see this he'd go out of his mind . . . I never saw anyone so hung up on books and painting."

"He's going to paint a picture of me this big . . ." and Good-Life showed the size by spreading out his arms.

Pedro Bala looked at the house again, moved a little closer to the garden, whistling. The maid was picking flowers and her white breasts were showing as she leaned over. Pedro Bala took a peek. They were white breasts, ending in red tips. Good-Life sighed beside him:

"There's gold in those hills, Bullet . . ."

"Shut up."

But the maid had already seen them and was looking at them as if to ask what they wanted. Pedro Bala took off his cap and asked:

"Could you give us a mug of water, please? The sun's knocking us out . . ." and he smiled, wiping his head with his cap as the sweat ran down. He was quite red in the sun, his long, blond hair hanging down over his ears in unkempt waves and the maid looked at him in a friendly way. Beside him Good-Life was smoking a cigar butt, with one foot on the garden fence. The maid first spoke to Good-Life with disdain:

"Get your foot off there . . ."

Then she smiled at Pedro Bala:

"I'll go get some water . . ."

She came back with two glasses of water and they were glasses such as they had never seen before, they were so pretty. They drank the water. Pedro Bala thanked her:

"Thanks a lot . . ." and in a low voice . . . "beautiful."

The maid also spoke in a low voice:

"Fresh kid . . ."

"What time do you get off work?"

"Watch your step. I've got my man. He waits for me at nine o'clock on that corner . . ."

"Well, tonight I'll be on the other one . . ."

They went down the street, Good-Life smoking his cigar butt, fanning his face with the straw hat he wore. Pedro Bala commented:

"I really am nice . . . It's all in the gab . . ."

Good-Life spat between his teeth again:

"With that female hair of yours too, all full of curls . . ."

Pedro Bala laughed and shook his fist at Good-Life:

"Don't be jealous, you halfbreed loafer . . ."

Good-Life changed the subject:

"What about the pile of gold?"

"First it's a job for Legless . . . Tomorrow he'll try to get into the house and spend a few days living there. After he finds out where the things are we'll come along, five or six of us, and get all the gold . . ."

"And you'll lose your little dish?"

"The maid? Tonight, right off . . . At nine o'clock sharp I'll be there . . ."

He turned around. He looked at the house. The maid was leaning over the fence. Pedro Bala waved. She answered. Good-Life spat:

"The damnedest luck, I've never seen the like of it."

The next day, around eleven-thirty in the morning, Legless put in an appearance at the front of the house. When he rang the bell the maid must have been still thinking about the night she'd spent with Pedro Bala in her room in Graça because she didn't hear the ringing. The boy rang again and in the window of a room on the second floor the gray head of a lady appeared as she squinted at Legless:

"What is it, son?"

"Lady, I'm a poor orphan . . ."

The lady signaled him to wait and in a few minutes she was at the door, not even listening to the maid's excuses for why she hadn't answered the bell:

"You can talk, son." She was looking at Legless's rags.

"Ma'am, I haven't got any father, my mother was called to heaven just a few days ago." He showed her a black ribbon on his arm, a ribbon he'd made from the band of Cat's new hat and Cat had raised hell. "I haven't got anybody in the world, I'm crippled, I can't do much work, I haven't set eyes on anything to eat for two days and I haven't got a place to sleep."

He looked as if he were about to cry. The lady watched him, very moved:

"Are you crippled, son?"

Legless showed her his lame leg, walked in front of her, exaggerating the defect. She looked at him with compassion:

"What did your mother die of?"

"I really don't know. She got something funny, poor thing, a bad fever, she kicked off in five days. And she left me alone in the world . . . If I could handle work I'd find something. But with this bad leg only in some private house. Don't you need a boy to run errands, help around the house? If you do, ma'am . . ."

And since Legless thought she was still undecided he finished it off cynically with a teary voice:

"If I wanted to I could join up with those boy bandits. With those Captains of the Sands as they're called. But I'm not like that, what I want is work. Except I can't take any heavy work. I'm a poor orphan, I'm hungry . . ."

But the lady wasn't undecided. She was remembering her son who had died at the same age as that one and who, when he died, had killed all her joy and that of her husband. The latter still had his art collection, but all she had was the memory of that son who'd left her so early. That's why she looked at ragged Legless with great warmth and when she spoke to him her voice had a sweetness different from her usual tone. There was something of a touch of joy in the softness of her voice that startled the servant:

"Come in, son. Let me find some work for you . . ." She put her thin aristocratic hand where a single stone flashed on Legless's dirty head and spoke to the servant. "Maria José, fix up the room over the garage for this boy. Show him the bathroom, give him a robe of Raul's, and then get him something to eat . . ."

"Before serving lunch, Dona Ester?"

"Before lunch, yes. He hasn't eaten for two days, poor thing."

Legless didn't say anything, he only dried his fake tears with the back of his hand.

"Don't cry . . ." the lady said, stroking the child's face.

"You're so good, ma'am. God will repay you . . ."

Then she asked what his name was and Legless gave the first name that came into his head:

"Augusto . . ." and as he repeated the name to himself so he wouldn't forget that his name was Augusto, at first he didn't see the emotion produced in the lady as she murmured:

"Augusto, the same name . . ."

As Legless was looking at her face now, she said aloud with emotion:

"My son's name was Augusto too . . . He died when he was just your size . . . But come in, son, go wash up for lunch."

Dona Ester went with him, deeply moved. She saw to it that the servant showed Legless the bathroom, gave him a robe, and went to the room over the garage to clean it up (the chauffeur had quit, the room was empty). Dona Ester came closer, said to Legless, who had stopped at the door of the bathroom:

"You can throw those clothes away. Maria José will bring you some clothes later . . ."

Legless watched the lady as she went away now and he was angry, but he didn't know whether at her or at himself.

Dona Ester sat down at her dressing-table, her eyes staring, anyone who saw her would have thought she was looking through the window at the sky. She really wasn't looking at anything, however, she didn't see anything. She was looking, yes, inside herself, at her memories of years ago and she saw a boy of Legless's age dressed in a sailor suit running in the garden of the other house, which they had moved out of after he died. He was a boy full of life and happiness, he liked to laugh and play. When he was tired of running with the cat, climbing on the seesaw in the garden, throwing the rubber ball in the yard for the German shepherd to catch, he would come and put his arms around Dona Ester's neck, kiss her cheek, and stay with her, looking at picture books, learning how to read and write the letters. In order to have him close to them for the longest time possible, Dona Ester and her husband had decided to teach their son his first lessons at home. One day (and Dona Ester's eyes filled with tears) the fever came. Then the small coffin went out the door and she watched it with eyes of horror, unable to comprehend that her son had died. His picture, an enlargement, is in her room but still covered by a cloth because she doesn't like looking at her son's face again so as not to revive her anguish. The clothes he wore are also all put away in his small trunk and they'll never be touched again. But now Dona Ester takes the keys out of her jewel box.

And slowly, very slowly, she goes to where the trunk is. She pulls over a chair and sits down in it. With trembling hands she opens the trunk, looks at the trousers and shirts, the sailor suit, the pajamas and nightshirts that he used to sleep in. She hugs the sailor suit to her breast as if she were embracing her son. Her tears pour forth.

Now a poor orphan boy had come knocking on her door. After the death of her son she hadn't wanted to have another, she didn't even like to see children playing so as not to renew the pain of her memories. But a poor orphan, crippled and sad, who said his name was Augusto, like her son's, had knocked at her door asking for food, shelter, and love. That's why she got up the courage to open the trunk where she kept the clothes her son had worn. Because for Dona Ester her son had come back today in the figure of this ragged, crippled child without father or mother. Her son had come back and her tears weren't only of grief. Her son had come back thin and hungry, with a crippled leg and dressed in rags. But in a short time he'll be the jolly, happy Augusto of those past years again, and once more he'll come and put his arms about her neck and read the big letters in his primer. Dona Ester gets up. She takes the blue sailor suit with her. And wearing it Legless eats the best lunch of his life.

If the sailor suit had been made to order for him it couldn't have been a better fit. It was perfect for Legless and when he saw himself in the hall mirror he didn't recognize himself. He'd washed, the maid had put lotion on his hair and perfume on his face. The sailor suit was great. Legless looked at himself in the mirror. He ran his hand over his head, then down his chest, smoothing the clothes, he smiled thinking about Cat. He would have given a million for Cat to have seen him looking so elegant. He had new shoes on too, but the truth is that he was a little put off by the shoes because they were tied with a ribbon and they looked a little like women's shoes. Legless found it strange to be dressed like a sailor wearing women's shoes. He went out into the garden because he wanted to have a smoke, he'd never given up having his puff after eating. Sometimes there hadn't been anything to eat but there'd always been a cigarette or cigar butt. He had to be careful there, he couldn't smoke openly. If they'd left him in the kitchen with the servants as they had in other houses he'd got into in order to rob them afterwards, he could have smoked, talked straight out in the language of the Captains of the Sands. But this time they'd washed him, dressed him up again, put lotion on his hair and perfume on his face. Then they'd fed him in the dining room. And during lunch the lady of the house had talked to him as if he'd been a properly brought up boy. Now she'd told him to go out into the garden and play where the yellow cat called Trinket was warming himself in the sun. Legless goes over to a bench, takes the packet of cheap cigarettes out of his pocket. When he'd changed clothes he hadn't forgotten the cigarettes. He lights one up and begins to savor a puff, thinking about his new life. He'd done that many times: going into a proper house as a poor, orphaned, crippled child and with those credentials spending the days needed to make a thorough inventory of the house, the places where valuables were kept, the easy exits for a getaway. Then the Captains of the Sands would raid the house one night, carry off the objects of value through the getaway exits and in the warehouse Legless would enjoy himself, overcome by a great joy, the joy of vengeance. Because in those houses even if they took him in, if they gave him food and a place to sleep, it was as though they were fulfilling a delicate duty. The owners of the house avoided coming close to him and left him in his filth, never had a good word for him. They would always look at him as if wondering when he was going to leave. And many times the lady of the house, who had been moved by his story told at the door in a weepy voice and who had taken him in, showed obvious signs of regret. Legless felt they were taking him in out of remorse. Because Legless thought that they were all to blame for the situation of all poor children. And he hated them all, with a deep hatred. His great and almost only joy was to calculate the despair of the family after the robbery, thinking that the hungry boy they had fed had been the one who had staked out the house for other hungry children to find its valuables.

But this time it was becoming different. This time they hadn't left him in the kitchen in his rags, they hadn't sent him out to sleep in the shed. They'd given him clothing, a room, fed him in the dining room. He was like a guest, like a beloved guest. And smoking his hidden cigarette (Legless was wondering why he was hiding to smoke), Legless is thinking and not understanding. He doesn't understand anything that's going on. His brow is wrinkled. He remembers the days in jail, the beating they gave him, the dreams that had never stopped pursuing him. And suddenly he has the fear that they'll be good to him in this house. He doesn't really know why, but he's afraid. And he gets up, comes out of his hiding place, and goes to smoke under the lady's window. In that way they'll see that he's a lost child, that he doesn't deserve a room, new clothes, food in the dining room. In that way they'll send him to the kitchen, he'll be able to carry out his work of vengeance, preserve the hatred in his heart. Because if that hatred disappears he'll die, he'll have no reason to live. And before his eyes passes the picture of the man in the vest who watches the policemen beat Legless and gives off a brutal laugh. That has to stop Legless from ever seeing Dona Ester's kind face, the protective gesture of Father José Pedro's hands, the solidness of the striker's muscles on João de Adão the stevedore. He will be all alone and his hatred will reach them all, black and white, men and women, rich and poor. That's why he's afraid for them to be good to him.

In the afternoon the master of the house, Raul, arrived home from his office. He was a well-known lawyer, he'd become wealthy in his profession, he was a professor at the Law School, but above all he was a collector. He had a fine gallery of paintings and he had some old coins, rare works of art. Legless saw him when he came in. At that moment Legless was looking at the picture in a children's book and laughing to himself at a silly elephant the monkey was tricking. Raul didn't see him, went upstairs. But then the maid came and called Legless and took him to Dona Ester's room, Raul was there in his shirtsleeves, smoking a cigarette, and he looked at the boy with an amused smile, now that Legless was putting on such a hangdog look on the threshold:

"Come in . . ."

Legless limped in, he didn't know where to put his hands. Dona Ester spoke in a kindly voice:

"Sit down, son, don't be afraid . . ."

Legless sat down on the edge of a chair and waited. The lawyer was studying him, looking at his face, but it was with sympathy and Legless was preparing his answers to the inevitable questions. He repeated the story he'd invented that morning, but when he began to weep abundant tears the lawyer ordered him to stop and got up, going over to the window. Legless saw that he'd been moved and the result of his art made him proud. He smiled to himself. But now the lawyer went over to Dona Ester and kissed her on the head and then on the lips. Legless lowered his eyes. Raul went over to him, laid his hand on his shoulder, and spoke:

"Stop it, you're not going to be hungry anymore. Go on . . . Go play, go look at your books. Tonight we're going to the movies. Do you like the movies?"

"Yes, sir, I do."

The lawyer sent him off with a wave. Legless went out but he still saw Raul go over to Dona Ester and say:

"You're a saint. We'll make a proper man of him . . ."

It was dusk, the lights were going on, and Legless thought that at that time the Captains of the Sands were running about the city looking for something to eat.

Too bad he couldn't cheer at the movies when the hero was beating the villain, the way he'd done the times he'd sneaked into the balcony at the Olímpia or at the movies in Itapagipe. There, at the Guarani, in the fine seats, he had to watch the film in silence and once, when he couldn't hold back a hiss, Raul looked at him. It's true that he was smiling, but it's also true that he gestured to Legless not to hiss anymore.

Then they took him to have an ice-cream soda at the stand across from the theater. While he was eating his ice cream Legless was thinking that he almost pulled an inevitable boner when the lawyer asked him what he wanted. He'd been about to ask for an ice-cold beer. But he caught himself in time and asked for a soda.

In the car the lawyer sat in the front driving and Legless sat in back with Dona Ester, who chatted with him. The conversation was difficult for Legless, who had to control his scant vocabulary, which was replete with dirty words. Dona Ester asked him things about his mother and Legless answered as best he could, making a great effort to remember the details he was inventing so that he wouldn't contradict himself afterwards. They finally got to the house in Graça and Dona Ester led Legless to the room over the garage:

"You aren't afraid to sleep alone, are you?"

"No, ma'am . . ."

"It'll only be for a few days. Then I'm going to put you up there in the room that should have been Augusto's . . ."

"You don't have to, Dona Ester, it's fine here."

She went over and kissed him on the cheek:

"Good night, son."

She went out, closing the door. Legless stood stock still, not moving, not even answering her "good night," his hand to his face at the spot where Dona Ester had kissed him. He wasn't thinking, wasn't seeking anything. Only the soft caress of the kiss, a caress such as he had never had, a mother's caress. Only the soft caress on his face. It was as if the world had stopped at the moment of the kiss and everything had changed. In the whole universe there was only the soft feel of that maternal kiss on Legless's face.

Afterwards came the horror of the dreams of jail, the man in the vest who laughed brutally, the policemen who were beating Legless, who ran around the small room on his crippled leg. But suddenly Dona Ester arrived and the man in the vest and the policemen died in infinite torture because now Legless was dressed in a sailor suit and had a whip in his hand like the hero in the movies.

A week had passed. Pedro Bala had come by the house several times to get news of Legless who was late in getting back to the warehouse. There had already been enough time for Legless to have found out where all the easy to carry objects in the house were and the exits they could use to facilitate their flight. But instead of Legless Pedro Bala saw the maid, who thought he'd come because of her. One day when he was chatting with the servant, Pedro Bala skillfully brought up the subject of Legless:

"The woman here has a son, doesn't she?"

"It's a boy she's taking care of. A nice fellow."

Pedro Bala smiled because he knew that when he wanted to, Legless could pass for the nicest boy in the world. And the maid went on:

"He's a little younger than you, but he's a boy just the same. He's not a no-good like you who's already sleeping with women . . ." and she laughed at Pedro Bala.

"You're the one who broke my cherry . . ."

"Don't be vulgar. Besides, it's a lie."

"I swear."

She would have liked it to have been that way and even if she was quite sure it wasn't, she liked his saying so. She not only felt like the boy's lover but a little like a mother too.

"Come today and I'll show you a nice way . . ."

"Tonight on the corner . . . But tell me something: haven't you been screwing with that boy there?"

"He doesn't know what it's all about . . . He's a booby. A spoiled child. You're out of your mind. You can't see that I wouldn't do it . . ."

Another time Pedro Bala managed to see Legless. He was stretched out in the garden (the cat was purring beside him), looking at a picture book and Pedro Bala was most startled when he saw him dressed in gray cashmere pants and a silk shirt. Legless's hair was even combed and Pedro Bala stood open-mouthed for a moment, not even whistling at Legless. Finally he came to and whistled. Legless stood up at once, saw the Bullet on the other side of the street. He signaled him to wait, went out through the gate after seeing that nobody from the house was around.

Pedro Bala walked to the corner and Legless accompanied him. When he got close Pedro Bala was even more surprised:

"Pew! You stink, Legless."

Legless made a face of distaste, but the Bullet went on:

"You're even more duded up than Cat. Jesus! If you ever

showed up like that at the den," that's what they called the warehouse, "the others would jump on you. You're a regular little sweetheart . . ."

"Lay off . . . I'm casing things. Pretty soon I'll take off and you can come with the others."

"You're taking your time this time . . ."

"It's because the things are better taken care of," Legless lied.

"Let's see if you can get things going."

Then he remembered:

"The Gringo was in bad shape. He was running almost a hundred and four. He almost kicked the bucket. If it hadn't been for Don'Aninha, who brewed up something for him that got him on his feet again, you wouldn't have seen him anymore. He's as skinny as a rail . . ."

And with that piece of news he went off, telling Legless again to hurry up.

Legless went back to lie down in the garden. But he wasn't seeing the pictures in the book now. He was seeing Gringo. Gringo was one of the ones in the gang that Legless teased the most. The son of Arabs, he spoke with a funny accent and that was cause for endless mocking on Legless's part. Gringo wasn't strong and he never got to be important among the Captains of the Sands, even though Pedro Bala and Professor tried to make it that way. They loved having a foreigner or near foreigner with them. But Gringo was content with petty thefts, he avoided risky attacks, and he thought up the idea of a trunkful of knick-knacks to sell on the street to maids from rich houses. Legless mistreated him mercilessly, making fun of him, of his tangled speech, of his lack of courage. But now, lying on the firm grass of the rich garden, wearing good clothes, combed and perfumed, a picture book beside him, Legless was thinking about Gringo's almost dying while he was eating well and wearing good clothes. It wasn't only Gringo who'd almost died. During that week the Captains of the Sands were still poorly clothed, poorly fed, sleeping in the rain in the warehouse or under the docks. During that time Legless was sleeping in a good bed, eating good food, he even had a lady who kissed him and called him son. He felt like a traitor to the group. He was just like that dockworker João de Adão talked about, spitting on the ground and rubbing it out as a sign of disgust. The dockworker who'd gone over to the other side during the big strike, to the side of the rich, had dropped out of the strike, had gone off to hire outsiders to work on the docks. No man on the waterfront had ever shaken his hand again, had ever treated him like a friend. And if anyone was an exception to Legless's hatred, which took in the whole world, it was the children who made up the Captains of the Sands. They were his comrades, they were just like him, they were the victims of all the rest, Legless was thinking. And now he felt that he was deserting them, going over to the other side. With that thought he jumped, sat up. No, he wouldn't betray them. Before anything else there was the law of the gang, the law of the Captains of the Sands. Those who broke it were expelled and nothing good awaited them in the world. And no one had ever broken it the way Legless was going to break it. In order to become a spoiled child, to become one of those children who were a perpetual source of mockery for them. No, he wouldn't betray them. Three days would have been enough for him to locate the objects of value in the house. But the meals, the clothes, the room, and more than the meals, the clothes, and the room, Dona Ester's love had made him stay a week already. He'd been bought by that love the way the stevedore had been bought with money. No, he wouldn't betray them. But then he thought that if he didn't he'd betray Dona Ester. She'd trusted in him. She, too, in her house had a law like the Captains of the Sands: she only punished when there was a wrong, she paid good with good. Legless was going to break that law, he was going to repay good with evil. He remembered that the other times when he ran away from a house so that it could be raided a great joy came over him. This time there was no joy at all. His hatred for everyone hadn't disappeared, that's true. But he'd made an exception for the people in that house because Dona Ester called him son and kissed him on the cheek. Legless was fighting with himself. He would have liked to have gone on in that life. But what good would that have been for the Captains of the Sands? And he was one of them, he would never cease being one of them because once the police had arrested him and had beaten him while a man in a vest laughed brutally. And Legless made up his mind. But he looked lovingly at the windows of Dona Ester's room and she, who was watching him, noticed that he was crying:

"Are you crying, son?" and she disappeared from the window to come over to him.

Only then did Legless see that he was indeed weeping, wiped away his tears, bit his hand. Dona Ester came over beside him:

"Are you crying, Augusto? Is something wrong?"

"No, ma'am. I'm not crying, I'm not . . ."

"Don't lie to me, son. I can see quite clearly . . . What happened? Are you thinking about your mother?"

And she pulled him over to her, sat down on the bench, rested Legless's head on her maternal breast.

"Don't cry for your mother. You've got another mamma now who loves you a lot and will do everything to take the place of the one you lost . . ." (. . . and he would do everything to take the place of the son she had lost, Legless heard inside himself).

Dona Ester kissed him on the cheek where the tears were streaming:

"Don't cry, your mamma will be sad."

Then Legless's lips opened wide and he sobbed, wept huddled against his mother's breast. And while he hugged her and let himself be kissed, he wept because he was going to abandon her and, worse than that, rob her. And she would never know perhaps that Legless felt he was going to rob himself too. As she didn't know that his weeping, his sobs were a way of asking forgiveness.

Events moved quickly because Raul had to take a trip to Rio de Janeiro on important legal business. And Legless thought there was no better time for the raid.

On the afternoon he left he looked all over the house, petted Trinket the cat, chatted with the maid, looked at the picture

books. Then he went to Dona Ester's room, said that he was
going to take a walk to Campo Grande. She told him then that
Raul was bringing a bicycle back from Rio for him and then
every afternoon he could ride in Campo Grande instead of
walking. Legless lowered his eyes but before going out he went
over to Dona Ester and kissed her. It was the first time he'd
kissed her and she was very happy. He spoke in a low voice,
pulling the words out of himself:

"You're very good. I'll never forget you . . ."

He left and didn't come back. That night he slept in his corner in the warehouse. Pedro Bala had gone with a group to
the house. The others had surrounded Legless admiring his
clothes, his neat hair, the perfume that evaporated off his
body. But Legless shoved one of them away, went mumbling to
his corner. And there he stayed, biting his nails, not sleeping,
in anguish until Pedro Bala returned with the others, bringing
the results of their burglary. He told Legless that no one was the
wiser in the house, that they'd all kept on sleeping. Maybe the
next day they'd discover the robbery. And he displayed the gold
and silver objects:

"Tomorrow González will give us a pile for this . . ."

Legless closed his eyes so as not to see. After they'd all gone
to sleep he went over to Cat:

"Do you want to make a deal with me?"

"What is it?"

"I'll swap these clothes for yours . . ."

Cat looked at him in surprise. His clothes were the best
without any doubt. But they were old clothes, far from being
worth as much as the fine cashmere clothing Legless was wearing. "He's nuts," Cat thought while he answered:

"Swap? Don't even ask."

They exchanged clothes. Legless went back to his corner,
tried to sleep.

On the street Doctor Raul was coming along with two
policemen. They were the same ones who had beaten him in
jail. Legless ran but Doctor Raul pointed him out and the soldiers took him to the same room. The scene was the same as
ever: the police who amused themselves by making him run on

his gimpy leg and beat him and the man in the vest who was laughing. Except that Dona Ester was also in the room and looking at him with sad eyes and saying that he was no longer her son, that he was a thief. And Dona Ester's eyes made him suffer more than the soldiers' blows, more than the man's brutal laughter.

He woke up bathed in sweat, he fled from the night of the warehouse, dawn found him wandering over the sand.

The next day, in the evening, they came to bring him his share in the theft. But Legless refused it without any explanation. Then Dry Gulch arrived with a paper that had news of Lampião. The Professor read the item for Dry Gulch and stayed looking at other things in the paper. Then he called:

"Legless! Legless!"

Legless came over. Others came with him and formed a circle. Professor said:

"This here is about you, Legless . . ."

And he read an item in the paper:

Yesterday the son of the householders at number . . . street, Graça, Augusto by name, disappeared. He must have got lost in the city, with which he was unfamiliar. He limps on one leg, is thirteen years of age, very shy, and wearing gray cashmere clothes. The police are looking for him to bring him back to his afflicted parents, but so far they have failed to find him. The family would be grateful for any news of little Augusto and for his return home.

Legless was silent. He was biting his lip. Professor said:

"They still haven't discovered the robbery . . ."

Legless nodded. When they discovered the robbery they wouldn't be looking for him as a lost son anymore. Outrigger put on a merry face and shouted:

"Your mommy's looking for you, Legless. Your mommy's looking for you so she can suckle you . . ."

But he didn't say anything else because Legless was already on top of him and raising his knife. And doubtless he would have stabbed the little black boy if Big João and Dry Gulch hadn't pulled him off. Outrigger ran off in fright. Legless went back to his corner with a look of hatred for everyone. Pedro Bala followed him, put his hand on his shoulder:

"Maybe they'll never discover the robbery, Legless. Never find out about you . . . It doesn't matter."

"When Doctor Raul gets back they'll find out . . ."

And he burst into sobs that left the Captains of the Sands puzzled. Only Pedro Bala and the Professor understood and the latter threw up his hands because he couldn't do anything. Pedro Bala started up a long conversation on a completely different subject. Outside the wind ran over the sand and its sound was like a moan.

PICTURE-BOOK MORNING

Pedro Bala, as he goes up the Montanha slope, is thinking that there's nothing better in the world than walking like that, with no set destination, through the streets of Bahia. Some of those streets are paved with asphalt, but most of them, the great majority, are paved with black stones. Girls lean out the windows of former mansions and no one can tell if it's a seamstress romantically waiting to marry a rich sweetheart or a prostitute looking at him from an ancient balcony with some very few floral decorations. Women with black veils are going into churches. The sun beats down on the stones or the asphalt of the pavement, it illuminates the tile roofs. On the terrace of a big town house flowers thrive in sad tin cans. They're of different colors and the sun is giving them their daily ration of light. The bells of the Conceição Praia church are calling the veiled women who hurry past. Halfway up the slope a black man and a mulatto are bent over a pair of dice that the black has just rolled. Pedro Bala greets him as he passes:

"How are things, White Owl?"

"What about you, Bullet? How's the sweet talk going?"

But the mulatto had already thrown the dice and the black man turned back to the game. Pedro Bala goes on his way. The Professor goes with him. His thin figure leans forward as if he had difficulty in climbing the slope. But he's still smiling at the

festive day. Pedro Bala turns to him and catches his smile. The
city is happy, full of sun. "Bahia days are like holidays," Pedro
Bala thinks as he too is filled with happiness. He whistles
loudly, gives a smiling pat on the Professor's shoulder. And the
two of them give off a laugh that turns into a cackle. But they
only have a few coins in their pockets, they're dressed in rags,
don't know what they'll eat. They're full of the beauty of the
day, however, of the freedom to walk through the streets of
the city. And they go along laughing with nothing that they
have to do, Pedro Bala with his arm over Professor's shoulder.
From where they are they can see the market and the sloop
dock and even the old warehouse where they sleep. Pedro Bala
leans against a wall on the slope and says to the Professor:

"You should paint a picture of this . . . It's wild."

Professor's face tightens:

"I know it'll never be . . ."

"What?"

"Sometimes I catch myself thinking . . ." and the Professor
looks at the docks down below, the sloops looking like toys,
the tiny men carrying sacks on their backs.

He goes on in a harsh voice, as if someone had struck him:

"I've thought about doing a little painting from here someday . . ."

"You've got the gift. If you could have gone to school . . ."

". . . but it can't ever be a happy piece, no . . ." (Professor
doesn't seem to have heard Pedro Bala's interruption. His eyes
are looking far away now and he seems even frailer.)

"Why?" Pedro Bala is startled.

"Can't you see that all this is really something beautiful?
Everything so happy . . ."

Pedro Bala points at the roofs of the lower city:

"It's got more colors than the rainbow . . ."

"That's right . . . But if you look at the people everything is
sad. I'm not talking about the rich ones. You know. I'm talking about the others, the ones on the docks, in the market. You
know . . . All of them with hungry faces, I don't know how to
say it. It's something I can feel . . ."

Pedro Bala wasn't surprised anymore:

"That's why João de Adão had a little strike on the docks. He says that things are going to change someday, everything's going to be just the opposite . . ."

"I read that in a book too . . . One of João de Adão's books. If I could have gone to school like you say it would have been good. I would have painted a nice picture someday. A nice day, happy people walking, laughing, falling in love just like the people in Nazaré, you know. But what school? I try to draw a happy picture, the day all pretty, everything pretty, but the people come out sad, I don't know . . . I was trying to draw something happy."

"Who can say, maybe it's better that you drew what you did. It might even be prettier, get more attention."

"What do you know about it? What do I know? We never went to school . . . I want to draw people's faces, the layout of the streets, but I never had any school, there's a whole lot I don't know . . ."

He paused, looked at Pedro Bala who was looking at him, went on:

"Have you ever taken a look at the School of Fine Arts? It's a real beauty, kid. One day I sneaked in, went into a room. They were all wearing smocks, they didn't even see me. And they were painting a naked woman . . . If only someday I could . . ."

Pedro Bala remained thoughtful. He was looking at the Professor as if thinking. Then he spoke in a very serious vein:

"Do you know how much it costs?"

"How much what costs?"

"The school. The teacher."

"What's this all about?"

"We could chip in, pay your . . ."

Professor laughed:

"You've got no idea . . . It's all so complicated . . . It can't be done, no, stop being foolish."

"João de Adão said that one day there'll be schools for everybody . . ."

They kept on walking. The Professor seemed to have lost the joy of the day. As if it had got far away from him. Then Pedro Bala gave him a soft punch:

"Someday you're going to have a couple of paintings in a gallery on the Rua Chile, buddy. Without school or anything else. None of those shitty schools can stand up to you . . . You've got it in you . . ."

Professor laughed. Pedro Bala laughed too:

"And you'll paint my picture, eh? Put my name underneath, right? Captain Pedro Bala, brave man."

He took a boxer's pose, one arm stuck out. Professor laughed, Pedro Bala laughed too, then the laugh turned into a cackle. And he only stopped laughing to go over to a group of idlers who'd gathered around a guitar player. The man was playing and singing a Bahian song:

> When she said goodby to me . . .
> My heart became a cross . . .

They joined the group. A while later they were singing along with the man. And everybody sang along with them, there were sloopmen, drifters, stevedores, even a prostitute was singing. The man with the guitar was completely given over to his music, he didn't even see anyone.

If the man hadn't got up to go away, still playing his guitar and singing, they would have forgotten to keep on climbing to the upper city. But the man went away, taking the joy of his music along. The group dispersed, a newsboy went by hawking the morning papers. The Professor and Pedro Bala went on up the hillside. From the Largo do Teatro they went up the Rua Chile. The Professor took the chalk out of his pocket, sat down on the sidewalk. Pedro Bala stood next to him. When they saw the couple coming Professor began to sketch. He drew as quick a picture as he could. The couple was very near now, Professor was drawing their faces. The girl was smiling, they were sweethearts no doubt. But they were so involved in their conversation that they didn't even notice the drawing. Pedro Bala had to step in front of them:

"Don't step on the young lady's face, sir . . ."

The man looked at Pedro Bala and was just about to curse

him when the girl saw the Professor's sketch and called his attention to it:

"That's good . . ." and she clapped her hands like a little girl who had just been given a present of a doll.

The young man spotted it and smiled. He turned to Pedro Bala:

"Did you draw that, kid?"

"My buddy here did, Professor, the painter . . ."

Professor was giving the last touches to the man's stylish mustache. Then he went on to perfect the girl's sketch. She stood like someone who was posing then. They both laughed, she leaned on her boyfriend's arm. The man took out his change purse, tossed a two *milreis* silver coin that Pedro Bala caught in midair. They went on their way. The drawing stayed behind in the middle of the sidewalk. Some young women coming from shopping saw it from a distance and one of them said:

"Hurry up, that looks like an ad for Barrymore's new movie . . . They say it's great . . . And he's a dream . . ."

Pedro Bala and the Professor heard that and burst out laughing. And hugging each other they went off together in the freedom of the streets.

Almost alongside the government palace they stopped again. Professor stood with the chalk in his hand waiting for a "mark" to get off the trolley. Pedro Bala was whistling beside him. In a while they had enough money for a good lunch and enough left over for a gift for Clara, God's-Love's girlfriend, whose birthday it was.

A big old woman gave ten cents for her picture. The old woman was ugly and the Professor had preserved her ugliness in the picture. Pedro Bala observed:

"If you'd made her younger and prettier she would have given you more."

Professor laughed. That's how they spent the morning, Professor sketching the faces of those who came down the street, Pedro Bala picking up the silver pieces and coins they tossed them. Almost by noontime a man was coming along smoking

with an expensive-looking cigarette holder. Pedro Bala ran to
tell the Professor:

"Draw the guy coming along, he looks like a first-class
'mark.'"

Professor began to sketch the man's thin face. The long cigarette holder, the curly hair showing under his hat. The man was
also carrying a book in his hand and Professor had an irresist-
ible urge to draw the man reading the book. The man was
passing by, Pedro Bala caught his attention:

"Look at your picture, sir."

The man took the long cigarette holder out of his mouth,
asked the Bullet:

"What, son?"

Pedro Bala pointed to the drawing the Professor was working on. The man was seen to be sitting down (there wasn't a
chair or anything, he was sitting on air), smoking through his
holder and reading his book. His curly hair flowed out from
under his hat. The man examined the sketch carefully, looked
at it from several angles, didn't say anything. When the Professor finished his work, he asked him:

"Where did you learn to sketch, my boy?"

"Nowhere . . ."

"Nowhere? What do you mean?"

"Just that, sir . . ."

"So how is it you can draw?"

"I feel like it, I pick up a piece of chalk, I draw."

The man was a little incredulous, but he no doubt thought
about other examples deep in his memory:

"Do you mean you never studied drawing?"

"Never, no, sir."

"I can guarantee it," Pedro Bala put in. "We live together
and I know."

"Then you've got a real talent . . ." the man murmured.

He examined the sketch again. He took a long drag on
his cigarette holder. Both boys were looking at the holder,
bewitched. The man asked Professor:

"Why did you draw me sitting down and reading a book?"

Professor scratched his head as if it were a difficult question to answer. Pedro Bala tried to speak, but he didn't say anything, he was perplexed. Finally the Professor explained:

"I thought it suited you better . . ." he scratched his head again. "I really don't know . . ."

"It's a real talent . . ." the man murmured in a lower voice, like someone who'd made a discovery.

Pedro Bala was waiting for the coin because the policeman on the corner was looking at them mistrustfully. Professor was looking at the man's cigarette holder, forged, a metal wonder. But the man went on:

"Where do you live?"

Pedro Bala didn't give the Professor a chance to answer. It was he who spoke:

"We live in the Cidade de Palha . . ."

The man put his hand into his pocket and took out a card:

"Can you read?"

"We can, yes, sir," Professor answered.

"Here's my address. I want you to come look me up. Maybe I can do something for you."

Professor took the card. The policeman was walking toward them. Pedro Bala took his leave:

"So long, doctor."

The man was taking out his coin purse, but he saw the Professor's gaze on his cigarette holder. He threw the cigarette away, handed the holder to the boy.

"That's for my picture. Come to my place . . ."

But they had both run off down the Rua Chile because the policeman was almost beside them already. The man was watching as if he only half understood when he heard the policeman's voice:

"Did they steal anything from you, sir?"

"No. Why?"

"Because since those hoodlums were here beside you . . ."

"They were two children . . . One of them has a wonderful gift for painting."

"They're thieves," the policeman retorted. "They're two of the Captains of the Sands."

CAPTAINS OF THE SANDS

"Captains of the Sands?" the man said, remembering. "I read something about it . . . Aren't they abandoned children?"

"Thieves is what they are . . . Be careful when they get close to you, sir. Check and see if anything is missing . . ."

The man shook his head no and looked down the street. But there was no trace of the two boys. The man thanked the policeman, saying once more that he hadn't been robbed and he went down the street murmuring:

"That's the way great artists are lost. What a painter he would make!"

The policeman was watching him. Then he said to the buttons on his uniform:

· "They're right when they say poets are crazy . . ."

Professor was showing off the holder. He was behind a tall building where there was a fashionable restaurant now. Pedro Bala knew how to get lunch leftovers from the chef. They were waiting for their lunch on the deserted street. After they ate, Pedro Bala offered the Professor a cigarette and he got ready to smoke it with the holder the man had given him. He tried to clean it:

"The guy was skinny as a rail. He might be a big shot . . ."

Since he couldn't find anything better to clean it with, he rolled up the man's card and shoved it through the holder. When he was through he tossed the card into the street. Pedro Bala asked:

"Why don't you keep it?"

"What do I want it for?" And the Professor laughed. Pedro Bala laughed too and for a moment their laughter filled the street. They laughed that way with no other reason than just for the pleasure of laughing.

But Pedro Bala became serious:

"The man looked like he might have been able to help you be a painter . . ." He picked up the card and read the man's name. "You should keep it. Who can tell?"

Professor lowered his head:

"Don't be a fool, Bullet. You know damned well that the only thing we'll ever get to be is thieves . . . Who cares about

us? Who? Nothing but thieves, just thieves . . ." and his voice
grew louder, now he was shouting with hate.

Pedro Bala nodded agreement, his hand dropped the card,
which fell into the gutter. They weren't laughing anymore now
and they were sad in the joy of the morning full of sun, of the
morning just like a painting in an art museum.

Workmen passed on their way to work after their meager
lunch, and that was all they saw, all they managed to see in the
morning.

MILK POX

Omolu sent the black pox into the city. But the rich people up above there got vaccinated and Omolu was a goddess from the jungles of Africa, she didn't know about things like vaccines. And the smallpox descended to the poor people's city and made people sick, laid black people full of sores onto their beds. Then the men from public health came, put the sick people into bags, carried them off to the distant pesthouse. The women stayed behind weeping because they knew they would never see them again.

Omolu had sent the black pox to the upper city, the city of the rich. Omolu didn't know about vaccines, Omolu was a goddess from the jungles of Africa, what could she know of vaccines and scientific things? But since smallpox had already been turned loose (and the black pox was terrible), Omolu had to let it go down to the city of the poor. Since she had already turned it loose she had to let it get on with its work. But since Omolu felt sorry for her poor little children, she reduced the strength of the black pox, turned it into milk pox, which is a white and mild pox, almost like measles. In spite of that the men from public health came and carried the sick off to the pesthouse. There the families couldn't visit them, they had nobody, only the visits from the doctor. They died without anyone's knowing and when one of them managed to return

he was looked upon as a corpse that had risen. The newspapers talked about a smallpox epidemic and the need for
vaccination. The *candomblés* beat their drums night and
day, in honor of Omolu, to placate the fury of Omolu. The
pai-de-santo priest of Paim, from Pineapple Hill, a favorite of
Omolu's, embroidered a white silk scarf with spangles to offer
Omolu and placate her wrath. But Omolu rejected it, Omolu
was fighting against the vaccine.

Women were weeping in houses of the poor. Out of fear of
the milk pox, out of fear of the pesthouse.

Almiro was the first of the Captains of the Sands to come
down with milk pox. One night when the little black boy Outrigger went to look for him in his corner to make love (the love
Pedro Bala had forbidden in the warehouse), Almiro told him:

"I've got a devilish itch."

He showed Outrigger his arms, already full of blisters:

"I seem to be burning up with fever too."

Outrigger was a brave little boy, the whole gang knew that.
But Outrigger had a crazy fear of smallpox, Omolu's ailment,
a fear accumulated inside him by many African races. And
without worrying about his sexual relations with Almiro being
discovered he ran among the groups shouting:

"Almiro's got smallpox . . . People, Almiro's got smallpox."

The boys soon got up and moved cautiously away from the
place where Almiro was. He began to sob. Pedro Bala hadn't
come in yet. Professor, Cat, and Big João were also out. Therefore it was Legless who took charge of the situation. Legless
had been more withdrawn than ever lately, he spoke to practi-
cally no one. He was wild in his mocking of everybody, he
started fights everywhere, he only respected Pedro Bala. Lollipop prayed for him more than for anyone and sometimes he
thought that Satan had got into Legless's body. Father José
Pedro was patient with him, but Legless had withdrawn from
the priest too. He didn't want to have anything to do with anyone, a conversation begun with him was a conversation that
ended up in a fight.

When Legless went through the groups they all backed off.

They were almost afraid of him as of the smallpox. During those days Legless had picked up a dog to whom he dedicated himself entirely. At first, when the dog appeared in the warehouse, famished, Legless mistreated him as much as he could. But he ended up petting him and taking him under his wing. Now it seemed that he only lived for the dog. And, therefore, he only went back to remove the dog, who'd come along, far from Almiro. Then he returned to where the boys were. They were surrounding Almiro from a distance. They pointed at the pustules that were showing on the boy's chest. Before anything else Legless spoke to Outrigger in his nasal voice:

"Now you're going to have smallpox on your prick, you black jackass."

Outrigger looked at him in terror. Then Legless spoke to everybody, pointing to Almiro:

"Nobody here's going to come down with smallpox just because of this fairy."

They all looked at him, waiting for what he was going to say. Almiro was sobbing, his hands to his face, huddled against the wall. Legless was speaking:

"He's getting out of here right now. He can go stick himself in some alley until the dogcatchers from public health pick him up and take him off to the pesthouse."

"No, no," Almiro roared.

"Yes, you're going," Legless said. "We're not calling the dogcatchers here for the police to find out where we're hiding out. You can go nicely or by force, and take your rags with you. You can go to hell because we're not going to catch smallpox because of you. Because of any love for you, faggot . . ."

Almiro said no, no, and his sobs filled the warehouse. Little black Outrigger was trembling, Lollipop proclaimed it to be the punishment of God because of their sins, the rest didn't know what to say. Legless was getting ready to force him to leave. Lollipop hugged a picture of Our Lady and said:

"Let's everybody pray because this is a punishment of God for our sins. We've done a lot of sinning, God is punishing us. Let's ask for forgiveness . . ." and his voice was like a great outcry sounding the arrival of vengeance.

Some clasped their hands and Lollipop started an Our Father. But Legless shooed him off with his hand:

"Beat it, sexton . . ."

Lollipop kept on praying in a low voice, still hugging the saint. It was a strange-looking picture. In the background Almiro was sobbing and saying no. Lollipop was praying, the others were indecisive, not knowing what to do. Outrigger trembled with fear, thinking that he'd caught it. Legless spoke again:

"People, if he doesn't want to leave we'll kick him out with a good clubbing. If not we'll all die of smallpox, all of us . . . Can't you see, damn you? Kick him out into the street where they can pick him up for the pesthouse."

"No. No," Almiro was saying. "For the love of God."

"This is a punishment," Lollipop said.

"Shut your mouth, you son of a priest," Legless went on. "Let's carry him out, people, since he refuses to go peacefully."

When he saw that the others were still undecided he marched over beside Almiro and put out his foot to give him a kick:

"So you're going out, pocky."

Almiro huddled all the more:

"No. You can't do this. I'm a member of the gang. Wait till the Bullet gets here."

"It's punishment . . . It's punishment . . ." Lollipop's voice annoyed Legless all the more and he gave a kick to Almiro.

"Get out, pocky. Get out, faggot."

But at that instant a hand grabbed him and pushed him away. Dry Gulch planted himself between Almiro and Legless. The Halfbreed had a revolver in his hand and his eyes were flashing:

"I swear it's loaded and if anybody so much as touches Almiro . . ." He looked at them all with a somber face.

"What business is it of yours, bandit?" Legless tried to regain control of the situation.

"He's not a cop for people to treat that way. He's a member of the gang, he was telling it straight. We're going to wait till Pedro Bala gets here. He'll decide. And if anybody touches him I'll shoot him down just like he was a stinking cop," and he clutched the revolver.

The others withdrew after a while. Legless spat:

"They're all cowards . . ." and he went over to where the dog was waiting for him. He lay down beside him and those closest heard him mutter: "Cowards, cowards."

Dry Gulch remained in front of Almiro with the revolver in his hand. Almiro was sobbing, and he cried out in a loud voice when he saw the blisters spreading over his body. Lollipop was praying, asking God to become supreme goodness again, not to be supreme justice.

Later Lollipop remembered that he ought to call Father José Pedro. He slipped out the door of the warehouse, went to the priest's home. But along the way he kept on praying, his eyes wide, full of the fear of God.

Pedro Bala arrived in the company of the Professor and Big João. They were coming back from some business they had to attend to and were commenting on their success amidst loud laughter. Cat had gone with them but he didn't come back. He'd stayed at Dalva's. The three of them came into the warehouse and the first thing they caught sight of was Dry Gulch with the revolver in his hand.

"What's all this?" Pedro Bala asked.

Legless got up out of his corner, the dog followed him:

"This bastard acting like a *cangaceiro* won't let us do what we've got to do," and he pointed to Almiro. "That fairy's got smallpox . . ."

Big João recoiled. Pedro Bala looked at Almiro, the Professor went over to Dry Gulch. The Halfbreed didn't put away his revolver. Then Pedro Bala asked:

"What happened, Dry Gulch?"

"This one's got the damned thing . . ." He pointed to the sobbing boy. "And that bastard, just like a cop, wanted to kick him out into the street so the public health people could take him off to the pesthouse. I wouldn't have got involved. But he didn't want to go. And all of them there," he spat, "tried to make him go. That was when he said he was a member of the

gang and that they should wait till you got back. I thought he
was right, I took his side . . . He's no cop to be treated like
that . . ."

"You did right, Dry Gulch." Pedro Bala patted the Halfbreed
on the back. Then he looked at Almiro. "Have you really got it?"

The boy lowered his head and burst into sobs. Legless shouted:

"The only thing to do is what I said. We can't call public
health here because everybody will find out where we're hanging out. All we can do is leave him on some street where there
are people. Let's do it whether he wants to or not . . ."

Pedro Bala shouted:

"Who's in charge here, you or me? Do you want me to bust
you one?"

Legless went off muttering. The dog came over to lick his
feet but he gave him a kick. But then he was sorry and petted
the dog while he looked at the others.

Pedro Bala went over to Almiro. Big João was trying to
overcome his fear and go over to Almiro too. But the fear of
smallpox was something big in him, it was almost bigger than
his goodness. Only Professor went with Pedro Bala. The latter
said to Almiro:

"Let me see . . ."

Almiro showed his arms full of boils. Professor said:

"It's milk pox. Black pox gets dark right away . . ."

Pedro Bala was thinking. There was silence all through the
warehouse. Big João managed to conquer his fear and went
over. But he was dragging his feet. He seemed to be going
against his own will getting close to Almiro. That was when
Lollipop came in accompanied by Father José Pedro. The
priest said good evening and asked which one was sick. Lollipop pointed to Almiro, the priest went over to him, went up
close, picked up his arm, examined it. Then he said to Pedro
Bala:

"We've got to get him to public health . . ."

"To the pesthouse?"

"Yes."

"No, he's not going," Pedro Bala said.

Legless got up again and came over to them:

"I've been saying that all along. He's got to go to the pest-house."

"He's not going," Pedro Bala repeated.

"Why, my son?" Father José asked.

"You know, Father. Nobody comes back from the pesthouse. Nobody comes back. And he's one of us, a member of the gang. We can't do that . . ."

"But it's the law, my son . . ."

"To die?"

The priest looked at Pedro Bala with wide eyes. Those boys always seemed to surprise him, always more advanced in intelligence than he thought. And underneath it all, the priest knew that they were right.

"He's not going, no, Father . . ." Pedro Bala asserted.

"Then what are you going to do, my son?"

"Take care of him here . . ."

"But how?"

"I'll call Don'Aninha . . ."

"But she doesn't know how to take care of anyone."

Pedro Bala was confused. After a moment he said:

"It's better for him to die here than in the pesthouse . . ."

Legless spoke up again:

"He's going to give us all smallpox . . ." He turned to the others. "He's going to infect everybody. We can't let him."

"Shut up, you bastard, or I'll lay you out," Pedro said.

But the priest intervened:

"He's right, Bullet."

"He's not going to the pesthouse, Father. You're a good man, you know very well that he can't go. It's awful there, everybody dies."

The priest knew quite well that it was true, he remained silent. That was when Big João spoke up:

"But doesn't he have a home?"

"Who?"

"Almiro. Yes, he's got one."

"I don't want to go there . . ." Almiro sobbed. "I ran away."

Pedro Bala went over to him and spoke very calmly:

"Take it easy, Almiro. I'll go first, talk to your mother. Then

we'll take you. You'll be all right there, you won't have to go to
the pesthouse. And Father will find a doctor to take care of
you, won't you, Father?"

"I'll find one, yes," Father José Pedro promised.

There was a law that obliged all citizens to report to public
health all cases of smallpox they knew about so that those
infected could immediately be taken to houses of quarantine.
Father José Pedro knew the law, but, more than once, he was
with the Captains of the Sands and against the law.

Pedro Bala went to Almiro's house, the boy's mother acted
crazy, she was a poor washerwoman living with a workman
from beyond the Cidade de Palha. They came to get Almiro
and the priest visited him and brought a doctor. But it turned
out that the doctor was after a position in public health and he
reported the case of smallpox. Almiro was taken to the pesthouse just the same and the priest was in a jam because the
doctor (who said he was a freethinker but really was a spiritu-
alist) reported the priest too as hiding the case. The authorities
didn't charge the priest but they complained to the Archdiocese. And Father José Pedro was called before the Canon Secretary of the Archbishop. He was frightened.

Heavy curtains, high-backed chairs, a portrait of Saint Igna-
tius on one wall. On the other a crucifix. A large table, expensive carpets. Father José Pedro came into the room with his
heart beating rapidly. He wasn't absolutely sure of the reasons
he'd received that message from the Canon Secretary of the
Archdiocese to appear at the Episcopal Palace. At first he
remembered the parish he'd been waiting for uselessly for two
years. Would it be his parish? He smiled with joy. Then, yes,
he was going to be a real priest, he was going to have souls
assigned to him, under his guidance. He would serve God. But
a certain sadness came over him: his children, the abandoned
children of the streets of Bahia, especially the Captains of the
Sands, what would become of them? He was one of their
few friends. No other priest had ever turned to those boys.
They were content to celebrate an occasional mass at the Re-

formatory, which made them even more hateful to the boys because it delayed the meager breakfast. Father José Pedro, while waiting for his parish, had dedicated himself to the abandoned boys. It couldn't be said that the results were great. But it was necessary to understand that he was conducting an experiment, that lots of times he had to start all over. It had only been a short time that the priest had gained the boys' complete trust. They treated him like a friend now, even though they didn't take him seriously as a priest. He had to overlook many things in order to gain the trust of the Captains of the Sands. But for José Pedro Lollipop and his vocation were enough to pay for his trouble. The priest had to do a lot of things that went against what he'd been taught. He had even made pacts with things that the Church had condemned. But it was the only way . . . At that point the priest remembered that it might be because of those things that he'd been summoned. It must have been because of that. A lot of church biddies were already gossiping about his relationship with children who lived by stealing. And there was that matter with Almiro. It must have been because of that. The first feeling Father José Pedro had when he realized the reason for the message was one of great fear. He was certainly going to be punished, he would lose all hope of a parish. And Father José Pedro needed a parish. He was supporting an old mother, a sister in Normal School. Then he thought that very possibly everything he'd done had been wrong, that his superiors wouldn't approve. And, at the seminary, they had taught him to obey. But he thought about the children. Through his memory passed the figures of Lollipop, Pedro Bala, Professor, Legless, Good-Life, Cat. It was necessary to save those little ones . . . Children were Christ's greatest concern. Everything had to be done to save those children. It wasn't their fault that they were lost . . .

The canon entered. In his thoughts the priest hadn't noticed that he'd been waiting a long time. Nor had he seen the canon enter with a soft step. He was tall and very thin, angular, with a clean cassock, what little hair he had left was carefully combed. His lips had a hard line. A rosary hung around his neck. Although his appearance gave an impression of purity, that impression didn't make his features any softer. There was no human kindness in his face, in his hard features. As if purity were a suit of armor that kept him away from the world. They said he was quite intelligent, a great preacher, famous for the strictness of his habits. There he was, standing in front of Father José Pedro, looking with observant eyes at the priest's short figure, his dirty cassock mended in two places, his frightened look, the lack of intelligence that, mixed with goodness, was reflected on the priest's face. He studied the priest for a few minutes. Enough to penetrate José Pedro's uncomplicated soul. He coughed. The priest saw him, got up, humbly kissed his hand:

"Canon . . ."

"Sit down, Father. We've got to have a talk."

He was looking at the priest's expressionless eyes. He sat down, carefully crossing his hands, drew his gleaming cassock away from Father José Pedro's dirty one. His voice contrasted with his person. It might be said that it was a soft voice, almost feminine, if there had not been a tone of decision that came out at every step along the way. Father José Pedro lowered his head and waited for the canon to speak. He began:

"This Archdiocese has received some serious complaints about you, Father."

Father José Pedro tried to put on the face of someone who didn't understand. But animosity was superior to his intelligence and at that moment he was thinking about the Captains of the Sands. The canon smiled slightly:

"I think you know what it's all about . . ."

The priest looked at him with open eyes, but then he lowered his head:

"Only if it's the children . . ."

"The sinner cannot hide his sin, it is visible in his conscience . . ." and the canon's voice had lost that note of softness.

Father José Pedro listened with terror. It was what he had feared. His superiors, those people who had the intelligence to understand God's desires, were not in agreement with the methods he had used with the Captains of the Sands. A fear was growing inside himself, not really a fear of the canon, of the Archbishop, but a fear of having offended God. And even his hands were trembling slightly.

The canon's voice took on its softness again. It was like a woman's voice, sweet and soft, but of one who denied a man her caresses:

"We've received a fair number of complaints, Father José Pedro. The Archbishop has closed his eyes in the hope that you would recognize your error and correct it . . ."

He looked at the priest with stern eyes. José Pedro lowered his head.

"Not long ago the widow Santos complained that you were helping a bunch of urchins on a square make fun of her. Rather, you were encouraging the urchins to make fun of her . . . What have you got to say, Father?"

"It's not true, Canon . . ."

"Are you telling me that the widow was lying?"

He ran the priest through with his eyes. But this time José Pedro didn't lower his head, he only repeated:

"What she said wasn't true . . ."

"You know that the widow Santos is one of the best supporters of religion in Bahia, don't you? You should see her gifts . . ."

"I can tell you the facts . . ."

"Don't interrupt me . . . Didn't they teach you to be humble and respectful to your superiors in the seminary? Maybe if you'd been one of the more brilliant students . . ."

Father José Pedro knew all that. It wasn't necessary to repeat to him that he was one of the worst students in the seminary in matters of study. For that very reason he'd been so afraid of having been in error, of having offended God. The canon was certainly right, he was more intelligent, he was much closer to God, who is the supreme intelligence.

The canon made a gesture with his hand like someone putting the business of the widow aside and his voice became soft again:

"Now, however, there is a much more serious matter. Because of you, Father, the authorities came to this Archdiocese. Do you know what you have done? Do you know?"

The priest didn't attempt to deny it:

"Was it the case of the boy with milk pox?"

"A boy with smallpox, yes, sir. And you concealed the case from the public health authorities . . ."

Father José Pedro had great faith in God's goodness. Many times he had thought that God approved what he was doing. He thought that now too. That thought had suddenly filled his heart. He raised his head, fixed his eyes on the canon:

"Do you know what the leprosarium is like?"

The canon didn't answer.

"It's rare for anyone to come back from there. Much less a child . . . Sending a child there is like committing murder . . ."

"That's not our business," the canon answered in an inexpressive voice but one full of decision. "That's the business of public health. But it's our role to respect the law."

"Even when it goes against the law of God's goodness?"

"What do you know of God's goodness? What great intelligence do you have to know the designs of God? Has the demon of vanity got hold of you?"

Father José Pedro tried to explain:

"I know that I'm an ignorant priest unworthy to serve the Lord. But these children have never had anyone to look after them. My intentions were . . ."

"Good intentions don't excuse evil acts . . ." the canon cut him off with a very soft voice as he pronounced sentence.

Father José Pedro felt doubt again. But the thought of God arose again, became part of his trust:

"Could they have been evil? They were boys who had never heard anyone speak seriously of God. They mix God up with black idols, they've got no idea of religion. I wanted to see if I could save those souls . . ."

"I already told you that your intentions were good, but that your actions didn't match your intentions . . ."

"You don't know those boys . . ." (The canon gave him a hard look.) "They're boys who are just like grown men. They live like men, they know all about life, everything . . . You have to deal with them carefully, make concessions."

"That's why you do what they want you to do . . ."

"Sometimes I have to do that in order to get good results . . ."

"Compromising with robbery, with the crimes of those hoodlums . . ."

"What fault is it of theirs?" The priest remembered João de Adão. "Who takes care of them? Who teaches them? Who helps them? What love do they get? He was excited and the canon drew back from him as he fastened his hard little eyes on him. "They steal in order to eat because all these rich people who've got enough to throw away, to give to churches, forget that hungry children exist . . . What fault . . ."

"Be still." The canon's voice was full of authority. "Anyone who heard you would think it was a communist speaking. And it's not so hard. In the midst of that rabble you must have picked up their ideas . . . You're a communist, an enemy of the Church . . ."

The priest looked at him in horror. The canon arose, held his hand out to the priest:

"May God be sufficiently good to forgive your acts and your words. You have offended God and the Church. You've dishonored the priestly vestments you wear. You've broken the laws of the Church and of the State. You've acted like a communist. That's why we see ourselves obliged not to be in any hurry to give you the parish you've asked for. Go" (now his voice had become soft again, but with a softness full of resolution, a softness that would not admit any reply) "and do penance for your sins, dedicate yourself to the faithful of the church where you work, and forget those communist ideas, if not we'll have to take more serious measures. Do you think that God approves of what you're doing? Remember that your intelligence is not very great, you can't penetrate the designs of God . . ."

He turned his back on the priest and was leaving. Father José Pedro took two steps toward him, spoke in a strangled voice:

"There's even one who wants to be a priest . . ."

The canon turned:

"The interview is over, Father José Pedro. You may with-draw and may God help you to think better . . ."

But the priest still stood there for a few minutes wanting to say something. But he didn't say anything, it was as if he had been kicked, looking at the door through which the canon had left. At that moment he couldn't think about anything. He was comical, his hand still held out, his body half-fallen to one side, his dirty, mended cassock, his eyes opened wide, terri-fied, his trembling as if wanting to say something. The heavy curtains kept the light from entering the room. The priest still lingered in the darkness.

A communist . . . A street band strangely in tune was playing an old waltz:

I was left joyless, O my God . . .

Father José Pedro went along hugging the wall. The canon had said that he couldn't understand the designs of God. He didn't have the intelligence, he was talking just like a commu-nist. That was the word that bothered the priest the most. From all pulpits all priests had spoken out against that word. And now he . . . The canon was very intelligent, he was close to God because of his intelligence, it was easy for him to hear God's voice. He was in error, he'd wasted those two years of so much work. He'd thought of bringing so many children to God . . . Lost children . . . Could it be their fault? Suffer the little children to come unto me . . . Christ . . . He was a radi-ant and young figure. The priests had said he was a revolution-ary too. He loved children . . . Woe to him who does harm to a child . . . The widow Santos was a pillar of the Church . . . Could it be that she could hear the voice of God too? Two years wasted . . . He made concessions, true, he had. Other-wise how could he have dealt with the Captains of the Sands? They weren't like other children . . . They knew everything, even the secrets of sex. They were like grown men, even though they were children . . . It wasn't possible to treat them like the children who attended the Jesuits' school after first communion. Those had fathers and mothers, sisters, confessors, and clothes and food, they had everything . . . But he wasn't the one to give lessons to the canon . . . The canon knew everything, he was very intelligent. He could hear God's voice . . . He was close to God . . . He wasn't one of the brightest students . . . He'd been one of the worst . . . God wasn't going to talk to an ignorant priest . . . He'd listened to João de Adão. A communist like João de Adão . . . But the communists are bad, they want to do away with everything . . . João de Adão was a good man . . . A communist . . . What about Christ? No, he couldn't for a moment think that Christ was a communist . . . The canon must have understood better than a poor priest in a dirty cassock . . . The canon was intelligent and God is the supreme intelligence . . . Lollipop wanted to be a priest. He wanted to be a priest, yes, his vocation was real. But he sinned every day, he stole, he assaulted. It wasn't their fault . . . He's talking like a communist . . . Why is that one driving in a car, smoking a cigar? Talking like a communist. The canon said that, will God forgive him?

Father José Pedro goes along hugging the wall. The last notes of the distant band reach his ears. The priest's eyes are bulging.

Yes, Father José Pedro, God sometimes talks to the most ignorant. To the most ignorant . . . He was ignorant . . . But, God, listen . . . They're just poor boys . . . What do they know of good and evil? Since no one has ever taught them anything? Never a mother's hand on their heads. A good word from a father. Lord, they know not what they do . . . That's why I was with them, did what they wanted so many times . . .

The priest opened his arms, held them up to heaven.

Can it be that's how a communist acts? Giving a little comfort to those small souls. Saving them, bettering their lot . . . Otherwise they would only turn out to be thieves, pickpockets, burglars, the best were drifters . . . The worthiest profession . . . He wanted them to turn out to be working men, honest, worthy . . . There was so little for them to turn to . . . From the Reformatory they came out worse . . . It isn't with

brutal punishment, God, hear me . . . The punishment is brutal there . . . Only with patience, with goodness . . . Christ
thought that way too . . . Why like a communist? . . . God can
talk to an ignorant person . . . Abandon the children? The
parish is lost . . . An old mother who will weep . . . What
about the career of the sister in Normal School? She wants to
teach children too . . . But they'd be other children, children
with books, with a father and mother . . . They won't be the
same as these, abandoned in the street, sleeping in the moonlight, under docks, in warehouses . . . He can't abandon them.
Who can God be with? With the canon or with the poor
priest? The widow . . . No, God is with the priest . . . He's
with the priest . . . I'm too ignorant to hear the voice of
God . . . (He hides in the doorway of a church.) But sometimes
God talks to the ignorant . . . (He leaves the church door, continues his walk close to the wall.) He will continue, yes. If he's
wrong God will forgive him . . . "Good intentions don't forgive evil acts." But God is the supreme goodness . . . He'll
keep on . . . Maybe the Captains of the Sands won't turn out
to be just thieves . . . And wouldn't it be a great joy for
Christ? . . . Yes, Christ smiles. He's a radiant figure. He smiles
on Father José Pedro. Thank you, my God, thank you.

The priest kneels in the street, lifts up his hands to heaven.
But he sees the people smiling at him. He stands up, frightened, leaps onto a streetcar, filled with shame.

A man comments:

"Look at the drunken priest. Disgraceful . . ."

All the people at the car stop laughing?

Good-Life dug in his black nail, scratched the pimple. Then he
peeked at his arm: it was full. That was why he felt so warm, a
lethargy in his body. It was the fever of the smallpox. The city
of the poor was ravaged by smallpox. The doctors said that
the epidemic was on the decline now, but even so there were a
lot of cases, people were going to the pesthouse every day. People who didn't come back, Good-Life thought. Even Almiro,
the cause of such a ruckus in the warehouse, had gone to the

pesthouse. And he hadn't come back . . . He was a nice-looking boy, there were those who said that he and Outrigger . . . But he wasn't a bad boy, he didn't bother anybody. Legless had raised hell. Then when he found out he'd died he was even more withdrawn, seeming to take the blame for Almiro's death. He didn't talk to anyone. Only with the dog he'd picked up.

"He'll end up going nuts . . ." Good-Life thought.

He lighted a cigarette. He walked about the warehouse. Only the Professor was there. It was rare for anyone to be in the warehouse at that time in the afternoon. Professor saw him when he came in:

"Give me a cigarette, Good-Life."

Good-Life tossed him one. He went over to his corner, made a bundle of his clothes. Professor watched his movements:

"Are you going away?"

Good-Life went over to him with the bundle under his arm:

"Don't tell anybody . . . Just the Bullet . . ."

"Where are you going?"

The mulatto laughed:

"To the pesthouse . . ."

The Professor saw his arms full of pustules, his chest.

"Don't go, Good-Life . . ."

"Why not, buddy?"

"You know . . . It's the cemetery for sure . . ."

"Do you think I'm going to hang around here so the others will get it?"

"We'll take care of you . . ."

"Everybody would die. Almiro had a home, you know, I haven't got anyone."

The Professor didn't say anything. He wanted to say a lot of things. The mulatto was in front of him, the bundle under the arm that was full of smallpox sores. Good-Life spoke:

"You tell Pedro Bala. The others don't have to know."

Professor could only say:

"Are you really going?"

Good-Life said yes, they went out of the warehouse. Good-Life looked at the city, gestured with his hand. It was like a farewell. Good-Life was a drifter and no one loved his city like a drifter. He looked at the Professor:

"When you paint my picture . . . Are you still going to paint it?"

"I am, Good-Life . . ." (The wish to say loving words as to a brother.)

"Don't have me full of pockmarks, no . . ."

His shape disappeared over the sands. Professor stood with his words withheld, a knot in his throat. But he also thought it was nice of Good-Life to go off to his death like that so as not to infect the others. Men like that are the ones who have a star in place of a heart. And when they die their hearts stay in the sky, God's-Love says. Good-Life was a boy, he wasn't a man. But he already had a star in place of a heart. His shape had already disappeared. And the certainty that he would never see his friend again filled the Professor's heart. The certainty that the other was going to his death.

At the *macumbas* in honor of Omolu the black people, punished with smallpox, were singing:

> Change your course,
> barnacles sticking!
> Let the whiplash clatter!
> Inland, Omolu,
> let the smallpox scatter.

Omolu had scattered smallpox over the city. It was a vengeance against the city of the rich. But the rich had vaccines, what did Omolu know about vaccines? She was a poor goddess from the jungles of Africa. A goddess of poor blacks. What could she know about vaccines? Then the smallpox descended and devastated Omolu's people. All Omolu could do was change the smallpox into milk pox, a white and simple pox. So black people died, poor people died. But Omolu said it wasn't the milk pox that killed them. It was the pesthouse. Omolu only wanted the milk pox to mark her black children. The pesthouse was what killed them. But the *macumbas* asked her to take the smallpox away from the city, take it to the rich landowners in the backlands. They had money, leagues and leagues of land, but they didn't know about vaccines either. And Omolu said that she was going inland. And the blacks, the acolytes, the dancers, and the *macumba* priests sang:

> He truly is our father
> and he's the one to help . . .

Omolu promised to go. But so that her black children wouldn't forget her, in her farewell chant she told them:

> Goodby now, my children,
> I'm leaving but I'll be back . . .

And on a night while the drums were beating at the *macumbas*, on a night of mystery in Bahia, Omolu took off on a locomotive of the Leste Brasileira and went into the backlands of Joazeiro. The smallpox went with her.

Good-Life came back skinny, his clothes dancing on his body. His face was all pockmarked now. The others still looked at him suspiciously when he came into the warehouse that night. But Professor went right over to him:

"Are you all right, kid?"

Good-Life smiled. They came over to shake his hand, Pedro Bala gave him a hug:

"You're a good boy, you're a tough boy."

Even Legless came over, Big João stood beside Good-Life. The mulatto looked at his friends. He asked for a cigarette. His hand was fleshless, his face bony. He remained silent, looking lovingly at the old warehouse, the boys, the dog, who was sitting in Legless's lap. Then Big João asked:

"What was the pesthouse like?"

Good-Life turned around quickly. His face took on a bitter expression of distaste. He took a while to answer. Then the words came out with difficulty:

"You can't describe it, you can't. It's too much . . . It makes you sick. When people go in there it's like getting into a coffin . . ."

He looked at the others, who were hanging on his words. His voice was bitter:

"Just like getting into a box to go to the cemetery . . . Just the same . . ."

He couldn't find anything else to say. Legless asked between his teeth:

"What else?"

"Nothing. Nothing. I don't know . . . God, don't ask me . . ." He lowered his head as it rocked back and forth. His voice came out very low, as if he were still afraid. "It's just like going to the cemetery. Everybody is already dead."

He looked at them as if asking them not to ask any more questions. Big João spoke for the rest:

"We shouldn't ask any questions . . ."

Good-Life backed him up with a gesture of his hand. He said in a very low voice:

"Nothing . . . It's just too awful . . ."

Professor looked at Good-Life's chest. It was all pockmarked. But in the place of his heart the Professor saw a star.

A star in the place of his heart.

DESTINY

They were at a corner table. Cat pulled out his deck. But neither Pedro Bala, nor Big João, nor the Professor, nor even Good-Life was interested. They were waiting in the Gate of the Sea for God's-Love. The tables were full. For a long time the Gate of the Sea had been without customers. The smallpox wouldn't permit it. Now that it had gone away people began to talk about the deaths. Someone mentioned the pesthouse. "It's tough being poor," a seafarer said.

At one table they were ordering cane liquor. There was a flurry of glasses on the bar. Then an old man said:

"No one can change destiny. It's something done up there," and he pointed to the sky.

But João de Adão spoke up at another table:

"Someday people are going to change the destiny of the poor . . ."

Pedro Bala raised his head. Professor listened with a smile. But Big João and Good-Life seemed to support the words of the old man, who repeated:

"No one can change it, no. It's written up there . . ."

"Someday people are going to change things . . ." Pedro Bala said and everybody looked at the boy.

"What do you know about it, squirt?" the old man asked.

"He's the son of the Blond, the father's voice is talking,"

João de Adão answered, looking with respect. "His father died to change people's destiny."

He looked at everyone. The old man fell silent and he was looking with respect too. They were all getting their confidence back. Outside there a guitar began to play.

THE NIGHT
OF GREAT PEACE,
THE GREAT PEACE
IN YOUR EYES

DAUGHTER OF
THE SMALLPOX MAN

The music had already started again on the hill. The drifters were coming back to play the guitar, sing *modinhas*, invent sambas they would later sell to famous samba singers in the city. In Deoclécio's store there was a group every afternoon again. For some time everything had come to a halt on the hill, giving way to the weeping and lamentations of women and children. The men went by head down on their way home or to work. And the black coffins of adults, the white ones of virgins, the little ones of children went down the harsh slopes of the hill to the distant cemetery. When it wasn't a case of sacks going down with smallpox victims still alive being carried off to the pesthouse. The family wept as it would for a dead person, with the certainty that he would never return. No music from a guitar. No full voice of a black man cut through the sadness of the hilltop in those days. Only the call of the watchmen, the convulsive weeping of women.

That was what the hill was like when Estevão was taken to the pesthouse. He didn't return, one afternoon Margarida learned that he had died there. That afternoon she already had a fever. But the milk pox in the washerwoman's body seemed to be one of the milder forms and she hid the news from everyone, she succeeded in not getting put into a sack. In a short time she was getting better. Her two children went about the house doing what she told them. Zé Ferret wasn't much use, still unable to do anything at the age of six. But Dora was thirteen going on fourteen, her breasts had begun to appear under her dress, she looked like a little woman, very serious, finding medicine for her mother, taking care of her. Margarida got better when the guitars were already being played on the hill, because the smallpox epidemic was over. Music grew to dominate the hilltop nights and Margarida, if she wasn't completely well yet, went to the houses of some of her customers looking for clothes. She returned with the bundle on her back, heading for the water spigot. She worked all day in the sun and in the rain that fell that afternoon. The following day she didn't go back to work because she had a relapse of milk pox and a relapse is always terrible. Two days later the last smallpox coffin went down the hill. Dora didn't sob. The tears ran down her face but while the coffin was going down she was thinking about Zé Ferret who was asking for something to eat. Her little brother was weeping from grief and hunger. He was too small to understand that he'd been left without anybody in the immensity of the city.

The neighbors fed the orphans that afternoon. The next day the Arab who owned the shacks on the hill ordered them to spray alcohol on Margarida's in order to disinfect it. And then he rented it, because it was a well-located shack, high up on the slope. And while the neighbors were discussing the problem of the orphans, Dora took her brother's hand and went down into the city. She didn't say goodby to anyone, it was like a flight. Zé Ferret went along not knowing where, dragged by his sister. Dora was going along calmly. In the city she would have to find someone to give them something to eat, who could at least take care of her brother. She would set up a job as table maid in some house. She was still quite young, but there were many houses that really preferred a young girl because they wouldn't have to pay as much. Her mother had spoken about getting her a job as table maid in the house of a customer. Dora knew where it was and went there. The hill, the guitar music, the samba a black man was singing all were left behind.

Dora's bare feet burned on the hot asphalt. Zé Ferret went along merrily, looking at the city that was unknown to him, the streetcars going by full of people, the buses honking their horns, the crowds crossing the streets. Dora had gone to the house of that customer once with Margarida. It was in the Barra district, they'd gone on a cargo trolley, carrying the bundle of clean clothes. The lady of the house had fussed over Dora, had asked her if she wanted to work there. Margarida had agreed to bring her when she was older. That was where Dora planned to go. And by asking different people she found her way to Barra. It was a long way and the asphalt burned her shoeless feet. Zé Ferret began to ask for something to eat and complained about being tired. Dora calmed him down with promises and they continued on. But at Campo Grande Zé Ferret couldn't go any farther. The distance was too much for him, for his six years. Then Dora went into a bakery, broke the only five hundred *reis* she had, bought two loaves of day-old bread, left Zé Ferret sitting on a bench with the bread:

"Eat and wait for me, you hear? I'm going over there, I'll be right back. But don't budge from here or else you'll get lost . . ."

Zé Ferret promised with a very solemn face, biting into the hard bread. She kissed him and continued on.

The policeman who told her the way looked at her breasts that were forming. Her blond hair, ill-treated, was waving in the breeze. The soles of her feet were burning and she felt fatigued all over her body. But she went on. The number was 611. When she reached 53 she stopped a bit to rest and think about what she would say to the lady of the house. Then she started up again. Now hunger was helping to weaken her body, that terrible hunger of children of thirteen, a hunger that demands immediate food. Dora felt like crying, like letting herself drop onto the street in the sun and not moving. A memory of her dead parents came over her. But she reacted against everything and continued on.

Number 611 was a big house, almost a small palace, with trees in front. In a playground a swing where a girl Dora's age was playing. A boy in his late teens was pushing her and both of them were laughing. They were the children of the owners of the house. Dora stood looking at them enviously for a few minutes. Then she rang the bell. The boy looked but continued pushing his sister. Dora rang again and the maid answered. She explained that she wanted to speak to Dona Laura, the lady of the house. The maid looked at her with mistrust. But the boy stopped pushing his sister and came over to the door. He was looking at Dora's breasts that were beginning to show, the thighs under her dress. He asked:

"What do you want?"

"I'd like to talk to Dona Laura. I'm the daughter of Margarida, who used to be her laundress . . . She doesn't know that she died . . ."

The boy didn't take his eyes off Dora's breasts. She was pretty, the girl, big eyes, very blond hair, the granddaughter of an Italian and a mulatto woman. Margarida said she took after her grandfather, who also had blond hair along with a big, well-cared-for mustache. Dora lowered her eyes because the boy wasn't taking his off her breasts. He also became flustered, spoke to the maid:

"Go call Mother . . ."

"Yes, sir."

The boy took out a cigarette, lighted it. He blew smoke into the air, pursing his lips, took another peek at Dora's breasts:

"Are you looking for work?"

"Yes, sir."

The breeze lifted her dress a little. He got lewd thoughts when he saw the piece of thigh. He was already thinking about bed, Dora bringing breakfast, the messing around that would follow:

"I'll see if I can get Mother to arrange something for you . . ."

She thanked him. But she was a little frightened, even if she had missed a lot of the malice in his eyes. Dona Laura came, graying hair, her daughter behind her, looking at Dora with big eyes. She was freckly but kind of cute.

Dora told her that her mother had died:

"You'd promised me a job . . ."

"What did Margarida die of?"

"Pox, ma'am."

Dora didn't know that by saying that she had lost all possibility of a job.

"Smallpox."

The girl drew back suspiciously. Even the boy withdrew a little, thinking about Dora's little breasts all pockmarked. He spat in disgust. Dona Laura took on a sad tone:

"The fact is I've already taken on another maid. I don't need anybody right now . . ."

Dora thought of Zé Ferret:

"Would you be needing a little boy to do shopping, run errands, things like that? He's my brother . . ."

"No, child, I wouldn't."

"Do you know of anybody?"

"No. If I did I'd recommend you . . ."

She wanted to end the conversation. She turned to her son:

"Have you got two *milreis* on you, Emanuel?"

"What for, Mother?"

"Give them to me."

The boy gave them to her, she put them on the railing. She was afraid of touching Dora, she wanted her away from there before she infected the house:

"Take this. God be with you . . ."

Dora went back down onto the street. The boy was still watching the buttocks that were nice and round under the tight dress. But Dona Laura's voice interrupted him. She was talking to the maid:

"Dos Reis, take a cloth and some alcohol and wipe the part of the door the girl touched. You can't fool around with smallpox."

The boy went back to playing with his sister on the swing among the mango trees. But every so often he would sigh to himself: "She had a nice pair of breasts . . ."

Zé Ferret wasn't on the bench. Dora had a fright. Her brother was capable of wandering off in the city and getting lost. And how would she find him there? She didn't know the city well. Besides, she was overcome by a great weariness, a listlessness, a longing for her dead mother, an urge to weep. Her feet hurt and she was hungry. She thought about buying bread (she now had two thousand four hundred), but instead of that she went off in search of her brother. She found him under some trees in the park eating green plums. She slapped his hand:

"Don't you know that can give you a bellyache?"

"I'm hungry . . ."

She bought some bread, they ate. The whole afternoon was going back and forth looking for work. At every house they said no, the fear of smallpox was stronger than any goodness. At nightfall Zé Ferret couldn't take any more, he was so tired. Dora was sad and thought about going back to the hill. She would be a burden on their poor neighbors. She didn't want to go back. Her mother had left the hill in a coffin, her father in a sack. Once more she left Zé Ferret alone in a park to go buy something to eat in a bakery before it closed. She spent her last coins. The lights went on and at first she thought it was very pretty. But then she felt that the city was her enemy, that it only burned her feet and tired her out. Those pretty houses didn't want her. She came back hunched over, wiping away the tears with the back of her hand. And once more she couldn't find Zé Ferret. After walking around the park she found her brother watching a game of *good* between two boys: a strong black one and a skinny white one. Dora sat down on a bench, called her brother. The boys who were playing got up too. She unwrapped the bread, gave a piece to Zé Ferret. The boys were looking at her. The black one was hungry, it was easy for her to see. She offered them some. The four of them sat in silence eating the day-old bread (it was the cheapest). When they finished the black boy clapped his hands, spoke:

"Your brother says your mother died of smallpox . . ."

"Papa too . . ."

"One of ours died too . . ."

"Your father?"

"No, it was Almiro, one of the gang."

The skinny white boy, who had been quiet, asked:

"Did you find any work?"

"Nobody wants the daughter of a smallpox man . . ."

She was weeping now. Zé Ferret was playing on the ground with the balls the others had left near the trees. The black boy shook his head. The thin one looked at him, then at Dora:

"Have you got a place to sleep?"

"No."

The skinny boy spoke to the black one:

"We could take her to the warehouse . . ."

"A girl . . . What's Bullet going to say?"

"She's crying," the skinny one said in a low voice.

The black boy looked. She was obviously perplexed. The white boy slapped his neck, chasing a fly. He put his hand on Dora's shoulder, very slowly, as if afraid to touch her:

"Come with us. We sleep in a warehouse . . ."

The black boy made an effort to smile:

"It's not a palace but it's better than the street . . ."

They went. Big João and the Professor went ahead. They both wanted to chat with Dora but nobody knew what to say, they'd never been in a jam like that before. They looked at her blond hair where the electric light was falling.

On the sand Zé Ferret was unable to walk any farther. Big João picked up the child (in spite of his also being a child . . .) and put him on his back. The Professor went along with Dora, but they were silent in the night.

They went warily into the warehouse. Big João put Zé Ferret down onto the ground, stood there waiting for the Professor and Dora to come in. They all went to the Professor's corner where he lighted his candle. The others were looking toward the corner with surprise. Legless's dog barked:

"New people . . ." Cat murmured as he got ready to leave.

Cat went over to where they were:

"Who are they, Professor?"

"Their father and mother died of smallpox. They were in the street with no place to sleep."

Cat looked at Dora, putting on his best smile. It was a kind

of greeting (he'd seen a leading man do it in a movie) with his
body, trying out a phrase he'd heard once:

"A hearty welcome, madame . . ."

He couldn't remember the rest, was half-bashful, went out
to see Dalva. But the others came over. Legless and Good-
Life were in the lead. Dora looked with fright. Zé Ferret was
asleep from fatigue. Big João placed himself in front of Dora.
The light from the candle illuminated the girl's blond hair, at
times lighted on her breasts. Professor got up, leaned against
the wall. Now the light was showing through the hole in the
roof.

Good-Life was in front of them. Legless limped over, and
the others right behind, their eyes on Dora. Good-Life spoke:

"Who's this little piece?"

The Professor came forward:

"She was hungry. She and her brother. Smallpox killed her
father and mother . . ."

Good-Life gave off a long laugh. He bent over:

"She's a knockout . . ."

Legless laughed his mocking laugh, pointed to the others:

"They're all like vultures over a piece of meat . . ."

Dora moved closer to Zé Ferret, who had awakened and
was shaking with fear. A voice from among the boys said:

"Professor, do you think only you and Big João can have
something to eat? Leave some for us too . . ."

Another shouted:

"My iron's all hot . . ."

A lot of them laughed. One came forward and showed his
sex to Big João:

"Look at this baby, Big Man. Crazy . . ."

Big João put himself in front of Dora. He didn't say a word,
but he drew his knife. Legless shouted:

"You won't get anywhere that way. She's got to be for all
of us."

Professor answered:

"Can't you see she's just a girl? . . ."

"She's got teats already," a voice shouted.

Dry Gulch came out from the group. His eyes were all excited, a laugh on his somber face:

"Lampião didn't respect nobody. Let us have her, Big Boy . . ."

They knew that the Professor was weak, he couldn't stand up. They were crazy and excited but they were still afraid of Big João, who was gripping his knife. Dry Gulch saw himself as though in the middle of Lampião's gang, ready along with the rest to deflower the daughter of a landowner. The candle lighted up Dora's blond hair. There was fright on her face.

Big João wasn't saying anything but he clutched the knife in his hand. Professor opened his switchblade, stood beside him. Then Dry Gulch drew his knife too, started forward. The others came behind him, the dog was barking. Good-Life spoke once more:

"Stand aside, Big Boy. It's better that way . . ."

Professor thought that if Cat had been there he would have been on their side because Cat already had a woman. But Cat had left.

Dora watched the advance. Fear was conquering the listlessness and fatigue that had been over her. Zé Ferret was crying. Dora didn't take her eyes off Dry Gulch. The Halfbreed's somber face was open with one desire, a nervous laugh shook it. She also saw the pockmarks on Good-Life's face when he passed in front of the candle and then she remembered her dead mother. A sob shook her and held the boys back for a moment. Professor said:

"Can't you see she's crying?"

They stopped for a moment. But Dry Gulch spoke:

"What difference does that make for us? The pussy's all the same . . ."

They kept on coming. They were advancing slowly, their eyes fixed now on Dora, now on the dagger Big João was holding. Suddenly they speeded up, came much closer. Big João spoke for the first time:

"I'll cut the first one . . ."

Good-Life laughed, Dry Gulch swung his knife. Zé Ferret

was crying. Dora looked at him with frightened eyes. She hugged him, she saw Big João knock Good-Life down. The voice of Pedro Bala who was coming in made them stop:

"What the hell is going on?"

The Professor got up. Dry Gulch let go of him, he'd already cut him on the arm. Good-Life lay where he was, a cut on his face. Big João stood guard in front of Dora. Pedro Bala came forward:

"What's this all about?"

Good-Life spoke from the ground:

"These guys fixed themselves a meal and they want it all for themselves. We've got a right to it too . . ."

"That's right. I for one would like some screwing today," Legless croaked.

Pedro Bala looked at Dora. He saw her breasts, her blond hair.

"They're right . . ." he said. "Give up, Big João."

The black boy looked at Pedro Bala, surprised. The group advanced again, led by Pedro Bala now. Big João put out his arms, shouted:

"Bullet, I'll eat the first one who gets here."

Pedro Bala took a step forward:

"Get away, Big Boy."

"Can't you see she's just a girl? Can't you see?"

Pedro Bala stopped, the group stopped behind him. Now Pedro was looking at Dora with other eyes. He saw the terror in her face, the tears falling from her eyes. He heard Zé Ferret sobbing. Big João was speaking:

"I've always stood by you, Bullet. I'm your friend, but she's just a girl, the Professor and me brought her here. I'm your friend but if you come any closer I'll kill you. She's just a girl and nobody's going to hurt her . . ."

"We'll knock you down and then . . ." Dry Gulch said.

"Shut up," Pedro Bala shouted.

Big João went on:

"Her father, her mother died of smallpox. We ran into her, she had no place to sleep, we brought her here. She's no whore,

she's just a girl, can't you see that she's just a girl? Nobody
touches her, Bullet."

Pedro Bala said in a low voice:

"She's just a girl . . ."

He went over to Big João and the Professor's side:

"You're a good man, black boy. You're straight . . ." He
turned to the others. "Anyone who wants to, come ahead . . ."

"You can't do this, Bullet . . ." and Good-Life ran his hand
over the cut. "You want to have a taste of her now for yourself,
like Big Boy and the Professor . . ."

"I swear I don't want her, they don't want her either. She's
just a girl. But nobody touches her. Let anybody who wants to
try it . . ."

The younger ones, more fearful, were going away. Good-
Life got up, went to his corner, wiping off the blood. Dry
Gulch spoke to Pedro Bala slowly:

"I'm not going because I'm afraid. It's because you said she's
just a girl."

Pedro Bala went over to Dora:

"Don't be afraid. Nobody's going to touch you."

She came out of her corner, took a piece of cloth, began to
look after the Professor's wound. Then she went over to Good-
Life (who was all curled up), wet the drifter's wound, put a
bandage on it. All her fear, all her fatigue had disappeared.
Because she trusted Pedro Bala. Then she asked Dry Gulch:

"Are you wounded too?"

"No . . ." the Halfbreed said without understanding. And
he fled to his corner. He seemed to be afraid of Dora.

Legless was watching. The dog left his lap and came over to
lick Dora's feet. She petted him, asked Legless:

"Is he yours?"

"Yes, he is. But you can have him."

She smiled. Pedro Bala wandered through the warehouse.
Then he said to everyone:

"She leaves tomorrow. I don't want any girls here."

"No," Dora said. "I'm staying, I'll help you . . . I can cook,
sew, wash clothes."

"She can stay as far as I'm concerned," Dry Gulch said.

Dora looked at Pedro Bala:

"Didn't you say that no one would hurt me? . . ."

Pedro Bala looked at her blond hair. The moonlight was coming into the warehouse.

DORA, MOTHER

Cat came over with his body swaying in that characteristic walk of his. He'd been trying to thread a needle for an exceedingly long time. Dora had put Zé Ferret to sleep, now she was getting ready to listen to the Professor read that pretty story in the book with a blue cover. Cat came slowly swaying over:

"Dora . . ."

"What is it, Cat?"

"Would you like to do something?"

He was looking at the needle and thread he had in his hand. He seemed to be facing a grave problem. He didn't know how to solve it. Professor stopped reading. Cat changed the subject:

"You're going to go blind from so much reading, Professor . . . If we only had electric lights . . ." He looked at Dora without having made his decision.

"What is it, Cat?"

"This damned thread . . . I never saw anything so hard. Getting it into the eye of this needle . . ."

"Let me have it . . ."

She threaded the needle, made a knot at one end. Cat said to the Professor:

"Only a woman can do something like that . . ."

He held out his hand to take the needle, but Dora didn't give it back. She asked what Cat had to sew. Cat showed her his

jacket with a torn pocket. It was the cashmere item that had
belonged to Legless when he'd been playing little rich boy in a
house in Graça:

"Shitty piece of clothing," Cat said.

"It's really fine," Dora defended it. "Take your jacket off."

Professor and Cat watched her sew. She was no real marvel
at sewing, but they'd never had anyone to mend their clothes.
And only Cat and Lollipop were in the habit of mending theirs
themselves. Cat because he wanted to be elegant and because
he had a lover, Lollipop because he liked to be neat. The others let the rags they picked up get even more ragged, until they
became useless. Then they would beg or steal another jacket
and pair of pants. Dora finished the job:

"Anything else?"

Cat smoothed his slicked-down hair:

"The back of my shirt . . ."

He turned around. The shirt was torn from top to bottom.
Dora told him to sit down, began to sew it on him. When her
fingers touched him for the first time Cat had a shiver. As
when Dalva would run her long manicured nails over him,
scratching his back and saying:

"The pussy is scratching the tomcat . . ."

But Dalva didn't mend his clothes, maybe she didn't even
know how to thread a needle. What she liked to do was fool
around with him in bed, scratch his sides, but with an aim to
working him up and exciting him so the love he made would
be even better. Not Dora. That wasn't her aim. Her hand
(neglected and dirty nails, chewed down) didn't mean to excite
or stir up. It passed over him like the hand of a mother mending her son's shirts. Cat's mother had died young. She was a
fragile, pretty woman. She'd had neglected hands too because
a worker's wife doesn't have manicures. And that business of
mending Cat's shirts while he had them on was also her practice. Dora's hand touches him again. The sensation is different
now. It's no longer a wave of desire. It's that feeling of good
affection and security that his mother's hands gave him. Dora
is behind him, he can't see her. He imagines then that it's his
mother who's come back. Cat is a little boy again, dressed in a

burgarian smock and playing on the side of the hill, getting it torn to pieces. And his mother comes, makes him sit down in front of her, and her agile hands manipulate the needle, they touch him from time to time and give him a feeling of absolute happiness. No desire. Just happiness. She's come back, she's sewing Cat's shirts. A wish to lie down in Dora's lap and let her sing him to sleep as when he was small. He remembers that he's still a child. But only in age, because in everything else he's the equal of a man, stealing in order to live, sleeping every night with a woman of the street, taking money from her. But tonight he's completely a child, he forgets Dalva, her hands scratching him, lips that hold his in long kisses, sex that absorbs him. He forgets his life of a petty pickpocket, the owner of a marked deck, a gambling cheat. He forgets everything, he's just a fourteen-year-old boy with a little mother who mends his shirts. A wish for her to sing him to sleep . . . One of those lullabies that talk about the bogey man. Dora bites the thread, leans over him. Her blond hair touches Cat's shoulder. But he has no desire other than for her to keep on being his little mother. His happiness at that moment is almost absurd. It's as if his whole life after his mother's death didn't exist. It's as if he'd kept on being a child just like all other children. Because on that night his mother had come back. That's why the unconscious brush of Dora's blond hair doesn't excite his desire, but increases his happiness. And her voice that says: "All set, Cat," sounds to his ears just like the soft musical voice of his mother, who would sing lullabies with Cat's head resting on her lap.

He gets up, looks at Dora with thankful eyes:

"You're our little mother now . . ." but he remains bashful over what to say, he thinks that Dora probably doesn't even understand because she's laughing with her serious face of an almost little woman. But Professor understands and Cat, standing opposite Dora, speaking in a happy voice but without desire, calling her mother and she smiling with her maternal air of an almost little woman is fixed in the Professor's head as a painting.

Cat throws the coat over his shoulder and goes out with his

swaying walk. He feels that there's something new in the warehouse: they've found a mother, the love and care of a mother.
Dalva finds him strange that night:

"What's wrong with my little cat? What happened?"

But he keeps the secret. It's something too big, finding a
dead mother on earth again. Dalva wouldn't understand.

When the Professor was just starting the story Big João
arrived and sat down beside them. It was a rainy night. In
the story Professor was reading the night was rainy too and the
ship was in great danger. The sailors were being whipped, the
captain was an evil man. The sailing ship seemed about to keel
over, the officers' whips fell on the naked backs of the sailors.
Big João had an expression of pain on his face. Dry Gulch
arrived with a newspaper but he didn't interrupt the story,
stood listening. Now the sailor John was being caned because
he'd slipped and fallen in the midst of the storm. Dry Gulch
interrupted:

"If Lampião had been there he would have blown that captain away with his rifle . . ."

That was what the sailor James did, a big hulk of a man. He
flung himself on top of the captain, mutiny broke out on board
ship. Outside it was raining. It was raining in the story too, it
was the story of a storm and a mutiny. One of the officers took
the side of the sailors.

"He's all right . . ." Big João said.

He loved heroism. Dry Gulch was looking at Dora. Her eyes
were shining, she loved heroism too. That pleased the boy
from the backlands. Then the sailor James had a fierce
fight. Dry Gulch was so happy that he whistled like a bird.
Dora laughed too, from satisfaction. The two of them laughed
together, then there was a cackling from all four, as was the
custom with the Captains of the Sands. They cackled for a few
minutes, others came over in time to hear the rest of the story.
They looked at Dora's serious face, the face of an almost little
woman who was watching them with the affection of a mother.
They smiled when the sailor James threw the captain of the
ship into a lifeboat and called him "Snake without venom,"

they all laughed hard along with Dora and looked at her with love. The way children look at their beloved mother. When the story was over they went back to their corners, commenting:

"Great . . ."

"Tough guy . . ."

"He was screwed too . . ."

"The captain got what he had coming, eh?"

Dry Gulch held the newspaper out to Professor. Dora looked at the Halfbreed, he smiled, half-confused:

"It's got news of Lampião . . ." His somber face lighted up. "Did you know that Lampião is my godfather?"

"Godfather?"

"Well, he is . . . It was my mother who picked him because Lampião's a real man, he doesn't kowtow to anybody . . . My mother was a brave woman, a woman who could hold a rifle. One day she chased off two cops who were acting up. She was quite a woman . . . As good as a man."

Dora listened with fascination. Her serious face was looking with great sympathy at the mulatto's somber face. Dry Gulch was silent but in the manner of someone trying to say something. Finally he spoke:

"You're brave too . . . You know? My mother was a great big woman. She was a mulatto, she didn't have blond hair, hers was the kinkiest . . . She wasn't a girl anymore either, she could have been your grandmother . . . But you're like her . . ."

He looked at Dora, but he lowered his head:

"It may seem funny, but you remind me of her. It may seem funny, but you're like her . . ."

Professor looked with his myopic eyes. Dry Gulch was almost shouting, his somber face showed the joy of a discovery. "He's discovered his mother too," the Professor thought. Dora was serious, but her look was loving. Dry Gulch laughed, she laughed, then it became a cackle. But the Professor didn't accompany them in their cackle. He began to read the account in the newspaper very quickly.

Lampião had been taken by surprise going into a village. A truck driver who'd seen him on the road with his gang had set

out for the village to warn it. There'd been time to ask for rein-
forcements from neighboring towns and the flying column had
come too. When Lampião entered the town he ran into a lot of
shooting, shooting he hadn't expected. There was a big fire
fight, Lampião was only able to take off into the scrubland,
which is his home. One of the gang members was laid out with
a bullet in his chest. They cut off his head, which they sent to
Bahia in triumph. The picture was in the paper. Mouth open,
eyes staring, a man holding it by the thin hair. They'd cut the
throat with a knife. Dora commented:

"Poor thing . . . How cruel!"

Dry Gulch looked at her with thanks. His eyes were blazing,
his face even more somber. Painfully somber.

"Son of a bitch . . ." he said in a low voice. "Son of a bitch
of a truck driver . . . If I ever catch him someday . . ."

The word was out that Lampião must have had other men
wounded because the retreat of the gang was too quick. Dry
Gulch muttered. It was as though he were talking to himself:

"It's time I was going . . ."

"Where to?" Dora asked.

"To join up with my godfather. He needs me . . ."

She looked at him sadly:

"Are you really going, Dry Gulch?"

"I am, yes."

"What if the police kill you, cut off your head?"

"I swear they won't take me alive. I'll take one of them with
me, but they won't take me alive . . . Don't be afraid, don't . . ."

He swore by his mother, a strong and brave mulatto woman
of the backlands, capable of fighting with the police, a comrade of Lampião, mistress of a *cangaceiro*, that she could trust
in him, they wouldn't take him alive, he'd fight to the death . . .
Dora listened with pride.

Professor closed his eyes and also saw in place of Dora a
strong backlands woman defending her piece of land against
plantation colonels with the friendly help of the bandits. He
saw Dry Gulch's mother. And that was what the mulatto saw.
The blond hair was thin and kinky, the soft eyes were the ori-
ental ones of a backlands woman, the serious face was the

somber face of an exploited peasant woman. And the smile was the same proud smile of a mother for her son.

Lollipop had viewed her arrival with mistrust. For him Dora was sin. It had been some time since he'd lingered with little black girls on the sands, lost in the warmth of their bodies rolling on the ground. He'd got rid of his sins some time back in order to appear pure in the eyes of God and be able to merit the grace of putting on a priest's vestments. He even thought of getting work as a newsboy in order to get away from the daily sin of stealing.

He looked upon Dora with mistrust: woman was sin. In reality she was only a child, an abandoned child like them. She didn't smile like the little black girls on the sand, an insolent inviting smile, a smile of teeth tight with desire. Her face was serious, it looked like the face of a very proper little woman. But the small breasts that were taking shape pointed out under her dress, the bit of thigh that showed as white and rounded. Lollipop was afraid. Not so much of Dora's temptation. She didn't seem to be the kind that tempted, she was a child, it was too early for that. But he was afraid of the temptation that would come from within him, which the devil had put inside him. And he tried praying in a low voice when she approached.

Dora stood looking at the holy pictures. Professor stopped behind her, looking too. There were flowers under the image of the Christ Child that Lollipop had stolen one day. Dora came closer:

"It's so pretty . . ."

The fear began to disappear from Lollipop's heart. She was interested in his saints, saints that nobody in the warehouse paid any attention to. Dora asked:

"Are they all yours?"

Lollipop nodded and smiled. He went on to show her everything he owned. The pictures, the catechism, the rosary, everything. She looked on with satisfaction. She also smiled while the Professor looked on with myopic eyes. Lollipop told the story of Saint Anthony, who'd been in two places, at the same time. In order to save his father from the gallows, to which he'd been unjustly condemned. He told it in the same way that Professor told the heroic stories of courageous and mutineering sailors. Dora listened with the same sympathy. The two of them chatted, the Professor silent, listening. Lollipop told things about his religion, miracles of the saints, the goodness of Father José Pedro:

"When you meet him, you'll like him . . ."

He said that with certainty. He'd already forgotten that she might bring temptation with her girl's breasts, her chubby thighs, her blond hair, now he was speaking as to an older woman who was listening to him with affection. Like a mother. Only then did he understand. Because at that moment a wish came over him to tell her that he wanted to be a priest, that he wanted to follow that vocation, that he felt the call of God. He would only have had the courage to tell his mother that. And she's standing before him. He speaks:

"Do you know I want to be a priest?"

"How nice . . ." she said.

Lollipop's face lighted up. He looked at Dora, spoke with an exalted voice:

"Do you think I'm worthy? God is good, but he also knows how to punish . . ."

"Why?" There was shock in Dora's question.

"You don't see how full of sin our life is . . . Every day . . ."

"It's not you people's fault . . ." Dora stated. "You haven't got anybody."

But now Lollipop had her. His mother. He laughed with satisfaction:

"Father José Pedro said that too. It may be . . ."

He laughed again, she smiled too, animated.

". . . it may be that I'll be a priest someday."

"You will be, yes."

"Do you want this Christ Child for yourself?" he suddenly asked.

He was like a son bringing some of his candy to his mother, who'd given him a nickel to buy it.

And Dora accepted as a mother accepts part of her dear son's candy so he'll feel satisfied.

Professor saw Lollipop's mother, not knowing what she was

like, what she might have been like. But he saw her there in Dora's place. He was envious of Lollipop's happiness.

They found Pedro Bala stretched out on the sand. The leader of the Captains of the Sands hadn't gone into the warehouse that night. He'd stayed looking at the moon, lying on the good warmth of the sand. The rain had stopped and the breeze that was blowing was warm now. Professor lay down too, Dora sat between the two of them. Pedro Bala looked at her out of the corner of his eye, pulled his cap farther down his face. Dora said, turning to him:

"You were good to me and my brother yesterday . . ."

"You should have gone away . . ." the Bullet answered.

She didn't say anything, but became sad. Then Professor spoke:

"No, Bullet. She's like a mother . . . Like a mother, yes. For everyone . . ."

He repeated:

"She's like a mother . . . Like a mother . . ."

Pedro Bala looked at the two of them. He took off his cap, sat up on the sand. But Dora was looking at him with affection. For him . . . For him she was everything: wife, sister, and mother. He smiled at Dora in confusion:

"I thought you might be a temptation for everyone . . ."

She said no, he went on:

"Later on they could take advantage of a time when nobody was around . . ."

They laughed. The Professor repeated again:

"No. She's like a little mother . . ."

"You can stay," Pedro Bala said and Dora smiled at him, he was her hero, a figure she had never imagined but whom she would have to imagine one day. She loved him as a son without love, a brave brother, a lover handsome as no one else.

But Professor saw the smiles on them both. And he said yet again in a serious voice:

"She's like Mother!"

He said it with a sullen voice because for him she wasn't Mother either. For the Professor, too, she was the beloved.

DORA, SISTER AND
SWEETHEART

Since her dress made her movements difficult and since she wanted to be one of the Captains of the Sands in all ways, she put it aside for a pair of pants Outrigger had been given at a house in the upper city. The pants had been enormous for the little black boy, so he offered them to Dora. Even so they were too big for her, she had to cut the legs to make them fit. She tied them with a cord, following the example of them all, the dress served as a blouse. If it hadn't been for her long, blond hair and her nascent breasts everyone would have taken her for a boy, one of the Captains of the Sands.

One day when, dressed like a boy, she appeared before Pedro Bala, the boy began to laugh. He ended up rolling on the ground from laughing so much. Finally he managed to say:

"You're funny . . ."

She was sad, Pedro Bala stopped laughing.

"It isn't right for you people to feed me every day. Now I can take part in what you do."

His surprise knew no limits:

"You mean . . ."

She was looking at him calmly, waiting for him to finish the sentence.

". . . that you're going out with us on the streets, doing things . . . ?"

"That's right." Her voice was full of resolve.

"You're crazy . . ."

"I don't see why."

"Don't you see that you can't? This isn't anything for a girl. This is something for men."

"As if you were all great big men. You're all boys."

Pedro Bala searched for an answer:

"But we wear pants, not skirts . . ."

"Me too," and she showed her pants.

For the moment he couldn't find anything to say. He looked at her thoughtfully, he no longer had an urge to laugh. After some time he spoke:

"If the police grab us they haven't got anything. But what if they grab you?"

"It's the same thing."

"They'll put you in the Orphanage. You don't know what it's like . . ."

"No more to be said. I'm going with you people now."

He shrugged his shoulders in the gesture of someone who had nothing to do with it. He'd given his warning. But she knew very well that he was worried. That's why she still said:

"You'll see that I'm the equal of any one of them . . ."

"Have you ever seen a woman do what a man can do? You couldn't stand up under a shove . . ."

"I can do other things."

Pedro Bala accepted. Underneath it all he liked her attitude, even if he was afraid of the results.

She walked the streets with them, just like one of the Captains of the Sands. She no longer found the city her enemy. Now she loved it too, learned to go through its alleys, its hillsides, jump on moving trolley cars, on automobiles in her escape. She was as agile as the most agile. She always went with Pedro Bala, Big João, and Professor. Big João never left her, he was like Dora's shadow, and he drooled with satisfaction when in her friendly voice she called him "my brother." The black boy followed her like a dog and devoted himself completely to her. He lived in awe of Dora's qualities. He found her almost

as brave as Pedro Bala. He would say to the Professor with
amazement:
"She's brave like a man . . ."
Professor would have liked it to be otherwise. He dreamed
of a loving look from Dora's eyes. But not that maternal love
that she had for the younger and the more unfortunate ones,
Dry Gulch, Lollipop. Nor a fraternal look like the one she
gave Big João, Legless, Cat, himself. He wanted one of those
looks full of love that she gave Pedro Bala when she saw him
on the run, fleeing the police or a man shouting from the door
of a shop:
"Stop thief! Stop thief! I've been robbed . . ."
She only had those looks for Pedro Bala and he didn't even
notice. Professor listened to Big João's words of praise but he
didn't smile.

Pedro Bala arrived at the warehouse that night with a black
eye and a red, bleeding lip. He'd run into Ezequiel, the leader
of another gang of thieves and beggar boys, a much smaller
group than the Captains of the Sands and without as much
organization. Ezequiel was coming along with some three others of his gang, including one who'd been kicked out of the
Captains of the Sands for being caught stealing from a comrade. Pedro Bala had gone to leave Dora and Zé Ferret at the
foot of the Ladeira do Taboão so they could go to the warehouse. Big João had a job to do and couldn't go with Dora.
Pedro Bala thought of going with her, not leaving her alone on
the sands. But since night still hadn't fallen there was no danger of any black man grabbing her. Besides, he had to go pick
up some pennies from the hand of González of the "14,"
money owed from a raid the gang had made for some leather
goods belonging to a rich Arab.
    While he was heading for the "14" Pedro Bala was thinking
about Dora. The blond hair that fell around her neck, her
looks. She was pretty, she was just like a girlfriend. Girlfriend . . . He shouldn't even think about that . . . He didn't
want the others in the gang to feel the right to think about dirty
things with her. And if he told Dora she was like a girlfriend to

him, somebody else might judge that he had a right to say so too. And then there wouldn't be any law and order among the Captains of the Sands. Pedro Bala remembers that he's the leader.

He goes along so lost in thought that he almost bumps into Ezequiel. The four of them are standing in front of him. Ezequiel is a tall mulatto, he's smoking a cigar butt. Pedro Bala stands there too, waiting. Ezequiel spits:

"Can't you see where you're going? . . . Are you blind or something?"

"What do you want?"

The boy who'd been with the Captains of the Sands asks:

"How are things with those faggots?"

"Do you still remember the beating you got there? You should keep your mouth shut."

The boy grinds his teeth, tries to step forward. But Ezequiel makes a motion and warns Pedro Bala:

"One of these days I'm going to pay a visit to you people."

"A visit?" Pedro Bala asks mistrustfully.

"They say that you've got a little whore there for everybody now . . ."

"Bite your tongue, you son of a bitch."

Ezequiel dropped with the punch. But the other three were already on top of Pedro Bala. Ezequiel put his foot on Bullet's face. The one who'd been with the Captains of the Sands shouted:

"Hold him good," and he punched Pedro on the face.

Ezequiel kicked him twice in the face.

"Admit that I'm your boss."

"Four . . ." Pedro Bala began to complain, but a punch shut him up.

A policeman was coming toward them, they scattered. Pedro Bala picked up his cap, the tears of rage flowed along with the blood. He shook his fist at where Ezequiel and his people had disappeared. The policeman spoke:

"Look alive, kid. Beat it, before I run you in."

Pedro Bala spat pure blood. He went down the slope slowly, not even thinking about going to collect the money from González.

He went down muttering to himself: "They're only men when it's four against one." And he thought of revenge.

He went into the warehouse, Dora was alone with her brother, who was sleeping. The last rays of the sun were coming in through the roof, giving a strange brightness to the big house. Dora saw him come in and went over to him:

"Did you get the dough? . . ."

But she spotted Pedro's swollen eye, his split lip:

"What happened, brother?"

"Ezequiel and three others. They're only men when there are four or more . . ."

"Did he do that to you?"

"There were four of them. Even so, they hit me when I wasn't looking. I was dumb enough to think Ezequiel was alone. There were four of them."

She sat him down, went to Lollipop's corner, brought some water. With a piece of cloth she cleaned his wounds. Pedro was mapping out plans of revenge. She backed him up:

"We'll get rid of them once and for all."

Pedro laughed:

"Are you coming too?"

"I am . . ."

Now she was cleaning his lips, she was leaning over him, her face right next to Bullet's, her blond hair mingling with his.

"What was the fight about?"

"Nothing."

"Tell me . . ."

"He said some things . . ."

"It was because of me, wasn't it?"

He nodded his head. Then she brought her lips over to Pedro Bala's, kissed him, and then ran off. He ran out after her, but she was hiding, she wouldn't let herself be caught. In a while the others were returning. She was smiling at Pedro Bala from a distance. There was no malice in her smile. But her look was different from the sisterly look she gave the others. It was the soft look of a girlfriend, an innocent and timid girlfriend. They might not even know that it was one of love. In spite of its not being night there was romantic romance in the big colonial house. She was smiling and lowering her eyes, sometimes she winked because she thought that was making love. And her heart beat rapidly when she looked at him. She didn't know that it was love. Finally, the moon came out, spread its yellow light over the warehouse. Pedro Bala lay down on the sand and even through closed eyes he saw Dora. He felt it when she came over and lay down beside him. He said:

"You're my sweetheart now. Someday we'll get married."

He kept his eyes closed. She said in a very low voice:

"You're my boyfriend."

Not even knowing that it was love, they felt that it was good.

When Legless and Big João arrived, Pedro Bala got up off the sand and called the leaders together. They went over to the Professor's candle. Dora came too and sat down between Big João and Good-Life. The drifter lighted a cigarette, said to Dora:

"I'm learning how to play a wild samba. And I'm going to get me a guitar, sister."

"You really are playing good, brother."

"It went over big at parties . . ."

Pedro Bala interrupted the conversation. They were looking at his lip, his swollen eye. He told them about the episode:

"Four against one . . ."

"He needs a lesson," Legless was laughing. "I won't let the guy get away with it."

They worked out a plan of battle. And around midnight some thirty went out. Ezequiel's gang slept around the Pôrto da Lenha, in some overturned boats and on the dock. Dora went alongside Pedro Bala and she carried a switchblade too. Legless said:

"She even looks like Rosa Palmeirão."

There never had been a woman as brave as Rosa Palmeirão. She took on six policemen all at one time. Every sailor on the waterfront of Bahia knows her ABC ballad. That's why Dora likes the comparison and smiles:

"Thank you, brother."

Brother . . . It's a nice and friendly word. They'd grown accustomed to calling her sister. She calls them brother too.

For the younger ones she's a kind of little mother, just like a little mother. She takes care of them. For the older ones she's like a sister who says nice things and plays with them innocently and goes through the dangers of the adventurous life they lead. But no one knows that she's Pedro Bala's sweetheart. Not even the Professor knows. And in his heart Professor calls her sweetheart too.

The dog Legless got goes along barking. Dry Gulch imitates the barking of a dog, they all laugh. Big João whistles a samba. Good-Life begins to sing it aloud:

"My mulatta's gone and left me . . ."

They go along merrily. They carry switchblades and knives in their pants. But they'll only take them out if the others do. Because abandoned children have a law and a morality too, a sense of human dignity.

Suddenly Big João shouts:

"There they are."

With the uproar they make, Ezequiel comes out from under a boat:

"Who goes there?"

"The Captains of the Sands, who don't swallow any insults . . ." Pedro Bala answered.

And they pounce on the others.

The return was a triumphal procession. In spite of Legless's getting a cut and Outrigger's almost having to be carried from such a beating (a big fellow from Ezequiel's gang was beating him up until Dry Gulch knocked him down), they were all returning happily, talking about their victory. The ones who'd stayed behind in the warehouse cheered them. They stayed up for a long time talking, making comments. They talked about the courage of Dora, who fought just like a boy. "Just like a man," Big João said. She was like a sister, just like a sister . . .

Like a sweetheart, just like a sweetheart, Pedro Bala was thinking, lying on the sand. The moon was yellowing the sands, the stars were reflected in the blue Bahia sea. She came, lay down beside him. And they began to talk about silly things. Just like a sweetheart. They didn't kiss, they didn't embrace, sex didn't call them at that moment. Her blond hair only touched Pedro Bala lightly.

She laughed, looked at his hair:

"Yours too."

They both laughed and then it turned into a cackle. It was a habit of the Captains of the Sands. She began to tell about things on the hilltop, stories about her neighbors, he remembered things from the agitated life of the gang:

"I came here when I was five. Younger than your brother . . ."

They laughed innocently, happy to be beside each other. Then sleep came. They were separated. Pedro took her hand, squeezed it. They slept like brother and sister.

REFORMATORY

The *Jornal da Tarde* carried the news in large letters. A headline across the front page read:

LEADER OF "CAPTAINS OF THE SANDS" CAPTURED

Then came the headings over a picture where Pedro Bala, Dora, Big João, Legless, and Cat were seen, surrounded by policemen and detectives:

A GIRL IN GROUP—HER STORY—SENT TO ORPHANAGE— LEADER OF "CAPTAINS OF THE SANDS" IS SON OF STRIKER— OTHERS ABLE TO GET AWAY—REFORMATORY WILL STRAIGHTEN THEM OUT DIRECTOR STATES.

Under the picture came this: "After this picture was taken, the leader of the vagrants started an argument and an uproar that enabled the rest of the urchins arrested to escape. The leader is the one marked by an X and alongside him is Dora, the new lady-friend of the Bahia urchins."

The story followed:

Yesterday the police of Bahia struck a blow. They succeeded in apprehending the leader of the gang of juvenile delinquents known as the "Captains of the Sands." More than once this newspaper has dealt with the problem of juveniles who live on the streets of the city and dedicate themselves to thievery.

We have also reported several times raids carried out by this same gang. The city has really been living under a constant fear of these boys. No one knew where they lived or who their leader was. Some months back we had occasion to publish letters from the Chief of Police, the Juvenile Judge, and the Director of the Reformatory of Bahia with regard to this problem. They all promised to initiate a campaign against juvenile delinquents and in particular against the "Captains of the Sands."

This worthy campaign bore its first fruit yesterday with the arrest of the leader of this pack and several members of the gang, including a girl. Unhappily, due to a wise ruse on the part of Pedro Bala, the leader, the rest managed to escape from the hands of the police. In any case, the police have already accomplished a great deal by catching the leader and the romantic inspiration for the robberies: Dora, a most interesting figure of a juvenile delinquent. With these commentaries let us go on to the facts:

ATTEMPTED ROBBERY

Late yesterday afternoon five boys and a girl entered the mansion of Dr. Alcibíades Meneses on the Ladeira de São Bento. They were heard by the son of the owner, however, a medical student who let them get into a room where he locked them in. He then called police and detectives and handed them over.

Reporters from the *Jornal da Tarde*, informed of the circumstances, went to Dr. Alcibíades's house. When they arrived they found the minors ready to be taken to Police Headquarters. We then asked permission to take a picture of the group. The police very kindly consented. At the moment when the photographer exploded the magnesium and took the picture, Pedro Bala, the fearsome leader of the "Captains of the Sands" made possible the

ESCAPE

Putting into use an unusual agility, Pedro Bala freed himself from the hands of the detective who was holding him and knocked him down with a *capoeira* kick. He did not flee, however. It is clear that the other policemen and detectives landed on him to prevent his flight. Only then were they able to understand the plan of the leader of the "Captains of the Sands," because he shouted to his comrades:

"Beat it, you guys . . ."

A single policeman managed to grab two others and one of them, very agile, knocked him down too with a *capoeira* kick. And they ran off down the Ladeira da Montanha.

AT THE POLICE STATION

At Police Headquarters we wanted to hear from Pedro Bala. But he would not tell us anything, nor would he tell the authorities the place where the "Captains of the Sands" slept and kept their loot. He only gave his name, said that he was the son of an old striker who had been killed at a rally during the famous dock strike of 191_, and that he had no one in the world. As for Dora, she is the daughter of a washerwoman who died of small-pox during the epidemic that swept the city. She has only been with the "Captains of the Sands" for four months, but has already taken part in many attacks. And she seems to take great pride in this.

SWEETHEARTS

Dora declared to our reporters that she was the sweetheart of Pedro Bala and that they were going to be married. She is still an ingenuous girl, more worthy of pity than punishment. She speaks of her engagement with the greatest innocence. She is not more than fourteen years old,

while Pedro Bala is around sixteen. Dora was taken to Our Lady of Mercy Orphanage. In those holy surroundings she will soon forget Pedro Bala, the romantic bandit-boyfriend and her criminal life with the "Captains of the Sands."

As for Pedro Bala, he will be remanded to the Reformatory for Juveniles as soon as the police are able to get him to reveal the gang's hiding place. The police have great hopes of getting the information today.

WORDS OF THE DIRECTOR OF THE REFORMATORY

The director of the Bahia Reformatory for Juvenile Delinquents and Abandoned Boys is an old friend of the *Jornal da Tarde*. One of our reporters once put an end to a series of libels brought against that educational establishment and its director. Today he was at the police station, waiting to take the minor Pedro Bala with him. To our question he replied:

"He'll reform. Remember the title of the institution I direct: 'Reformatory.' He'll reform."

And to another question of ours he smiled:

"Escape? It's not easy to escape from the Reformatory. I can guarantee that he won't."

That night the Professor read the news to everybody. Legless said:

"He's in the Reformatory now. I saw him when he left the police station."

"And she's in the Orphanage . . ." Big João added.

"We'll get them out," Professor stated. Then he turned to Legless. "Until Pedro Bala gets out, you're leader, Legless."

Big João held his arms out to the others, spoke:

"People, until Bullet comes back, Legless is leader . . ."

Legless said:

"He stayed behind so we could be free. We have to free him. Isn't that right?"

They all agreed.

When they took him into that room, Pedro Bala imagined what was waiting for him. He didn't see any guard. Two policemen, a detective, and the director of the Reformatory came in. They closed the door. The detective said in a laughing voice:

"Now that the reporters have gone, kid, you're going to tell us what you know, whether you like it or not."

"Talk now . . ."

The detective asked:

"Where do you sleep?"

Pedro Bala looked at him with hatred:

"If you think I'm going to tell . . ."

"You will . . ."

"You can stand on your head."

He turned his back. The detective signaled to the policemen. Pedro Bala felt two clubs at the same time. And the detective's boot on his face. He rolled on the ground, cursing.

"You still won't talk?" the Reformatory director asked. "This is just the beginning."

"No," was all that Pedro Bala said.

Now they were hitting him on all sides. Whacks, punches, and kicks. The director of the Reformatory got up, kicked him, Pedro Bala fell to the other side of the room. He didn't get up. The policemen twirled their clubs. He saw Big João,

Professor, Dry Gulch, Legless, and Cat. They all depended
on him. The safety of all of them depended on his courage.
He was the leader, he couldn't betray them. He remembered the scene in the afternoon. He had managed to let the
others get away in spite of being caught too. Pride filled his
chest. He wouldn't talk; he'd escape from the Reformatory,
he'd free Dora. And he'd get his revenge . . . He'd get his
revenge . . .

He cries out with pain. But not a word comes from his lips.
It's getting to be night for him. Now he doesn't feel the pain
anymore, he doesn't feel anything. But the policemen are still
beating him, the detective punching him. But he doesn't feel
anything else.

"He's fainted," the detective says.

"Leave him to me," the director of the Reformatory explains.
"I'll take him to the Reformatory, he'll open his mouth there. I
guarantee it. I'll let you know."

The detective agrees. With the promise that the next day
he'd come for Pedro Bala, the director left.

In the pre-dawn, when Pedro came to, the prisoners were
singing. It was a sad *moda*. It spoke of the sunlight there was
on the streets, how great and beautiful freedom is.

Ranulfo, the beadle, who'd gone to pick him up at Police
Headquarters, brought him into the presence of the director.
Pedro felt his body aching all over from the beating of the day
before. But he was satisfied because he hadn't said anything,
because he hadn't revealed the place where the Captains of the
Sands lived. He remembered the song the prisoners were singing at daybreak. It said that freedom is the best thing in the
world. That there was sunlight on the streets and there was
eternal darkness in the cells, because freedom was unknown
there. Freedom. João de Adão, who was on the street, in the
sunlight, talked about it too. He said that it wasn't just for pay
that they went on those strikes on the docks and would go on
others. It was for freedom, because the dockworkers didn't
have much of it. Pedro Bala's father had died for freedom. For
freedom—Pedro was thinking—for his friends, he'd taken a

beating from the police. Now his body was soft and painful, his ears full of the *moda* the prisoners were singing. Outside there, the old song said, is sunlight, freedom, life. Pedro Bala sees the sun through the window. The street goes right in front of the main gate of the Reformatory. Inside here it's like eternal darkness. Outside it's freedom and life. And revenge— Pedro Bala thinks.

The director comes in. Beadle Ranulfo greets him and shows him the Bullet. The director smiles, rubs his hands, sits down in front of a tall cabinet. He looks at Pedro Bala for a few minutes:

"At last . . . I've been waiting a long time for this pigeon, Ranulfo."

The beadle smiles approval of the director's words.

"He's the leader of those so-called Captains of the Sands. Look at him . . . The born criminal type. It's true you haven't read Lombroso . . . But if you'd read him, you'd understand. He has all the marks of the criminal on his face. At his age he has a scar already. Look at his eyes . . . He can't be treated like an ordinary person. We're going to give him special honors . . ."

Pedro Bala is looking at him with his sunken eyes. He feels a weariness, a mad urge to sleep. Beadle Ranulfo essays a question:

"Shall I put him with the others?"

"What? No. Put him in the hole to start. Let's see if he comes out of there a little reformed . . ."

The beadle bows and goes out with Pedro Bala. The director then orders:

"Diet number 3."

"Black beans and water . . ." Ranulfo mutters. He sneaks a look at Pedro Bala, shakes his head. "You're going to come out a lot thinner."

Outside there is freedom and sunlight. Jail, the prisoners in jail, the beating had taught Pedro Bala that freedom is the greatest thing in the world. Now he knows that it wasn't just for his story to be told on the waterfront, in the Market, at the Gate of the Sea, but that his father had died for freedom. Freedom is like the sun. It's the greatest thing in the world.

He heard the beadle Ranulfo snap the padlock outside. He'd
been thrown into the hole. It was a small room underneath the
stairway, where he couldn't stand because it wasn't high
enough, nor could he lie down fully because it wasn't long
enough. He could either sit or lie with his legs up in a very
uncomfortable position. That was precisely how Pedro Bala
lay. His body gave a turn and his first thought was that the
hole was only good for the snake-man he'd seen in the circus
once. The room was shut up tight, the darkness was complete.
The air came in through the thin, rare cracks in the steps of
the staircase. Pedro Bala, lying as he was, couldn't make the
slightest movement. The walls stopped him on all sides. His
limbs ached, he had a mad urge to stretch his legs. His face
was full of bruises from the beating at the police station and
this time Dora wasn't there to bring him a cool cloth and take
care of his wounded face. Freedom was Dora too. It wasn't just
sunlight, walking freely in the streets, laughing on the waterfront with the great guffaw of the Captains of the Sands. It
was also feeling Dora's blond hair next to him, listening to her
tell stories about up on the hilltop, feeling her lips on his
wounded lips. Sweetheart. She was without freedom too.
Pedro Bala's limbs are aching and now his head aches too.
Dora is with him, without sunlight, without freedom. She was
taken to an orphanage. Sweetheart. Before she appeared, he'd
never thought about that word: sweetheart. He liked to pull
little black girls down onto the sand. Lie chest to chest, head
to head, legs to legs, sex to sex. But he'd never thought of lying
on the sand beside a girl, a girl like him, and talking about
foolish things and playing hide-and-seek the same as other
children, without pulling her down to make love. He'd always
thought that love was the pleasant moment when a black or
mulatto girl moaned under his body on the waterfront sand.
He learned that early, when he wasn't thirteen years old yet.
All the Captains of the Sands knew that, even the smallest
ones, the ones who still weren't strong enough to pull a halfbreed girl down. But they already knew it and thought joyfully
about the day when they could. Pedro Bala's limbs and head

hurt. He's thirsty, he still hasn't drunk or eaten that day. With
Dora it was different. As soon as she arrived, he, just like all of
them in the warehouse, thought about pulling her down, possessing her, using her, because she was pretty, for the only kind
of love they knew. But since she was just a girl, they'd respected
her. Then she became like a mother to all of them. And like a
sister, Big João said that was for sure. But for him it was different from the first moment. She'd been a playmate, the same as
for the others, a beloved sister too. But it had been a different
joy from what a sister gives. Sweetheart. He'd like to, yes. Even
when he tries to deny it to himself he can't. It's true that that's
why he doesn't do anything, content to chat with her, listen to
her voice, timidly take her hand. But he'd like to possess her
too, see her moan with love. Not, though, just for a night. For
every night of a whole lifetime. The way other people have a
wife, a wife who's mother, sister, and friend. She was mother,
sister, and friend to the Captains of the Sands. For Pedro Bala
she's a sweetheart, one day she'll be his wife. They can't keep
her in an orphanage like a girl who hasn't got anybody. She
has a boyfriend, a legion of brothers and children she takes
care of. The weariness leaves Pedro Bala's limbs. He needs
movement, walking, running, to be able to think up a plan to
free Dora. There in that darkness, he can't. He's of no use,
thinking that maybe she's in a hole too. But he's too used to
rats to be bothered. But Dora is probably afraid of that continuous noise. It's maddening for anyone who isn't the leader
of the Captains of the Sands. All the more so for a girl . . . It's
true that Dora is the bravest of all women born in Bahia,
which is the land of brave women. Braver than even Rosa Palmeirão, who took on six policemen, than Maria Cabaçu, who
respected no guy, than Lampião's companion, who can handle
a rifle just like a *cangaceiro*. Braver because she's just a girl,
she's just beginning to live. Pedro Bala smiles with pride in
spite of his aches, his weariness, the thirst that's almost squeezing him. How nice a glass of water would be! Beyond the sand
by the warehouse is the sea, never-ending water. A sea that
God's-Love, the great *capoeira* fighter, cuts with his sloop
when he goes fishing in the southern sea. God's-Love is a good

fellow. If Pedro Bala hadn't learned Angola *capoeira* from him, the prettiest fighting in the world because it's also a dance, he wouldn't have been able to help Big João, Cat, and Legless get away. Now, there in the hole, unable to move, *capoeira* would be of no use to him. He'd like to have a drink of water. Can Dora be thirsty right now too? She must be in a hole too, Pedro Bala imagines the Orphanage as just like the Reformatory. Thirst is worse than a rattlesnake. It's scarier than smallpox. Because it starts tightening your throat, mixing up your thoughts. A little water. A little light too. Because if there's a little light maybe he'll see Dora's smiling face. In the darkness like that he sees it full of suffering, full of pain. A dull, impotent rage grows inside him. He rises up a little, his head resting against the steps of the stairway that serves as a ceiling. He pounds on the door of the dungeon. But it seems there's no one to hear him out there. He sees the director's evil face. He'll bury his knife in the director's heart up to the hilt. Without any trembling of his hand, without any remorse, enjoying it. His knife was at the police station. But Dry Gulch would give him his, he has a pistol. Dry Gulch wants to go join the band of Lampião, who's his godfather. Lampião kills policemen, kills bad men. Pedro Bala at this moment loves Lampião as his hero, as his avenger. He's the armed hand of poor people in the backlands. Someday he'll be able to join Lampião's gang too. And, who knows, maybe they'll be able to invade the city of Bahia, split open the head of the director of the Reformatory. What a face he'd put on seeing Pedro Bala coming into the Reformatory at the head of some *cangaceiros* . . . He'd let go of the bottle of liquor, the present from a friend in Santo Amaro, and Pedro Bala would open his head. No. First he'd leave him in that same hole, with nothing to eat, nothing to drink. Thirst . . . Thirst is mistreating him. It makes him see Dora's sad and mournful face on the darkness of the wall. The certainty that she's suffering . . . He closes his eyes. He tries to think about Professor, Dry Gulch, Big João, Cat, Legless, Good-Life, all of them at the warehouse except Dora. But he can't. Even with his eyes closed he sees her face, embittered by thirst. He pounds on the door again.

He shouts, curses names. No one comes, no one sees him, no one hears him. That must be what hell is like. Lollipop is right to be afraid of hell. It's too terrible. Suffering with thirst and darkness. The prisoner's song said that outside there's freedom and sunlight. And water too, nice clear rivers running over stones, cascades falling, the great mysterious sea. Professor, who knows a lot of things, because he reads stolen books at night (he's ruining his eyes . . .), told him once that there's more water in the world than land. He'd read it in a book. But not even a drop of water in his hole. There mustn't be any in Dora's either. Why pound on the door the way he is at that moment? No one hears him, his hands hurt already. The night before the police had beaten. His sides are black and blue, his chest hurts, his face is swollen. That's why the director said he had the face of a criminal. He doesn't. What he wants is freedom. One day an old man said you can't change anyone's destiny. João de Adão said it could be changed, he'd believed João de Adão. His father had died to change the destiny of the dockworkers. When he got out he'd be a dockworker too, fight for freedom, for sunlight, for water and food for everyone. He spits a big wad. Thirst is tightening around his throat. Lollipop wants to be a priest in order to get away from that hell. Father José Pedro knew that the Reformatory was like that, he spoke out against putting children there. But what can a poor priest without a parish do against them all? Because they all hate poor boys, Pedro Bala thinks. When he gets out he'll ask the priestess Don'Aninha to make a strong fetish to kill the director. She has power with Ogun, and once he got Ogun away from the police. He'd done a lot for someone his age. Dora had done a lot in those few months with them too. Now they were thirsty, Pedro Bala pounds uselessly on the door. Thirst is gnawing inside him like a legion of rats. He falls kneeling onto the floor and weariness overcomes him. In spite of the thirst, he sleeps. But he has terrible dreams, rats gnawing at Dora's beautiful face.

Now he awakens because someone is tapping lightly on one of the steps. He gets up, curved over, he can't stand up straight because the stairs won't let him. He asks in a low voice:

"Is someone out there?"

A mad joy comes over him when they answer:

"Who's in there?"

"Pedro Bala."

"Are you the leader of the Captains of the Sands?"

"I am."

He hears a whistle. The voice goes on, rapid now:

"I've got a message for you, someone brought it today . . ."

"Let me have it . . ."

"Someone's coming now. I'll be back later."

Pedro Bala hears the steps going away. But he's happier. He thinks immediately that the message is from Dora, but he can see that it's foolish to think that. How could Dora have sent a message to him? It must be from the gang. They must be trying to get him out of there. But first he has to get out of the hole. As long as he's in there the Captains of the Sands won't be able to do anything. After he's got the run of the Reformatory escape will be easy. Pedro Bala sits down to think. What time can it be, what day is it? It's always night there, the sunlight never shines. He waits impatiently for his informant to return. But there's a delay and he gets worked up. What can the others be doing without him? Professor will think up some plan to get him out of there. But while he's in the hole it's useless. And as long as they don't get him out he won't be able to get Dora out of the Orphanage. The door is opened. Pedro Bala leaps forward, thinking that they're going to let him out. A hand holds him back:

"Hey, take it easy . . ."

He sees Ranulfo, the beadle, in the door. He has a mug with water that Pedro Bala snatches from his hands and drinks with great gulps. But it's so little . . . It doesn't get to kill his thirst. The beadle gives him a clay dish with water where a few black beans are floating. Pedro Bala asks:

"Could you give me a little more water?"

"Tomorrow . . ." the beadle laughs.

"Just another mug."

"You'll have more tomorrow. And if you keep on pounding

on the door and hollering, instead of one week you'll spend two." He pushes the door shut in Pedro Bala's face.

He hears the key locking it. He feels in the darkness until he finds the plate. He drinks the dark bean water. He doesn't notice that it's quite salty. Then he eats the hard grains. But thirst attacks him again. The salty beans stir up his thirst. What good is a mug of water for that thirst, which calls for a whole jar? He lies down. He no longer thinks about anything. Hours pass. He can barely see Dora's sad face in the darkness. And he feels aches all over his body.

Much later he hears someone rapping on the stairs again. He asks:

"Are you there?"

"A crippled guy said to tell you they're going to get you out of here. As soon as you come out of the hole . . ."

"Is it nighttime yet?" Pedro Bala asks.

"It's just starting . . ."

"I'm dying of thirst."

The voice doesn't answer. Pedro thinks with despair that maybe the boy has gone off. But he doesn't hear any steps on the stairs . . . And the voice comes back:

"I can't give you any water. There's no way to pass it to you. But do you want a cigarette?"

"Yes, I do."

"Wait, then."

Minutes later the rapping is very light on the door. The voice comes from underneath the door:

"I'm going to pass the cigarette through here. Put your hands underneath, right in the middle of the crack under the door."

Pedro Bala does as he's told. A squashed cigarette reaches his hands. He pulls it from under the door. Then a match that comes with a piece of the box, the part where it's scratched.

"Thanks a lot," Pedro Bala says.

But at that moment there's a scuffle outside. The sound of a blow, a body falling. And a voice he doesn't know speaks to him:

"If you try to communicate with people outside, your punishment will be increased."

Pedro huddles up. Now someone is going to be punished because of him. When he escapes, he'll take him to the Captains of the Sands. For sunlight and freedom. He lights the cigarette. Very carefully, so as not to lose the match, which is the only one he has. He hides the glow of the cigarette under his hand so no one will see it through the cracks in the stairs. Silence enwraps him again and with the silence, thoughts, visions.

When he finishes smoking, he curls up on the floor. If he could only sleep . . . At least he wouldn't see Dora's face filled with suffering.

How many hours? How many days? The darkness is always the same, the thirst is always unchanged. They've brought him water and beans three times now. He learned not to drink the liquid from the beans, because it made him thirstier. Now he's much weaker, a listlessness all over his body. The pail where he defecates gives off a horrible smell. They still haven't taken him out. And his belly hurts, it's horrible when he defecates. It's as if his insides were coming out. His legs don't help him. What keeps him up is the hate that fills his heart.

"Sons of bitches . . . Bastards . . ."

It's all he can manage to say. Even then in a low voice. He no longer has the strength to shout, to pound on the door. Now he's sure that he's going to die there. Each time it's more painful to defecate. He sees Dora stretched out on the ground, dying of thirst, calling for him. Big João is beside her, but separated by bars. Professor and Lollipop are crying.

They brought him water and beans for the fourth time. He drinks the water, but delays eating the beans. He only knows how to say in a low voice:

"Sons of bitches . . . Sons of bitches . . ."

Before the meal (if that could be called a meal) arrived that day (it was always night for Pedro), the voice called him again on the stairs. He asked, without even rising up:

"How many days have I been here?"

"Five."

"Give me another cigarette."

The cigarette bolsters his spirits a little. He can think that with five more days he'll die. That's punishment for a man, not for a boy. The hatred in his heart doesn't grow anymore. It's reached its maximum.

It's always night. Dora is slowly dying before his eyes. Big João beside her, the bars separating them. Professor and Lollipop are crying. Is he asleep or awake? His stomach hurts terribly.

How long will the darkness go on? And Dora's agony? The smell from the pail is unbearable. Dora is dying before his eyes. Can he be dying too?

The face of the director appears beside Dora's face. Has he come to torture her agony even more? How long will it take her to die . . . Pedro Bala asks for her to die quickly, quickly . . . It will be better. Now the director has come, has come to increase the torture. He hears his voice:

"Get up . . ." and a foot touches him.

He opens his eyes more. Now he doesn't see Dora anymore. Only the face of the director, who smiles:

"Let's see if you're a little tamer now."

He can't stand the light coming through the windows. He can barely use his legs. He falls down in the middle of the corridor. Can Dora have died or not?—he thinks as he falls.

He's in the director's office once more. The latter looks at him with a smile:

"Did you like your apartment? Do you still feel like stealing? I know how to teach and break young hoodlums here."

Pedro Bala is unrecognizable, he's so thin. He looks all skin and bones. His face is greenish from intestinal complications. The beadle Fausto, owner of the voice he'd heard one time at the door to the hole, is beside him. He's a strong guy, he has the reputation for being just as mean as the director. He asks:

"The blacksmith's shop?"

"I think the field is better. Digging in the ground . . ." He laughs.

Fausto says all right, the director advises:

"Keep your eye on him. He's a bad bird. But I'll teach him . . ."

Pedro Bala bears his look. The beadle pushes him.

Now he takes a slow look at the mansion. In the middle of the courtyard the barber shaves his head down to nothing. He sees the blond hair curling on the ground. They give him some pants and jackets of mixed blue. He gets dressed right there. The beadle takes him to a blacksmith shop:

"Have you got a machete, a sickle?"

He gives the items to Pedro Bala. They walk to the cane field where other boys are working. On that day, from being so weak, Pedro Bala can barely hold the machete. For that reason the beadles punch him. He doesn't say anything.

At night, standing on line, he looks at everyone, trying to figure out who talked to him and gave him cigarettes. They go up the stairs, go to the dormitory that's on the fourth floor so as to discourage any idea of escape. The door is closed. The beadle Fausto says:

"Graça, start the prayers."

A yellowish boy makes the Sign of the Cross. They all repeat the words and the gestures. Then an Our Father and a Hail Mary, said in a strong voice in spite of their fatigue. Pedro Bala throws himself onto his bed. A dirty bedcover awaits him. They change the bedclothes every two weeks. And the bedclothes are only a cover and a case for a rock-hard pillow.

He's already asleep when someone touches him on the shoulder.

"You're Pedro Bala, aren't you?"

"Yes."

"I'm the one who brought you the message."

Pedro looks at the mulatto beside him. He could be ten years old:

"Have they come back?"

"Every damned day. They only wanted to know when you were getting out of the hole."

"Tell them I'm in the cane field . . ."

"Would you like a little ass tonight? We've got some boys here, at night we . . ."

"I'm dead tired . . . How long was I in there?"

"A week. Somebody died there once."

The boy goes away. Pedro didn't ask his name. All he wants is to sleep. But the ones going to the pederasts' beds make noise. The beadle Fausto comes out of his walled-off room:

"What's going on there?"

Silence. He claps his hands:

"Everybody on your feet."

He looks at them all:

"Nobody knows anything?"

Silence. The beadle rubs his eyes, walks among the beds. A huge clock strikes ten on the wall.

"Nobody has anything to say?"

Silence. The beadle grinds his teeth:

"Then you can all stand for an hour . . . Until eleven o'clock. And the first one who tries to go to bed goes into the hole. It's empty now . . ."

The voice of a boy cuts the silence:

"Mister beadle . . ."

It's a little half-yellowish boy.

"Speak, Henrique."

"I know . . ."

All eyes are on him. Fausto encourages his informing:

"Tell us what you know."

"It was Jeremias who was going to Berto's bed to do something dirty."

"Mr. Jeremias, Mr. Berto!"

The two come out from their beds.

"Stand by the door. Until midnight. The rest can go to bed." He looks at all of them again. The ones being punished are standing by the door.

When the beadle withdraws, Jeremias threatens Henrique. The others comment. Pedro Bala sleeps.

In the mess hall, while they drink the watered coffee and chew the hard, stale bread, his tablemate speaks:

"Are you the leader of the Captains of the Sands?" His voice is very low.

"Yes, I am."

"I saw your picture in the paper . . . You've got guts! But they did you in." He looks at Bullet's thin face.

He chews the roll. Goes on:

"Are you going to stay here?"

"I'm getting out . . ."

"Me too. I've got a plan . . . When I take off can I join your gang?"

"Sure."

"Where's your hideout?"

Pedro Bala looks at him mistrustfully:

"You'll find the guys at Campo Grande every afternoon."

"Do you think I'll tell?"

The beadle Campos claps his hands. They all get up. They go to the different shops or to the cultivated fields.

In the middle of the afternoon Pedro Bala sees Legless going by on the road. He also sees a beadle, who touches him.

Punishment . . . Punishment . . . It's the word that Pedro Bala hears most in the Reformatory. They're beaten for any reason, they're punished for trifles. Hatred is growing in all of them.

At the end of the cane field he passes a note to Legless. The next day he finds the rope in the cane brush. They must have put it there during the night. It's a roll of strong, thin rope. It's brand new. Inside it the knife that Pedro puts into his pants. The hard thing is getting the roll to the dormitory. Running away during the day is impossible because of the watchfulness of the beadles. He can't carry the roll in his clothing because they would notice.

Suddenly a fight starts. Jeremias jumps on the beadle Fausto with his machete in his hand. Other boys jump on him too, but a group of beadles comes armed with clubs. They're getting Jeremias down. Pedro puts the rope under his jacket, takes off for the dormitory. A beadle is coming down the stairs with a revolver in his hand. Pedro hides behind a door. The beadle comes along fast, passes by.

He shoves the rope under his mattress, goes back to the cane field. Jeremias was taken to the hole. The beadles are counting the boys now. Ranulfo and Campos have gone off after Agostinho, who went over the wall during the confusion of the fight. The beadle Fausto has a cut on his shoulder and has gone to the infirmary. The director is among them, his eyes flashing with rage. A beadle counts the boys. He asks Pedro Bala:

"Where were you hiding?"

"I left so I wouldn't get mixed up in it."

The beadle looks at him suspiciously, but goes on.

Ranulfo and Campos come back with Agostinho. The runaway is beaten in front of everybody. Then the director says:

"Put him in the hole."

"Jeremias is already there," Ranulfo says.

"Put them both in. They can talk that way . . ."

Pedro Bala has a shudder. How are both of them going to fit into the small space of the hole?

That night vigilance is tight, he doesn't try anything. The boys gnash their teeth with rage.

Two nights later, after the beadle Fausto had already retired to his partitioned room for a long time and they were all asleep, Pedro Bala got up, took the rope from under his mattress. His bed was beside a window. He opened it. He tied the rope to one of the hammock hooks there were on the wall. He let the rope fall out the window. It was short. There was still a long way to go. He pulled it up. He tried to make as little noise as possible, but even so, one of his neighbors woke up:

"Are you running away?"

That one didn't have a good reputation. He was in the habit of squealing. That's exactly why he'd been put next to Pedro Bala. Bullet grabbed his knife, showed it to him:

"Look, stooly, try to sleep. If you so much as peep I'll cut your throat, I swear as I'm Pedro Bala. And if you say anything after I've gone . . . Have you heard tell of the Captains of the Sands?"

"I have."

"Well, they'll get even for me."

He lays the knife within reach. He pulls up the rope all the way, ties the sheet to it at one end with one of the knots God's-Love had taught him. He threatens the boy once more, tosses the rope out, puts his body out the window, starts his descent. Halfway down he already hears the squealer's shouts. He lets himself slide down the rope, leaps to the ground. The drop is long, but he takes off running. He jumps over the wall then to avoid the police dogs that are loose. He runs down the road. He has a few minutes head start. The time for the beadles to get dressed and come out after him, turning the dogs out too. Pedro Bala puts the knife between his teeth, takes off his clothes. In that way the dogs won't know him by the scent. And, naked, in the cold dawn, he starts running toward the sunlight, toward freedom.

The Professor reads the headline in the *Jornal da Tarde*:

LEADER OF CAPTAINS OF THE SANDS MANAGES ESCAPE FROM REFORMATORY

It carried a long interview with the furious director. The whole warehouse laughs. Even Father José Pedro, who's with them, laughs in a cackle, as if he were one of the Captains of the Sands.

ORPHANAGE

A month of Orphanage was enough to kill Dora's joy and health. She'd been born on the hilltop, a childhood of running about the hill. Then the freedom of the streets of the city, the adventurous life of the Captains of the Sands. She wasn't a hothouse flower. She loved the sunlight, the streets, freedom.

They'd made two braids out of her hair, tied it with ribbons. Pink ribbons. They gave her a dress of blue cloth, an apron of a darker blue. They made her attend classes with girls five or six years old. The food was bad, there was also punishment. Fasting, losing play period. A fever came over her, she was in the infirmary. When she got out she was skinny. She still had a fever, but she didn't say anything because she hated the silence of the infirmary, where the sunlight never entered and all hours seemed like the dying hour of sunset. When she could, she got close to the fence because sometimes she spotted Professor or Big João, who made their rounds out there. One day they passed her a note. Pedro Bala had escaped from the Reformatory. He would come get her out of there. She didn't even feel the fever she had.

They told her in another note that the Professor wrote and threw to her for her to arrange some means of going to the infirmary. But it wasn't necessary, because a Sister noticed that her cheeks were flushed. She put her hand on her face:

"You're burning with fever."

It was always sunset in the infirmary. It was like an anteroom to the tomb, with the heavy curtains that stopped the light from entering. The doctor who saw her shook his head sadly.

But the light came in with them. How thin Pedro Bala is, Dora thought when he came up by her side. Big João, Cat, Professor were with him. Professor showed his knife to the Sister, who smothered a cry. The girl who had chickenpox in the other bed was shivering under the sheets. Dora was burning with fever, she could barely stand. The Sister murmured:

"She's very sick . . ."

Dora answered:

"I'm coming, Pedro."

They went out through the door. Dry Gulch was holding the big dog by the collar. They'd brought along a piece of meat too. Cat opened the gate. On the street, he said:

"Duck soup . . ."

Professor warned:

"Let's get out of here before they give the alarm."

They ran down a hillside. Dora didn't feel the fever because she was going along with Pedro Bala. He was holding her hand.

Dry Gulch brought up the rear, his hand on his knife, a smile on his somber face.

NIGHT OF GREAT PEACE

The Captains of the Sands look at little mother Dora, little sister Dora, Dora, sweetheart, Professor sees Dora, his beloved. The Captains of the Sands look in silence. The *mãe-de-santo* Don'Aninha says a strong prayer so that the fever that's eating Dora will disappear. With a branch of elder she orders the fever to go away. Dora's feverish eyes are smiling. It seems that the great peace of the Bahia night is in her eyes too.

The Captains of the Sands look in silence at their mother, sister, and sweetheart. No sooner had they got her back than fever laid her low. Where is her joy, because she can't play hide-and-seek with her younger children, can't go into the streets with her black, white, and mulatto brothers? Where is the joy in her eyes? Only a great peace, the great peace of the night. Because Pedro Bala squeezes her hand with warmth.

The peace of the Bahia night is in the heart of the Captains of the Sands. They tremble with the fear of losing Dora. But the great peace of the night is in her eyes. Eyes that softly close while the priestess Aninha banishes the fever that's devouring her.

The peace of the night envelops the warehouse.

DORA, WIFE

The dog barks at the moon on the sand. Legless leaves the warehouse, takes Don'Aninha across the sands. She said the fever wouldn't be long in leaving. Lollipop goes off too, goes to get Father José Pedro. He has faith in the priest, he might know a cure.

Inside the warehouse, the Captains of the Sands are quiet. Dora asked them to go to bed. They lay down on the ground, but few of them are sleeping. In the immense peace of the night they're thinking about the fever that's consuming Dora. She kissed Zé Ferret, told him to go to sleep. He doesn't understand too well. He knows that she's ill, but he doesn't think for a moment that she'll abandon him. But the Captains of the Sands are afraid of that happening. Then they will be without a mother once again, without a sister, without a sweetheart.

Now only Big João and Pedro Bala are by her side. The black boy smiles, but Dora knows his smile is forced, it's a smile to cheer her up, a smile forcibly pulled out of the sadness that the black boy feels. Pedro Bala holds her hand. Farther off, the Professor is doubled over, his head buried in his hands.

Dora says:

"Pedro?"

"What is it?"

"Come closer."

He goes over. His voice is just a thread. Pedro speaks with love:

"Do you want something?"

"Do you love me?"

"You know I do . . ."

"Lay down here."

Pedro lies down beside her. Big João goes away, goes over by Professor. But they don't talk, they stay given over to their sadness. But it's a night of peace that envelops the warehouse. And the peace of the night is in Dora's eyes too.

"Closer . . ."

He moves closer, their bodies are together. She takes his hand, brings it to her breast. It's burning with fever. Pedro's hand is on her young girl's breast. She makes him stroke it, says:

"Do you know that I'm a woman now?"

His hand is resting on her breast, their bodies together. A great peace in her eyes:

"It was at the Orphanage . . . Now I can be your wife."

He looks at her, startled:

"No, you're sick . . ."

"Before I die. Come . . ."

"You're not going to die."

"Not if you come to me."

They embrace. The desire is abrupt and terrible. Pedro doesn't want to hurt her, but she doesn't show any signs of pain. A great peace in all her being.

"You're mine now," he says with an agitated voice.

She doesn't seem to feel the pain of possession. Her face lighted by the fever swells with joy. Now the peace is only from the night, joy is with Dora. Their bodies come apart. Dora murmurs:

"It's good . . . I'm your wife."

He kisses her. Peace returns to her face. She looks at Pedro Bala with love.

"Now I'm going to sleep," she says.

He lies down beside her, grasps her burning hand. Wife.

The peace of the night envelops husband and wife. Love is always sweet and good, even when death is near. Their bodies

no longer sway in the rhythm of love. But in the hearts of the
two children there's no more fear. Only peace, the peace of
the Bahia night.

In the early morning, Pedro puts his hand on Dora's forehead.
Cold. She hasn't any pulse, her heart is no longer beating. His
cry cuts through the warehouse, awakens the boys. Big João
looks at her with wide-open eyes. He says to Pedro Bala:
"You shouldn't have done it . . ."
"She was the one who wanted to," he explains, and goes out
so as not to burst into sobs.
Professor comes over, stands looking. He doesn't have the
courage to touch her body. But he feels that for him life in the
warehouse is over, there's nothing left for him to do there. Lollipop comes in with Father José Pedro. The priest takes Dora's
pulse, puts his hand on her head:
"She's dead."
He starts a prayer. And almost all of them pray aloud:
"Our Father, who art in heaven . . ."
Pedro Bala remembers the prayers at night in the Reformatory. He hunches his shoulders, covers his ears. He turns,
looks at Dora's body. Lollipop has put a purple flower between
her fingers. Pedro Bala breaks into sobs.

The *mãe-de-santo* Don'Aninha has come, God's-Love has come
too. Pedro Bala doesn't take part in the conversation. Aninha
says:
"She was like a shadow in this life. She became a saint in the
other. Zumbi of Palmares is a saint in halfbreed *candomblés*,
Rosa Palmeirão too. Brave men and women become saints for
blacks . . ."
"She was like a shadow . . ." Big João repeats.
She was like a shadow for all of them, a happening that had
no explanation. Except for Pedro Bala, who had her. Except
for Professor, who loved her.
Father José Pedro speaks:
"She's gone to heaven, she had no sins. She didn't know
what sin was . . ."

Lollipop prays. God's-Love knows what they expect of him. To take the body in his sloop and throw it into the sea, beyond the old fort. How can a funeral leave from the warehouse? It's hard to explain all that to Father José Pedro. Legless does it in a hurried voice. The priest is horrified at first. It's a sin, he can't consent to a sin. But he consents, he won't tell where the Captains of the Sands live. Pedro Bala doesn't say anything.

The peace of night is all around. In Dora's dead eyes, the eyes of a mother, a sister, a sweetheart, and a wife, there is a great peace. Some of the boys are weeping. Dry Gulch and Big João will carry the body. But, facing it, Dry Gulch can't reach out his hands, Big João is crying like a woman.

Don'Aninha wraps her in a white shawl:

"She's going to Iemanjá," she says. "She's going to become a saint too . . ."

But no one can carry the body. Because Pedro Bala is hugging it, won't let go of it. Professor calls to him:

"Let go. I loved her too. Now . . ."

They carry her into the peace of the night, into the mystery of the sea. The priest prays, it's a strange procession that goes through the night to God's-Love's sloop. From the sands, Pedro Bala watches the sloop as it goes away. He bites his hands, stretches out his arms.

They go back into the warehouse. The white sail of the sloop is lost at sea. The moon lights up the sands, the stars are both in the sky and in the sea. There is peace in the night. A peace that comes from Dora's eyes.

LIKE A STAR WITH
BLOND HAIR

On the waterfront of Bahia, they say that when a brave man dies, he becomes a star in the sky. That's how it was with Zumbi, with Lucas da Feira, with Beetle, all brave black men. But there was never a case of a woman, brave as she might be, becoming a star after death. Some, like Rosa Palmeirão, like Maria Cabaçu, became saints in halfbreed *candomblés*. None of them ever became a star.

Pedro Bala jumps into the water. He can't stay in the warehouse, amidst the sobbing and laments. He wants to go with Dora, join her in Iemanjá's Lands of the Endless Way. He keeps swimming forward. He's following the wake of God's-Love's sloop. He swims, keeps on swimming. He sees Dora before him, Dora, his wife, her arms out to him. He swims until he has no more strength. He floats then, his eyes turned up to the stars and the great yellow moon in the sky. What does dying matter when we're going in search of the beloved, when love awaits us?

What does it matter either that astonomers say that it was a comet that passed over Bahia that night? What Pedro Bala saw was Dora, changed into a star, going to heaven. She was braver than all women, braver than Rosa Palmeirão, than Maria Cabaçu. So brave that, before dying, while still a girl, she gave herself to his love. That's why she became a star in the sky. A star with long, blond hair, a star like none other ever in the Bahia night of peace.

Happiness lights up Pedro Bala's face. The peace of the night came for him too. Because now he knows that she will shine for him among a thousand stars in the unmatched sky of the black city.

God's-Love's sloop picks him up.

SONG OF BAHIA, SONG OF FREEDOM

VOCATIONS

Not much time had passed since Dora's death, the image of her presence, so swift and yet making such a mark, of her death, too, still filled the warehouse nights with visions. Some, when they came in, would still look toward the corner where she used to sit alongside Professor and Big João. Still with the hope of finding her there. It had been something without explanation. It had been something completely unexpected in their lives, the appearance of a mother, a sister. Reason for them to look for still in spite of having seen God's-Love take her away in his sloop to the bottom of the sea. Only Pedro Bala didn't look for her in the warehouse. He looked for her in the sky where there were so many stars, a star with long, blond hair.

One day Professor came into the warehouse and didn't light his candle, didn't open a story book, didn't chat. For him that whole life had ended, ever since Dora had been carried off by fever. When he'd seen the warehouse fill up with her presence. For Professor, everything had a new meaning. The warehouse was like the frame of a picture: now the blond hair falling over Cat, who saw his mother. Now the lips that kissed Zé Ferret to put him to sleep. Or the voice that sang lullabies. Also proud smiles for Dry Gulch's bravery, as if she were a fearless backlands mulatto woman. Or her entrance into the warehouse, hair flying, her face all laughter, back from the day's adventure on the streets of the city. Or eyes full of love, fever burning her face, hands calling her beloved for the first and last possession. Now the Professor looks upon the warehouse as a frame without a picture. Useless. For him it had ceased having meaning or had too terrible a meaning. He'd changed a great deal in those months after Dora's death, he went about silently, his face serious, and he struck up a relationship with that gentleman who once on the Rua Chile had chatted with him, given him a cigarette holder and his address.

That night, Professor didn't light a candle, didn't open a story book. He kept silent when Big João came over beside him. He was gathering his belongings in a bundle. They were almost all books. Big João was looking at him, not saying anything, but he understood a lot, even if everybody said there was no bigger black boob than Big João the black boy. But when Pedro Bala arrived and sat down beside him too and offered him a cigarette, Professor spoke:

"I'm going away, Bullet . . ."

"Where to, buddy?"

Professor looked at the warehouse, the boys going about, laughing, moving among the rats like shadows:

"What's this life going to get us? Just a beating at the police station when they catch us. Everybody says it might change someday . . . Father José Pedro, João de Adão, even you. Now I'm going to change mine . . ."

Pedro Bala didn't say anything, but the question was in his eyes. Big João didn't ask anything, he understood it all.

"I'm going to study with a painter in Rio. Dr. Dantas, the one with the cigarette holder, wrote to him, sent him some of my sketches. He sent word to send me down . . . Someday I'm going to show what our life was like . . . I'm going to paint everybody's picture . . . You talked about it once, remember? Well, I'm going to do it . . ."

Pedro Bala's voice backed him up:

"You're going to change our lives too . . ."

"How?" Big João asked.

Professor didn't understand either. And Pedro Bala didn't know how to explain it. But confidence in the Professor, in the pictures he would paint, in the stamp of hate he carried in his heart, in the stamp of love for justice and freedom he carried inside himself. A childhood lived among the Captains of the Sands isn't anything useless. Even when later on you're going to be an artist and not a thief, murderer, or drifter. But Pedro Bala didn't know how to explain all that. He only said:

"We'll never forget you, buddy . . . You read us stories, you were the sharpest of the group . . . The sharpest . . ."

Professor lowered his head. Big João got up, his voice was a call, it was a farewell shout too:

"People, people!"

They all came, stood around. Big João held out his arms:

"People, Professor's going away. He's going to be a painter in Rio de Janeiro. People, let's give a cheer for the Professor."

The cheer tightened the boy's heart. He looked around the warehouse. It wasn't like a picture without a frame. It was like the frame of any number of pictures. Like the pictures on a reel of movie film. Lives of struggle and courage. Misery too. An urge to stay. But what use was there in staying. If he left, he could be of more help. He'd exhibit those lives . . . They shake his hand, embrace him. Dry Gulch is sad, as sad as if a *cangaceiro* from Lampião's gang had died.

That night on the dock the man with the cigarette holder, who was a poet, gives the Professor a letter and some money:

"He'll meet you at the pier. I sent a telegram. I hope you won't betray the trust I've put in your talents."

Never had a third-class passenger had so many people seeing him off. Dry Gulch gives him a dagger as a present. Pedro Bala does everything he can to laugh, say pleasant things. But Big João can't hide the sadness inside himself.

From far off, Professor can still see Pedro Bala's cap waving on the dock. And in the midst of those strangers, officers in uniform, businessmen, and young ladies, he's timid, doesn't know what to do, feels that all his courage has stayed behind with the Captains of the Sands. But inside his chest there's the stamp of a love for freedom. A stamp that will lead him to leave the old painter who teaches him academic things and go paint pictures on his own, ones which, more than causing admiration, frighten the whole nation.

Winter passed, summer passed, another winter came and this one was full of long rains, the wind didn't stop blowing on the sands a single night. Now Lollipop was selling newspapers, working as a bootblack, carrying passengers' luggage. He'd managed to give up stealing to make a living. Pedro Bala let him stay on at the warehouse in spite of his not leading the same life as the others. Pedro Bala doesn't understand what's going on inside Lollipop. He knows that he wants to be a priest, that he wants to get away from that life. But he doesn't think that will solve anything, won't straighten out their lives at all. Father José Pedro did everything to change their lives. But only one of them, the others didn't think he'd done too well. What had it got him? Only if all of them were united, as João de Adão would say.

But God was calling Lollipop. In the night, in the warehouse, the boy heard the call of God. It was a powerful voice inside him. A voice as powerful as the voice of the sea, as the voice of the wind that blows around the big old house. A voice that doesn't speak to his ears, that speaks to his heart. A voice that calls him, that makes him happy and frightened at the same time. A voice that demands everything of him in order to give him the happiness of serving. God is calling him. And God's call inside Lollipop is as powerful as the voice of the wind, as the powerful voice of the sea. Lollipop wants to live for God, entirely for God, a life of withdrawal and penance, a life that will cleanse him of his sins, will make him worthy of the contemplation of God. God calls him and Lollipop thinks about his salvation. He'll be a penitent, he won't look at the spectacle of the world anymore. He doesn't want to see anything that's going on in the world in order to have his eyes sufficiently clean to see the face of God. Because for those who don't have their eyes completely clean of all sin, the face of God is as

terrible as the infuriated sea. But for those who have their eye
and heart clean of all sin, the face of God is calm, like the waves
of the sea on a morning of sunlight and tranquility.

Lollipop is stamped by God. But he's also stamped by the
life of the Captains of the Sands. He withdraws from their
freedom, from seeing and hearing the spectacle of the world,
the stamp of adventure on the Captains of the Sands in order
to hear the call of God. Because the voice of God that speaks
in his heart is powerful beyond comparison. He'll pray for the
Captains of the Sands in his penitent's cell. Because he has to
hear and follow the voice that's calling him. It's a voice that
transfigures his face on the winter night in the warehouse. As
if it were springtime there.

Father José Pedro was called to the Archdiocese again. This
time the canon is accompanied by the superior of the Capuchins. Father José Pedro is trembling, thinking that they're
going to scold him again, are going to talk about his sins. He's
done many things against the law in order to help the Captains
of the Sands. He fears he failed, because in almost no way has
he bettered their life. But at certain cruel moments he derived
a bit of comfort from those small hearts. And he had Lollipop . . . He was a conquest for God. Although he hadn't done
everything, although he hadn't transformed those lives as he
wanted, he hadn't lost completely either. He'd managed something for God. He was happy in spite of his sadness over how
little he'd accomplished for the Captains of the Sands. Even so,
at certain moments he'd been like the family they didn't have.
At certain moments he'd been father and mother. Now the
leaders were big boys, almost men. Professor had already gone
off, others wouldn't be long in leaving. Even if they went off to
be thieves, to live a life of sin, at certain moments the priest
had succeeded in lessening the spectacle of misery in their lives
with a little comfort and love. And solidarity.

But this time the canon doesn't scold. He announces that the
Archbishop has decided to give him a parish. He concluded:

"You've given us a lot of trouble, Father, with your mistaken

ideas on upbringing. I hope that the Archbishop's goodness in
giving you this parish will make you think about your obliga-
tions and give up those Bolshevik innovations."

The parish had never had a priest because the Archbishop
had never found one prepared to go among *cangaceiros* in a
village lost far in the backlands. But the name of the hamlet
gladdens Father José Pedro's heart. He was going among bandits. And *cangaceiros* are like big children. He thanked him,
was going to speak, but the superior of the Capuchins interrupted him:

"The canon tells me that among those boys there's one who
has a priestly vocation . . ."

"I was going to mention that very same thing," the priest
said. "I've never seen such a firm vocation."

The missionary smiled:

"Because we're in need of a brother. It isn't the same as
being a priest, I know that full well. But it's quite close to it.
And if his vocation is real, the order might have him study and
even have him ordained."

"He'll be wild with happiness."

"Will you answer for him?"

Lollipop was going to be a monk. Someday he might be
ordained. The priest leaves, thanking God.

They take the priest to the station. The train whistle is like a
lament. Several of the Captains of the Sands are there. Father
José Pedro looks at them with love. Pedro Bala says:

"You were good to us, Father. A good man. We're not going
to forget you . . ."

They don't recognize Lollipop when he arrives dressed in a
monk's robe, a long cord hanging down the side. Father José
Pedro says:

"Do you know Brother Francisco of the Holy Family?"

They look at Lollipop with a certain shame. He's thinner,
has an ascetic look. He looks very tall in the Capuchin habit.

"He'll pray for you . . ." Father José Pedro says.

He says goodby. Gets into the coach. The train whistles, it's
like a farewell. From the window the priest sees the boys waving

their hands and their caps, old hats, rags that serve as handkerchiefs. An old woman across from him, dying to start a conversation, is startled to see the priest weeping.

Good-Life doesn't come to the warehouse very much. He has a guitar, composes sambas, he's great, he's one more drifter on the streets of Bahia. No one leads a life like that of the drifters. He spends the day chatting on the docks, at the market, goes to parties on the hilltops and at the Cidade da Palha at night or to *macumbas*. He plays his guitar, eats and drinks the very best, rouses up halfbreed girls with his voice and his music. He raises rows at parties, and when the police chase him he takes refuge in the warehouse among the Captains of the Sands.

Then he plays for them, laughs with them in great guffaws, as if he were still one of them. Good-Life slowly moves away as he grows. When he's nineteen, he won't be coming back anymore. He'll be a thoroughgoing drifter, one of those mulattoes who love Bahia above all, who live a perfect life on the streets of the city. The enemy of wealth and work, the friend of parties, music, the bodies of halfbreed girls. A drifter. A rowdy. A *capoeira* fighter, switchblade artist, thief when necessary. Good-hearted, the way Good-Life sings in an ABC ballad that he put together about another drifter. Promising the girls to reform and go to work, always staying a drifter. One of the rowdies of the city. A figure that future Captains of the Sands will love and admire, just as Good-Life loved and admired God's-Love.

One day, after a long time had passed, Pedro Bala was going along the streets with Legless. They went into a church in Piedade, they liked to look at gold objects, it was even easy to snatch the purse of a lady at prayer. But there was no lady in the church at that time. Only a group of poor boys and a Capuchin who was teaching them catechism.

"It's Lollipop . . ." Legless said.

Pedro Bala stood looking. Shrugged his shoulders:

"What's it got him?"

Legless looked:

"Barely enough to eat . . ."

"Someday he'll be a priest too. He has to go all the way."

Legless said:

"Goodness isn't enough."

He finished the thought:

"Only hate . . ."

Lollipop didn't see them. With extreme patience and goodness, he was teaching the unruly children their catechism lessons. The two Captains of the Sands went out shaking their heads. Pedro Bala put his hand on Legless's shoulder:

"Not hate, not goodness. Only the struggle."

Lollipop's kind voice crossed through the church. Legless's voice of hate was next to Pedro Bala. But he didn't hear either one. What he heard was the voice of João de Adão, the dockworker, the voice of his father, dying in the struggle.

THE SPINSTER'S
LOVE SONG

Cat said that the old maid was loaded with money. She was the last of a rich family, going on forty-five, ugly and nervous. The word went around that she had a parlor full of gold objects, diamonds and jewels accumulated by the family over generations. Pedro Bala thought it might render up a little taste of money. González, the pawnbroker at the "14," would pay for those items. He asked Legless:

"Think you can get in?"

"I can . . ."

"Then we'll raid."

They laughed in the warehouse. Cat left to see Dalva. Legless told him:

"I'll go over tomorrow."

The old maid opened the door. She had only one servant, an old black woman who seemed to be part of the inheritance, for she'd been with the family for fifty years. The old maid looked very haughtily at Legless:

"Do you want something?"

"I'm a poor crippled orphan." He showed her his game leg. "I don't want to live by stealing or begging. Have you got any work for me to do? I could do your shopping."

The old maid didn't take her eyes off him. A boy . . . It wasn't kindness speaking inside her. It was the voice of a sex that was giving its last beats. In a short time her sex would become useless, the doctors had said that her nervousness would stop then. Much earlier, when she was still a young lady, there'd been a boy in the house to do the shopping. It had been good . . . But her brother had found out, sent the boy away. Now the brother was dead, another boy had come to ask if he could do her shopping:

"All right."

She told him to take a bath. In the afternoon she gave him money for the shopping and also for some clothes for himself. Legless managed to add a thousand two hundred to the bills. He thought:

"I'm going to make some money while I'm here . . ."

In the kitchen the black woman told ancient stories in her mixed-up language. Legless listened, showing excessive interest in order to win the woman's confidence. But when he asked her about the gold objects, the woman didn't answer. Legless didn't insist. He knew how to be patient, he was used to that kind of work. In the parlor the old maid was embroidering a shawl, watching Legless through the door with interest. She had an ugly face, but her oldish body still had something attractive about it. She called Legless over to look at the work she was doing. When Legless took a look, she bent over, he saw her large breasts. But he didn't think she was showing them to him. He found the work very nice, he said:

"You're a very smart lady . . ."

He even seemed to be a well-brought-up boy. In spite of his game leg and ugly face, the old maid found him handsome. It would have been better if he hadn't been quite so grown. But even so . . . She bent over again, showed her breasts to Legless. Legless averted his eyes, didn't think that she did it on purpose. When he praised the work again, she passed her hand over his face:

"Thank you, son." Her voice was languid.

The black woman laid out a mattress in the dining room for Legless to sleep on. She covered it with a sheet, got a pillow.

The old maid was visiting the house of a friend on the same street, and when she returned, Legless was already lying down. He heard her taking leave of someone:

"Forgive me for making you take a spinster home."

"Dona Joana, don't say that . . ."

She came in, locked the street door, removed the key. The black woman had already gone to bed in her room off the kitchen. The old maid came into the dining room, took a peek at Legless, who pretended to be asleep. She sighed. Went into her room.

The lights were all out in the house. In spite of its being very early in comparison with the time they went to bed in the warehouse, Legless fell asleep.

That's why he didn't know what time it was when the spinster came. What he felt was a hand running through his hair. He thought it was a nice dream. The hand slid down, passed over his chest, onto his stomach, now it was softly gripping his sex. Legless woke up completely, but he kept his eyes shut. The old maid was squeezing his sex, lying next to him. She had a nightgown on. She put Legless's hand on her body. Legless got close to her. He tried to speak, she put her hand on his mouth, pointed to the kitchen:

"She might hear . . ."

Then she said in a softer voice:

"You're going to be nice to me, aren't you?"

She squeezed against him. She pulled Legless's pants down. Then she covered them both with the sheet. But when Legless wanted to go all the way, she said:

"No. Only on the outside."

It was an incomplete affair that enraged Legless.

The old maid was softly moaning with love. She was squeezing Legless's head against her enormous breasts, his sex against her thighs, the boy's hand on her sex.

Legless gets up bewildered. A great weariness in his limbs. Those nights are like a battle. It's never a complete pleasure, a full satisfaction. The old maid wants a crumb of love. She's

afraid of complete love, the scandal of a child. But she's hungry and thirsty for love, she doesn't care if it's only the crumbs.
But Legless wants full love, it bothers him, makes his hate
grow. At the same time, he feels drawn to the body of the old
maid, the half-caresses, exchanged in the night. One thing
keeps him in that house. Even though he feels hatred for Joana
when he wakes up, an impotent rage, an urge to strangle her
since he can't possess her fully, even though he finds her ugly
and old, when night approaches he gets eager for the spinster's
caresses, for the hand that manipulates his boyish sex, for her
breasts, where he rests his head, for her thick thighs. He thinks
up plans to possess her, but the old maid frustrates them, fleeing at the last moment and scolding him in a low voice. A dull
rage comes over Legless. But her hand goes back to his sex and
he can't fight against desire. And there's a return to that tremendous struggle from which he emerges nervous and exhausted.

During the day he scarcely answers the old maid, says brutal
things, the old maid weeps. He calls her spinster, says he's going
away. She gives him money, asks him to stay. But he doesn't stay
because of the money. He stays because desire holds him back.
He already knows which key opens the room where Joana
keeps her gold objects. He knows how to lift the key to bring to
the Captains of the Sands. But desire holds him there, along
with the spinster's breasts and thighs. Along with the spinster's
hand.

He'd always been unfortunate on the woman side. When he
managed to get a little black girl on the sand, it was with the
help of the others, by force. No one looked at him, inviting him
with her eyes. Others were ugly, but he was repulsive, with his
game leg, walking like a crab. Besides, he'd ended up being
nasty and was in the habit of possessing the black girls by force.
Now along comes a white woman, with money, too, old and
ugly, it's true, but quite screwable still, and she was going to
bed with him. He stroked her sex with his hand, lay thigh to
thigh, rested his head on her big breasts. Legless couldn't leave
there, even if he was getting more brutish and more restless
every day. His desire demanded a complete possession. But the
spinster was content to gather up the crumbs of love.

During the day Legless hates her, hates himself, hates the whole world.

Pedro Bala complained about the delay. It was time enough already for Legless to know the secrets of the house. Legless says yes, he won't take any longer. And that night the battle of love is even stronger. The old maid moans with love, picking up the crumbs of love. But she won't cede "her honor." That gives Legless the courage to take off with the key the next day.

The spinster is waiting for him for love. She's like a wife who's been abandoned by her husband. She weeps and pities herself. Her love isn't coming, she needs love too, just like all those girls who pass on the street in their pretty dresses.

But the robbery infuriates her. Because she thinks that Legless only loved her on the long nights of sin in order to rob her. Her thirst for love is humiliated. It's as if he'd spat in her face, saying it was because of her ugliness. She weeps, she doesn't moan a song of love anymore. She feels enough anger to strangle Legless if she were to find him. Because he'd mocked her love, the thirst for love that's in her blood. Her misfortune is even more thorough because for a whole week she was completely happy with the crumbs of love. She rolls on the floor with an attack.

In the warehouse, Legless laughs, telling about his adventure. But underneath he knows that the old maid had made him even worse, with her vices had increased the hate that dwelt latent in his heart. Now an unsatisfied desire fills his nights. A desire that interferes with his sleep, that brings on rage.

HITCHING A RIDE
ON A TRAIN

The ships reach Ilhéus loaded with women. Women who come
from Bahia, from Aracaju, the complete womandom of Recife,
the same for Rio de Janeiro. The fat plantation colonels watch
the arrival of the women from the docks. Black, blond, mulatto
women, they've come in search of them. Because the news of
the rise in cacao prices has spread all over the country. The
news that in a relatively small city like Ilhéus four cabarets had
opened. That the colonels squandered their money in nights of
gambling and champagne, five hundred thousand *reis* notes.
That in the wee small hours of the morning they would go out
naked into the streets of the city to form the so-called Y
ox-team. The news ran through the streets of lost women.
Traveling salesmen carried the news. The Brama cabaret in
Aracaju was depopulated of women. They went to the El-Dorado,
a cabaret in Ilhéus. The women from Recife came down on ships
of the Lóide Brasileiro Line. The Pernambucans were left without women, they'd all gone to the Bataclan cabaret, nicknamed the School by students on vacation. Some had come
from Rio de Janeiro, and these went to the Trianon, formerly
the Vesúvio, the most luxurious of the four cabarets in the
cacao city. Even Rita Tanajura, famous for her great rolling
behind, left the peace of her city of Estância, where she was
queen of the women of easy virtue and where she took on

everyone, and came to be the queen of the Far-West, the cabaret on the Rua do Sapo, where kisses and the pop of champagne bottles mingled with pistol shots, the noise of brawls.
Because the Far-West was the cabaret of the foremen, the small
landowners who were suddenly wealthy.

On Dalva's street, in the district of lost women in Bahia, the
houses were depopulated. Women had gone to the Bataclan, to
the El-Dorado, mulatto women to the Far-West. A few had
gone to the Trianon, where they danced with the colonels. At
the Bataclan, Pernambucan and Sergipean women gave part of
the money they got from the colonels to students, who gave them
love in return. Travelers filled the El-Dorado. Even in the Far-
West women got jewels. Sometimes they got a bullet too, like
a strange red jewel on their breast. Rita Tanajura danced the
Charleston on top of a table in the midst of champagne and
pistol shots. All of that took place during that rise in cacao
prices many years ago.

When Dalva learned that Isabel had necklaces and a dia-
mond ring and, yet, wasn't at the Trianon, which was the most
luxurious of the cabarets, but was at the Bataclan, she couldn't
resist. She packed her bags. What couldn't she do at the Trianon, she, who was the best of the women on her street? She
decked Cat out in an elegant cashmere suit, made to order,
suddenly Cat wasn't a boy anymore, he was the youngest con
man in Bahia.

On the night when, decked out in his new suit, black polished
shoes, bow tie, Panama hat, he appeared at the warehouse, Big
João let out an exclamation of surprise:

"Say, isn't that Cat?"

Cat still wasn't eighteen. He'd been making love to Dalva
for four years. He turned to Big João:

"Life's about to begin . . ."

He passes around cigarettes from an expensive case, smooths
his slick hair. He puts his hand on Pedro Bala's shoulder:

"Buddy, I'm going to Ilhéus. The old lady is going to try out
life there. I'm going with her. I might even get rich. Where
there are plantation owners, you can pull a big swindle."

Pedro smiled. It was another one leaving. They wouldn't be

boys all their lives . . . He knew quite well that they'd never seemed like children. Since very small, in the risky life on the streets, the Captains of the Sands were like men, were the equal of men. The only difference was in size. In everything else they were equal: they loved and pulled down black girls onto the sand from an early age, they stole in order to live, like the thieves of the city. When they were caught, they were beaten like men. Sometimes they made armed attacks, like the most feared bandits in Bahia. Nor did they talk like children either, they talked like men. They felt the same as men. When other children were only concerned with playing, studying books in order to learn how to read, they found themselves involved in happenings that only men knew how to resolve. They'd always been like men in their life of misery and adventure, they'd never been completely children. Because what makes a child is the environment of a home, father, mother, no responsibility. They'd never had a father or mother in the life of the street. And they'd always had to take care of themselves, had always been responsible for themselves. They'd always been the same as men. Now the oldest ones, those who'd been the leaders of the gang for years, were big boys, beginning to go off to their destinies. Professor had already gone away, he was painting pictures in Rio de Janeiro. Good-Life had broken away from the warehouse a while back, playing guitar at parties, going to *candomblés*, raising hell at fairs. He's one more drifter in the city. His name is already well known, even in the newspapers. Like other vagabonds, he's known to police detectives, who always keep their eyes on drifters. Lollipop is a monk in a monastery, God called him, they'll never hear anything more from him. Now it's Cat who's leaving, going to squeeze money out of the colonels in Ilhéus. God's-Love once said that Cat would get rich. Because life on the street, abandonment, had made Cat a crooked gambler, a swindler, a gigolo. It won't be long before the others leave. Only Pedro Bala doesn't know what to do. In a while he'll be more than a big boy, he'll be a man and he'll have to turn the leadership of the Captains of the Sands over to someone else. Where will he go? He can't be an intellectual like Professor, whose hands were made to paint, he wasn't born to be a drifter like Good-Life, who doesn't feel the spectacle of men's daily struggle, who only likes to wander around the streets, chat squatting on the docks, drink at celebrations on the hilltops. Pedro feels the spectacle of men, he doesn't think this freedom is enough for the thirst for freedom he has inside. Nor does he feel the call of God as Lollipop felt it. For him, the preachings of Father José Pedro never said anything. He liked the priest as a good man. Only João de Adão's words found a place in his heart. But even João de Adão knows very little. What he's got are strong muscles and a commanding voice, and he still isn't big enough to lead a strike. Nor does Pedro Bala want to go off like Cat to trick the colonels of Ilhéus, suck money out of them. He wants something that he still can't figure out, and that's why he lingers among the Captains of the Sands.

The warehouse shouts, saying goodby to Cat. He smiles, so elegant, smoothing his hair, on his finger that wine-colored ring he'd stolen once.

From the pier Pedro Bala waves goodby to Cat. Dressed in his ragged clothes, waving his cap, he feels very far away from Cat, who, alongside Dalva, looks like a full-fledged man in his well-fitting suit. Pedro feels afflicted, an urge to flee, to go anywhere, on a ship or hitching a ride on a train.

But the one who is going to hitch a ride on a train is Dry Gulch. One afternoon the police caught him when the mulatto was relieving a businessman of his wallet. Dry Gulch was sixteen at the time. He was taken to the police station, they beat him because he cursed them all, patrolmen and officers, with that immense disdain a backlands man has for the police. He didn't utter a sound when they beat him. A week later they turned him out onto the street and he went away almost happy because now he had a mission in life: killing cops.

He spent a few days at the warehouse, his face somber, sunk in his thoughts. The backlands were calling him, the struggle of the bandits called him. One day he said to Pedro Bala:

"I'm going to spend some time with the Bandit Indians in Aracaju."

The Bandit Indians were the Captains of the Sands of

Aracaju. They lived under bridges, stole and fought in the
streets. The juvenile judge, Olímpio Mendonça was a good man,
he tried to resolve conflicts as best he could, pondered the intelligence of children who were just like men, understood that it
was impossible to resolve the problem. He told novelists things
about the boys, deep down he loved the boys. But he felt
afflicted because he couldn't solve their problems. When somebody new appeared among the Bandit Indians, he knew that it
was a Bahian who'd arrived by hitching a ride on a train. And
when one disappeared, he knew that he'd gone to be with the
Captains of the Sands in Bahia.

One day the train for Sergipe whistled at the Calçada station. No one came to bring Dry Gulch to the station because
he was leaving to come back, he was going to spend some time
with the Bandit Indians, to forget the Bahia police, who'd
stamped him. Dry Gulch got into an open boxcar, hid among
some bales. In a short while the train leaves the station. Then
it's the backlands route, the India Nordestina. Women and
girls appear in the adobe houses. The men, half-naked, are
working the land. On the animal road that runs parallel to the
railroad, ox teams pass. Drovers shout, goading the animals.
At the stations they sell corn sweets, manioc mush, rolled corn
paste, and grated coconut-corn mix. The backlands are getting into Dry Gulch's nose and eyes. Cheeses and raw sugar
blocks pass by on trays at the small stations, the never forgotten wild countryside fills the eyes of the backland boy once
more. Those many years spent in the city haven't taken away
his love for the miserable and beautiful backlands. He'd never
been a city child like Pedro Bala, Good-Life, Cat. He'd always
been out of place in the city, with a different way of speaking,
talking about Lampião, saying "my godpa," imitating the
voices of backlands animals. Formerly, he and his mother had
had a piece of land. She was a close friend of Lampião, the
colonels respected her land. But when Lampião went off into
the backlands of Pernambuco, the colonels took Dry Gulch's
mother's land. She went down to the city to ask for justice. She
died on the way. Dry Gulch continued the trip with his somber
face. He learned many things in the city among the Captains

of the Sands. He learned that it wasn't only in the backlands that rich men were bad to the poor. In the city, too. He learned that poor children are bad off everywhere, that the rich persecute and run things everywhere. He smiled sometimes, but never stopped hating. In the figure of José Pedro he discovered why Lampião respected priests. If he'd already thought that Lampião was a hero, his experience in the city, the hate acquired in the city, made him love the figure of his godfather above everything. Even above Pedro Bala.

Now it's the backlands. The smell of backland flowers. Friendly fields, friendly birds, skinny dogs in the doorway of houses. Old men who look like missionaries among the Indians, black men with long rosaries around their necks. The good smell of corn and manioc cooking. Thin men who work the land in order to earn a thousand five hundred from landowners. Only the brushland belongs to everyone, because Lampião freed the brushland, drove the rich men out of the brushland, made the brushland the home of the *cangaceiro* bandits who fight against the plantation owners. Lampião, the hero, the hero of all the backlands of five States. They say he's a criminal, a heartless bandit, murderer, rapist, thief. But for Dry Gulch, for the men, women, and children of the backlands he's a new Zumbi of Palmares, he's a liberator, the captain of a new army. Because freedom is like sunlight, the best thing in the world. And Lampião fights, kills, deflowers, and steals for freedom. For freedom and justice for the exploited men of the backlands of five States: Pernambuco, Paraíba, Alagoas, Sergipe, Bahia.

The backlands bring emotion to Dry Gulch's eyes. The train doesn't go fast, it goes along slowly, cutting through the backlands. Here everything is lyrical, poor, and beautiful. Only the misery of men is terrible. But these men are so strong that they've managed to create beauty within this misery. What won't they do when Lampião frees all the brushland, implanting justice and freedom?

Guitarists pass, improvisors of poetry. Herdsmen pass, driving cattle, men plant manioc and corn. At the stations, colonels get off to stretch their legs. They carry large revolvers. The blind guitarists sing, asking for alms. A black man in a short shirt and a rosary goes through the station saying strange things in an unknown tongue. He used to be a slave, now he's a madman at the station. Everybody is afraid of him, afraid of his curses. Because he suffered a lot, the factor's whip cut his back. The whip of the policeman, factor for the rich, had also cut Dry Gulch's back. They'll all be afraid of him, too, one day.

Brush of the backlands, smell of backland flowers, the slow movement of the backland train. Men in rope sandals wearing leather hats. Children who study to be *cangaceiros* in the school of misery and the exploitation of man.

The train stops in the middle of the brushland. Dry Gulch jumps out of the boxcar. The bandits are aiming their rifles, the truck that brought them is parked on the other side of the tracks, the telegraph wires have been cut. In the wild brush no one can be seen. A girl faints in one of the coaches, a traveling salesman hides his wallet with money in it. A fat colonel gets out of the coach, speaks:

"Captain Virgulino . . ."

The *cangaceiro* with glasses aims his rifle:

"Inside."

Dry Gulch thinks his heart is going to burst with joy. He's found his godfather, Virgulino Ferreira Lampião, the hero of backland children. He goes up to him, another *cangaceiro* tries to push him away, but he says:

"Godfather . . ."

"Who are you?"

"I'm Dry Gulch, the son of your good friend . . ."

Lampião recognizes him, smiles. The bandits are going into the first-class coaches, there aren't many of the *cangaceiros*, some twelve. Dry Gulch asks:

"Godfather, let me stay with you . . . Give me a rifle."

"You're still a boy . . ." Lampião looks at him with his dark glasses.

"Not anymore, no, I've already had a fight with a cop . . ."

Lampião shouts:

"Zé Bahia, give Dry Gulch a rifle . . ."

He looks at his godson:

"Guard this exit. If anyone tries to escape, shoot him."

He goes in to collect. Fainting and cries from inside, the sound of a shot. Then the group returns to the road. They bring along two policemen who were traveling on the train. Lampião divides up the money with the *cangaceiros*, Dry Gulch also gets a share. From a coach, a trail of blood is dripping. The good smell of the backlands penetrates Dry Gulch's nose. The policemen are stood up against some trees. Zé Bahia cocks his rifle, but the voice of Dry Gulch asks for a favor:

"Let me, godfather. They beat me in the police station, they beat a lot of kids."

He raises the rifle, what backlands boy doesn't know how to shoot straight?

His somber face has a smile that fills it completely. The first one falls, the second tries to run away, but the bullet catches him in the back. Then Dry Gulch runs over on top of them with his dagger, satisfies his revenge. Zé Bahia says:

"This kid is a good one . . ."

"His mother was a tough one, she was my good friend . . ." Lampião remembers proudly.

"A real wild beast . . ." the traveler thinks while the train moves along slowly after the trainmen have taken the sawhorses off the tracks. The group of *cangaceiros* is lost in the brushland. The air of the backlands fills Dry Gulch's lungs as with his knife he cuts two notches in the stock of his rifle. The first two. In the distance, the train whistles in anguish.

LIKE A CIRCUS
TRAPEZE ARTIST

It had been too daring to raid that house on the Rua Rui Barbosa. Near there, on the Praça do Palácio, there were a lot of guards, detectives, policemen. But they were thirsty for adventure, they were getting bigger and bigger and more and more daring. But there were a lot of people in the house, they gave the alarm, the guards came. Pedro Bala and Big João took off down the slope of the square. Outrigger got away too. But Legless was cornered on the street. He played hide-and-seek with the guards. They'd given up on the others, thought it would be enough to catch that cripple. Legless ran from one side of the street to the other, out-dribbled one of the guards, went down the hill. But instead of going down to take the Baixa dos Sapateiros, he headed for the Praça do Palácio. Because Legless knew that if he ran on the street they would catch him for sure. They were men with longer legs than his, and, besides, he was lame, he couldn't run very fast. And, above all, he didn't want them to catch him. He remembered the time he'd been taken to the police station. The dreams he had on his bad nights. They wouldn't catch him, and while he runs that's the only thought that goes with him. The guards are right on his heels. Legless knows they'd like to catch him, that the capture of one of the Captains of the Sands is a big thing for a guard. That will be his vengeance. He won't let them catch him, they won't lay a hand on his body. Legless hates them the way he hates the whole world, because he was never able to have any love. And the day he had it, he was obliged to leave it, because life had already marked him too much. He'd never had the happiness of a child. He'd become a man before he was ten years old in order to struggle for the most miserable of lives: the life of an abandoned child. He'd never come to love anyone, unless it was the dog who followed him. While the hearts of other children are still pure with feelings, Legless's is already full of hate. He hated the city, life, men. He only loved his hatred, the feeling that made him strong and courageous in spite of his physical defect. Once a woman had been good to him. But it really wasn't for him, but for the son she'd lost and thought had returned. At another time another woman had lain down with him in a bed, caressed his sex, taken advantage of him to collect the crumbs of love she'd never had. They'd never loved him for what he was, however, an abandoned boy, crippled and sad. A lot of people hated him. And he hated everybody. He'd been beaten at the police station, a man laughed when they beat him. For him, it's that man who's running after him in the figure of the guards. If they bring him in, the man will laugh again. They won't bring him in. They're right on his heels, but they won't bring him in. They think he's going to stop by the big elevator. But Legless doesn't stop. He climbs up over the small fence, turns his face to the guards, who are still running, laughs with all the strength of his hatred, spits in the face of the one who's approaching, holding out his arms, throws himself backward into space like a circus trapeze artist.

The whole square is suspended for a moment. "He jumped," a woman says and faints. Legless crashes onto the hillside like a circus trapeze artist who'd missed the other trapeze. The dog is barking between the bars of the fence.

NEWS ITEMS

The *Jornal da Tarde* publishes a wire from Rio reporting the success of an exhibition by a young painter unknown until then. Days later it reprints some art criticism published in a Rio de Janeiro newspaper. Because the painter is a Bahian, and the *Jornal da Tarde* is very mindful of the glories of Bahia. A portion of the criticism goes on to speak of the qualities and defects of the new social painter, using and abusing expressions such as setting, light, color, angles, strength, and others, it says:

. . . one detail was noticed by all who went to this strange exhibition of scenes and portraits of poor boys. It is the fact that all good feelings are always represented by the figure of a thin, blond girl with feverish cheeks. And that all evil feelings are represented by a man in a black overcoat and the look of a traveler. What interpretation would a psychiatrist find in the almost unconscious repetition of these figures in all the paintings? It is known that the painter João José has a history . . .

And the abuse of the words color, strength, setting, light, angles, and other more complicated ones continued.

Months later a news item passed this on to the readers of the *Jornal da Tarde* under the title of

A GREEK GIFT
SWINDLER "CAT" RETURNED BY BELMONTE POLICE

The Belmonte police received a real Greek gift from the Ilhéus police. A well-known young swindler who operated in Ilhéus under the name of "Cat," after having piled up some good money from a lot of landowners and businessmen, was shipped to Belmonte. There he continued conducting swindles, at which he was a master. He managed to sell an immense tract of land, the very best for the cultivation of cacao, to several plantation owners. When they went to look at the lands, they turned out to be the bed of the Cachoeira River, no less. The Belmonte police were able to lay their hands on the fearsome swindler and sent him back to Ilhéus.

"The Ilhéusans are a lot richer than we are," the informant ends with a certain irony, "they can support the elegant 'Cat' in more comfort than the sons of beautiful Belmonte, Princess of the South. Because if Belmonte is the Princess, Ilhéus is quite properly called Queen of the South."

Among police items of small importance, the *Jornal da Tarde* noted one day that a drifter known by the name of Good-Life had raised a tremendous row at a party in the Cidade da Palha, opening the skull of the master of the house with a beer bottle, and that he was being sought by the police.

During one Christmas season the *Jornal da Tarde* appeared with enormous headlines. A news item as sensational as the one that brought to light the story of the woman who traveled with Lampião's band, the *cangaceiro*'s mistress. Because the population of the five States of Bahia, Sergipe, Alagoas, Paraíba, and Pernambuco lives with its eyes fixed on Lampião. With hate or with love, never with indifference. The headline said in block letters:

16-YEAR-OLD CHILD IN LAMPIÃO'S GANG

Large type was also used for the heading of the story:

IS ONE OF THE MOST FEARED OF THE BANDITS—THIRTY-THREE NOTCHES ON HIS RIFLE—BELONGED TO THE "CAPTAINS OF THE SANDS"—DEATH OF AX-HEAD DUE TO DRY GULCH.

The story was long. It spoke of how in the villages sacked some time back people noticed a boy of sixteen among Lampião's band, who bore the name Dry Gulch. In spite of his age, the young *cangaceiro* had become feared all through the backlands as one of the cruelest of the group. It was said that his rifle had thirty-five notches. And each notch on the rifle of a *cangaceiro* stands for a dead man. Then came the story of the death of Ax-Head, one of the oldest veterans in Lampião's gang.

It so happened that the gang had caught an old police sergeant on the road. And Lampião had given him to Dry Gulch to "dispatch." Dry Gulch was "dispatching" him slowly, with the point of a dagger, cutting out small pieces with obvious satisfaction. It was so cruel that Ax-Head, horrified, raised his rifle to put an end to Dry Gulch. But before he could fire, Lampião, who was very proud of Dry Gulch, shot Ax-Head. Dry Gulch went on with his task.

The item went on to tell of various other crimes of the sixteen-year-old bandit. Then the author remembered that a boy with the name Dry Gulch had lived with the Captains of the Sands and that it was possible that it was the same one. Then came several considerations of a moral nature.

The edition sold out.

Months later the edition sold out again, because it carried the news of Dry Gulch's capture while he was sleeping by the flying column that covered the backlands in pursuit of Lampião. It announced that the *cangaceiro* would arrive in Bahia the following day. There were several pictures where Dry Gulch appeared with his somber face. The *Jornal da Tarde* said that it was the "face of a born criminal."

Which wasn't true, as the *Jornal da Tarde* itself observed some time later, when it related, in extra editions and supplements, the trial that condemned Dry Gulch to 30 years in prison for 15 known and proven killings. His rifle had 60 notches, however. And the newspaper recalled that fact, repeating that each notch was a dead man. But it also published part of the report by a forensic doctor, a gentleman of recognized honesty and education, already at that time one of the foremost sociologists and ethnologists in the nation, a report that proved that Dry Gulch was an absolutely normal type and that if he had become a *cangaceiro* and had killed so many men and with such extreme cruelty, it had not been because of an inborn vocation. It had been the environment . . . and the necessary scientific considerations followed.

Which, however, didn't arouse as much curiosity among the public as the description of the beautiful, vibrant, and impassioned speech of the State's Attorney, who had made the jury weep, and even the judge himself had brushed away tears as the attorney described with sublime oratorical force the suffering of the victims of the ferocious boy bandit.

The public was indignant because Dry Gulch didn't weep at the trial. His somber face was filled with a strange calm.

COMRADES

There's new movement in the city. Pedro Bala comes out of the warehouse with Big João and Outrigger. The waterfront is deserted, it looks as if everyone had abandoned it. Only a few policemen guarding the big warehouses. There's no unloading of ships this day. Because the stevedores, with João de Adão at their head, have shown solidarity with the streetcar motor-men, who are on strike. There seems to be a festival in the city, but a different kind of festival. Groups of men pass talking, automobiles cut through the street taking men to work, employees in businesses laugh, the Ladeira da Montanha is full of people going up and down, because the elevators have stopped too. The jitneys are jammed, with people hanging out the doors. The groups of strikers pass silently on their way to union headquarters, where they are going to hear the reading of the stevedores' manifesto that João de Adão carries in his big hand. At the door of the union hall, groups chat, police stand guard.

Pedro Bala goes along through the streets with Big João and Outrigger. He says:

"It's nice . . ."

Big João also smiles, little black Outrigger speaks:

"There's going to be a wing-ding today."

"I wouldn't want to be a motorman or a conductor. They don't get a pig's wages. They did the right thing . . ." Big João says.

"Shall we go have a look?" Pedro Bala proposes.

They go to the door of the union hall. Men are going in, blacks, mulattoes, Spaniards, and Portuguese. They watch while João de Adão and the other stevedores come out to the cheers of the streetcar workers. They cheer too. Big João and Outrigger because they like the dockworker João de Adão. Pedro Bala not only for that reason, but also because he finds the spectacle of the strike nice, it's like one of the nicest adventures of the Captains of the Sands.

A group of well-dressed men enters the union hall. From the door they hear a voice discoursing, one that interrupts: "Sellout," "scab."

"It's nice . . ." Pedro Bala repeats.

He has the urge to go in, mingle with the strikers, shout and fight alongside them.

The city goes to sleep early. The moon lights the sky, the voice of a black man comes from the sea opposite. He's singing about the bitterness of his life since his loved one left. In the warehouse the children are asleep already. Even black Big João is snoring, stretched out by the door, his knife within reach. Only Pedro Bala is awake, lying on the sand, looking at the moon, listening to the black man sing of his yearning for the mulatto girl who's gone away. The wind brings snatches of the song and it makes Pedro Bala look for Dora among the stars in the sky. She, too, had turned into a star, a strange star with long, blond hair. Brave men have a star in place of their hearts. But no one had ever heard tell of a woman who wore a star on her breast like a flower. The bravest women on the land and sea of Bahia, when they died, became saints for the blacks, the same as drifters who were also very brave. Rosa Palmeirão became a saint in a halfbreed *candomblé*, they pray to her in Yoruba. Maria Cabaçu is a saint in the *candomblés* of Itabuna, because it was in that town that she first showed her courage.

They were two great, strong women. With muscular arms like men, like strikers. Rosa Palmeirão was pretty, she had a sailor's swaying walk, she was a woman of the sea, at one time she owned a sloop, cut the waves at the entrance to the breakwater. The men on the waterfront loved her not only for her courage but for her body too. Maria Cabaçu was ugly, a dark-skinned mulatto, the daughter of a black man and an Indian woman, fat and hot-tempered. She attacked men who said she was ugly. But she gave herself over completely to a weak and sallow man from Ceará, who loved her as though she were a pretty woman with a beautiful body and sensuous eyes. They'd been brave, they'd become saints in halfbreed *candomblés*, which are *candomblés* that invent new saints from time to time, that don't have the purity of the Yoruba *candomblés* of blacks. They're mulatto *candomblés*. But Dora was braver than they. She was only a girl, she'd lived just like one of the Captains of the Sands and everybody knows that a Captain of the Sands is the equal of a brave man. Dora had lived with them, had been a mother to all of them. But she'd also been a sister, had run through the streets with them, raided houses, picked pockets, fought with Ezequiel's gang. Then for Pedro Bala, she'd been sweetheart and wife, wife when the fever was devouring her, when death was already stalking her that night of so much peace. A peace that came out of her eyes for all the night around. She'd been in the Orphanage, had run away from it, the same as Pedro Bala had run away from the Reformatory. She had the courage to die consoling her children, brothers, sweethearts, and husband, who were the Captains of the Sands. The *mãe-de-santo* Don'Aninha had wrapped her in a white shawl, embroidered as if for a saint. God's-Love had taken her out in his sloop to be with Iemanjá. Father José Pedro had prayed. They all loved her. But only Pedro Bala had wanted to go with her. Professor ran away from the warehouse because he could no longer stand the big house after she'd left. But only Pedro Bala had jumped into the water to follow Dora's destiny, take that marvelous journey with her, the one that brave men take with Iemanjá in the green depths of the sea. That's why only he saw when she became a star and crossed the sky. She came only for him, with her long, blond hair. She shined over his head of a near suicide by drowning. She gave him new strength, God's-Love's sloop was able to pick him up on the way back. Now he looks at the sky, seeking Dora's star. It's a star with long, blond hair, a star like no other in existence. Because no woman like Dora, who was just a girl, ever existed. The night is full of stars reflected on the calm sea. The black man's voice seems directed at the stars, as there is wailing in his full voice. He, too, is looking for his beloved, who'd fled in the Bahia night. Pedro Bala thinks that the star that's Dora may be running above the streets, alleys, and hillsides of the city now, looking for him. Maybe she thinks he's on some adventure on the slopes. But today it isn't the Captains of the Sands who are involved in a beautiful adventure. It's the motormen, strong black men, smiling mulattoes, Spaniards, and Portuguese who came from distant lands. They're the ones who are lifting their arms and shouting, the same as the Captains of the Sands. The strike is loose in the city. It's a nice thing, the strike is, nicer than adventures. Pedro Bala has an urge to join the strike, shout with all the strength of his chest, heckle speeches. His father made speeches in a strike, a bullet cut him down. He has the blood of a striker in him. Also, that life in the streets had taught him to love freedom. The song of those prisoners that said freedom is like sunlight: the greatest thing in the world. He knows that the strikers are fighting for freedom, for a little more to eat, for a little more freedom. The fight is like a festival.

The shapes approaching make him get up mistrustfully. But then he recognizes the enormous figure of the stevedore João de Adão. Along with him comes a well-dressed young man with unruly hair. Pedro Bala takes off his cap, speaks to João de Adão:

"You got a lot of cheers today, eh?"

João de Adão laughs. He stretches his muscles, his face opens into a smile for the leader of the Captains of the Sands:

"Captain Pedro, I'd like to introduce you to Comrade Alberto."

The young man holds out his hand to Pedro Bala. The leader

of the Captains of the Sands first wipes his hand on his ragged jacket, then he shakes the student's. João de Adão is explaining:

"He's a student at the University, but he's our comrade."

Pedro Bala looks at him without any mistrust. The student smiles:

"I've heard a lot about you and your gang. You're really something . . ."

"We're tough, that's for sure," Pedro Bala answers.

João de Adão comes closer:

"Captain, we've got to talk to you. We've got business with you. Something serious. Comrade Alberto here . . ."

"Shall we go inside?" Pedro Bala asks.

They awaken Big João as they pass. The black boy looks mistrustfully at the student, thinks he's from the police, moves his knife under his arm a little. Only Pedro Bala notices and says:

"He's a friend of João de Adão. Come with us, Big Boy."

The four of them go in. They sit down in a corner. Some of the Captains of the Sands wake up and watch the group. The student looks the warehouse over, the children sleeping. He shivers as if a cold wind had passed over his body:

"How awful!"

But Pedro Bala is telling João de Adão:

"What a great thing the strike is! I never saw anything so nice. It's like a big festival . . ."

"The strike is the poor people's festival . . ." the student says.

Alberto's voice is soft and kind. Pedro Bala listens to him, carried away as if it were the voice of a black man singing a sea chanty.

"My father died in a strike, did you know that? Ask João de Adão if you don't believe me . . ."

"It was a beautiful death," the student says. "He was a champion of his class. Wasn't he the Blond?"

The student knows his father's name. His father was a champion . . . They all know him. He had a beautiful death, he died in a strike, a strike is the poor people's festival . . . He listens to the student's friendly voice:

"Do you find the strike nice, Pedro?"

"Comrade, this fellow is a great one," João de Adão says. "You don't know the Captains of the Sands or Captain Pedro . . . He's a comrade . . ."

Comrade . . . Comrade . . . Pedro Bala thinks it's the nicest word in the world. The student says it the way Dora used to say the word brother.

"Well, Comrade Pedro, we need you and your gang."

"What for?" Big João asks curiously.

Pedro Bala introduces him:

"This black man here is Big João, a good man. Anyone good may be the equal of Big João, there isn't anyone better . . ."

Alberto shakes the black boy's hand. Big João is undecided for a moment, he's not used to handshakes. But then he shakes that hand, half-bashful. The student says again:

"You people are great . . ."

Suddenly he asks with interest:

"Is it true that Dry Gulch was one of you?"

"We'll get him out of jail someday . . ." is the Bullet's reply.

The student is half-startled. He takes a look around the warehouse, João de Adão makes a gesture as if reminding him, "Didn't I tell you?"

Pedro Bala wants to talk about the strike, find out what they want of him:

"Is it for the strike that you need us?"

"And if it is?" the student asks.

"If it's for helping the strikers my mind's already made up. You can count on us . . ." He gets up, he looks like a young man, his face ready for the fight.

"You don't see . . ." João de Adão begins to explain.

But he falls silent because the student is speaking:

"The strike is proceeding in a very orderly way. We want to do things in orderly fashion because that way we'll win and the workers will get their raises. We don't want to start any trouble, we want to show that the workers are capable of discipline." ("Too bad," thinks Pedro Bala, who likes disturbances.) "But it so happens that the directors of the Company are hiring strike-breakers to go to work tomorrow. If the workers break up the groups of strike-breakers, they'll give the police an excuse to intervene and everything will be lost . . . Then Comrade João de Adão thought about you people . . ."

"Break up the strike-breakers? Such a thing," Bullet says happily.

The student thinks about the argument that evening at the organization. When João de Adão proposed calling in the Captains of the Sands, a lot of comrades declared themselves against it. They smiled at the idea. João de Adão only said:

"You people don't know the Captains of the Sands."

That statement, that confidence had impressed Alberto and a few others. Finally the idea won out, nothing would be lost in trying. Now he was glad he'd come. And in his head he was already planning how to make use of the Captains of the Sands. In all the things those hungry and poorly dressed boys could be of use. He remembered other examples, the anti-Fascist struggle in Italy, Lusso's boys. He smiled at Pedro Bala. He explained the plan: the strike-breakers would come to the three large trolley yards before dawn to take over the cars. The Captains of the Sands had to split up into three groups, guard the entrances to the three yards. And, no matter what, prevent the strike-breakers from getting the streetcars moving. Pedro Bala nodded. He turned to João de Adão:

"If Legless was alive, if Cat was only here . . ."

Then he remembered the Professor:

"Professor would have thought up a good plan in a minute . . . Then he would have sketched a picture of the fight. He's in Rio now."

"Who's he?" the student asks.

"Somebody called João José, who we used to call Professor. He's painting pictures in Rio now."

"He's the painter João José?"

"The very same," Bullet says.

"I'd always thought that story was made up. Do you know that he's a good comrade?"

"He always was a good comrade," Pedro says forcefully.

The student was making plans for the Captains of the Sands. Now Pedro Bala was waking them all up and telling them what they had to do. The student was enthusiastic over the urchin's words. When he finished explaining, Bullet summed it all up in these words:

"The strike is a festival for the poor. The poor people are all comrades, our comrades."

"You're terrific," the student said.

"You'll see how we'll take care of those traitors."

He explained to Alberto:

"I'll go with one group to the main yard. Big João will take another. Outrigger will take a third one to the smaller yard. Nobody gets in. We know what to do. You'll see . . ."

"I'll be there to see," the student said. "So, at four in the morning?"

"That's right."

The student makes a gesture:

"See you later, Comrades . . ."

Comrades . . . A nice word, Pedro Bala thinks. Nobody sleeps at the warehouse anymore that night. They're preparing the most diverse weaponry.

In the breaking dawn the stars are beginning to disappear from the sky. But Pedro Bala seems to see Dora's star in a falling star, which gladdens him. Comrade . . . She would have been a good comrade too. The word leaps into his mouth, it's the prettiest word he's ever heard. He'll ask Good-Life to compose a samba about it, a samba for a black man to sing at night by the sea. They go as if to a festival. Armed with the most diverse weapons: switchblades, daggers, pieces of wood. They're going to a festival, because the strike is the festival of the poor, Pedro Bala repeats to himself.

At the foot of the Ladeira da Montanha, they divide into three groups. Big João heads one, Outrigger goes with another, the largest goes with Pedro Bala. They're going to a festival. The first real festival these children have had. Even so, it's a festival for men. But it's a festival for the poor, poor people like them.

The early morning is cold. At the corner of the yard, while Pedro Bala is placing the boys, Alberto comes over to him. Pedro turns, his face smiling. The student speaks:

"There they come, Comrade."

"Wait and see."

Now it's the student who's smiling. He's obviously enthusiastic over the boys. He'll ask the organization to work with them. They're going to do a lot of things together.

The strike-breakers come along in a closed group. An American with a tight face is leading them. They all head for the entrance. Out of the shadows, from alleys, no one knows from where, like demons out of hell, the ragged boys emerge with weapons in their hands. Knives, switchblades, clubs. They take the gate. The strike-breakers stop. Then the demons attack, it's one single blow. There are more of them than strike-breakers. The latter roll over from *capoeira* kicks, take a drubbing, some run away. Pedro Bala knocks down the American, with the help of another who punches him. The strike-breakers think they're demons out of hell.

The great, free guffaw of the Captains of the Sands resounds in the dawn. The strike hasn't been broken.

Big João and Outrigger are victorious too. The student laughs the guffaw of the Captains of the Sands with them.

At the warehouse, to the joy of the boys, he says:

"You're the greatest bunch I've ever seen . . ."

"Comrades, Comrades," says João de Adão.

The wind that passes says it, the voice in the heart of Pedro Bala says it. It's like the music of a song sung by a black man:

"Comrades."

THE DRUMS RESOUND
LIKE TRUMPETS OF WAR

After the strike is over, the student continues to come to the warehouse. He has long talks with Pedro Bala, transforms the Captains of the Sands into a shock brigade.

One afternoon Pedro Bala is going along the Rua Chile, his cap over his eyes, whistling as he scuffs his feet on the ground. A voice exclaims:

"Bullet!"

He turns. Cat is standing elegantly before him. A pearl stick-pin in his tie, a ring on his little finger, blue suit, a felt hat creased drifter style:

"Is that you, Cat?"

"Let's get out of here."

They turn down an uncrowded street. Cat explains that he got in from Ilhéus a couple of days ago. That he'd picked up a chunk of money there. He's a full-fledged man, all perfumed and elegant:

"I almost didn't recognize you . . ." Pedro Bala says. "What about Dalva?"

"She took up with a colonel. But I'd already left her. Now I've got a terrific little dark girl . . ."

"What about the big ring that Legless used to make fun of?"

Cat laughs:

"I pawned it off for five hundred on a colonel who had plenty . . . The clown swallowed it without a complaint . . ."

They chat and laugh. Cat asks about the others. He says that he's sailing for Aracaju the next day with his dark girl because sugar is bringing in money. Pedro Bala watches him go off in all his elegance. He thinks that if he'd stayed on a little longer in the warehouse maybe he wouldn't have been a thief. He would have learned with Alberto, the student, what nobody knew how to teach them. What the Professor had kind of guessed at.

The revolution calls Pedro Bala the way God called Lollipop at night in the warehouse. It's a powerful voice inside him, as powerful as the voice of the sea, as the voice of the wind, as powerful as a voice without comparison. With the voice of a black man on a sloop singing the samba that Good-Life had composed:

Comrades, the time has come . . .

The voice calls him. A voice that makes him happy, that makes his heart beat. Helping change the destiny of all poor people. A voice that goes through the city, that seems to come from the drums that resound in the *macumbas* of the blacks' illegal religion. A voice that goes with the sound of the street-cars with motormen and conductors. A voice that comes from the waterfront, from the docks, from the chest of stevedores, from João de Adão, from his father, dying in a rally, from sailors on ships, from sloopmen, from canoemen. A voice that comes from a group doing *capoeira* foot-fighting, that comes with the kicks that God's-Love applies. A voice that even comes from Father José Pedro, a poor priest with fearful eyes as he sees the terrible destiny of the Captains of the Sands. A voice that comes from the *filhas-de-santo*, dancers of Don'Aninha's *candomblé* on the night the police took Ogun away. A voice that comes from the warehouse of the Captains of the Sands. That comes from the Reformatory and the Orphanage. That comes from Legless's hatred as he jumps from the elevator so as not to be taken. That comes on the Leste Brasileira train through the backlands, from Lampião's gang, seeking justice for backlands people. That comes from Alberto, the student, asking for schools and freedom of culture. That comes from the Professor's paintings, where ragged boys fight in the exhibition on the Rua Chile. That comes from Good-Life and the drifters of the city, from the belly of their guitars, from the sad sambas they sing. A voice that comes from all the poor, from the chest of all poor people. A voice that speaks a beautiful word of solidarity, of friendship: "Comrades." A voice that invites everyone to the festival of the struggle. That's like the happy samba of a black man, like the pounding drums in *macumbas*. A voice that brings memories of Dora, a brave fighter. A voice that calls Pedro Bala. Like the voice of God calling Lollipop, Legless's voice of hate, like the voice of backlands people calling Dry Gulch to Lampião's gang. A voice powerful like no other. Because it's a voice that calls all to the struggle, to the destiny of all, without exception. A voice powerful like no other. A voice that crosses through the city and comes from all sides. A voice that brings a festival with it, that makes winter end out there and turn to spring. The springtime of the struggle. A voice that calls Pedro Bala, that brings him into the struggle. A voice that comes from all hungry chests in the city. A voice that brings the greatest good in the world, a good equal to the sunlight, even greater than the sunlight: freedom. The city on that spring day is dazzlingly beautiful. A woman's voice sings the song of Bahia. The song of the beauty of Bahia. A city black and old, church bells, streets paved with stones. The song of Bahia that a woman sings. Inside Pedro Bala a voice calls him: a voice that joins the song of freedom to the song of Bahia. A powerful voice that calls him. A voice of the whole poor city of Bahia, a voice of freedom. The revolution calls Pedro Bala.

Pedro Bala was accepted into the organization on the same day that Big João embarked as a sailor on a merchantman of the Lóide Line. On the pier he waves goodby to the black boy who is going off on his first trip. But it's not a farewell like the ones

he'd given those who left before. It's no longer a gesture of
goodby. It's a gesture of greeting to the comrade who's leaving:
   "Goodby, Comrade."

Now he commands a shock brigade made up of the Captains
of the Sands. Their destiny has changed, everything is different now. They take part in rallies, in strikes, in workers' struggles. Their destiny is different. The struggle has changed their
destinies.

Orders came to the organization from the highest quarters.
Alberto was to stay with the Captains of the Sands and Pedro
Bala was to organize the Bandit Indians of Aracaju into a
shock brigade too. And after that he was to go on changing
the destiny of other abandoned children in the country.

Pedro Bala comes into the warehouse. Night had covered the
city. The black man's voice is singing at sea. Dora's star is shining almost as brightly as the moon in the most beautiful sky in
the world. Pedro Bala comes in, looks at the children. Outrigger
comes along next to him, the little black boy is 15 years old now.
   Pedro Bala looks. They're lying down, some already asleep,
others are talking, smoking cigarettes, laughing the great guffaw of the Captains of the Sands. Bullet brings them all together,
has Outrigger come over:
   "People, I'm going away now, I'm going to leave you. I'm
going away, Outrigger is leader now. Alberto will still come to
see you, do what he says. And everybody listen: Outrigger is
leader now."
   The black boy Outrigger speaks:
   "People, Pedro Bala is going away. Three cheers for Pedro
Bala . . ."
   The fists of the Captains of the Sands are raised.
   "Bullet, Bullet," they shout as a farewell.
   The shouts fill the night, drown out the voice of the black
man singing on the sea, the sky trembles, as does Pedro Bala's
heart. Clenched fists of children who stand up. Mouths that
shout a farewell to their leader: "Bullet, Bullet."

Outrigger stands before them all. He's leader now. Pedro Bala seems to see Dry Gulch, Legless, Cat, Professor, Lollipop, Good-Life, Big João, and Dora, all at the same time among them. Now their destiny has changed. The voice of the black man on the sea is singing Good-Life's samba:

Comrades, let's go into the fight . . .

With their fists raised, the children salute Pedro Bala, who is leaving to change the destiny of other children. Outrigger shouts in front of them all, he's the new leader now.

From far off Pedro Bala can still see the Captains of the Sands. In the moonlight, in an old abandoned warehouse, they're raising their arms. They're on their feet, their destiny has changed.

In the mysterious night of the *macumbas* the drums resound like trumpets of war.

... A HOMELAND AND
A FAMILY

Years later, good newspapers, little newspapers, several of which existed illegally and were printed on clandestine presses, newspapers that circulated in factories, passed from hand to hand, and which were read by the light of a match, kept publishing news about a militant proletarian, Comrade Pedro Bala, who was sought by the police of five States as an organizer of strikes, as the director of illegal parties, as the dangerous enemy of the established order.

In the year that all mouths were prevented from speaking, in the year that was one whole night of terror, those newspapers (the only mouths still speaking) demanded the freedom of Pedro Bala, the leader of his class, who was imprisoned in a penal colony.

And the day he escaped, in numberless homes at the hour of their poor meal, faces lighted up when they heard the news. And in spite of the fact that the terror was out there, any one of those homes was a home that would be open for Pedro Bala, a fugitive from the police. Because the revolution is a homeland and a family.

THE END

In the house haunted by Doninha Quaresma (jugs and Doninha's soul were buried there), now the Captain's, in the peace of Estância, Sergipe, March 1937.

On board the *Rakuyo Maru*, going up the coast of South America en route to Mexico, June 1937.

Postface: The Bahian Novels

With the publication of *Captains of the Sands*, I bring to a close the cycle of works that I call "The Bahian Novels." They are six books in which I have tried to set down the life, the customs, the language of my State. In *Carnival Country* it is the restlessness of intellectual youth that seeks its way at a moment of definition. Various critics who have written about my work, unfamiliar, naturally, with that first novel of mine, are accustomed to see it as a satirical book about Brazilian intellectuals who live as an offshoot of European literature, especially that of France. There is, however, not the slightest intent at satire in that novel. There does exist a desire to bring into focus a moment lived by the more or less intellectual or intellectualized youth of Brazil, a moment in which social and political currents were beginning to show and be defined. *Cacao* tried to give a glimpse of the life of workers on plantations in the south of Bahia, its richest region. *Sweat* exposes the most failed aspect of the State, creatures who have already lost everything and expect nothing more from life. I had the action of that novel take place in one of those strange tenements on the Ladeira do Pelourinho, and I did it with an aim: not only because I had met most of the characters in one of those tenements (where I lived), but as much because it seems to me that only in that environment could the novel and characters of the novel take on a tone of revolt in the face of their anguish and misery, and in that way, with some healthy pamphleteering, save the novel from the futility of reactionary pessimism or false mysticism. *Jubiabá* is the life of the black race in Brazil, a life of adventure and poetry. *Sea of Death* is a new vision of the life of the sailors of small sailing vessels on the waterfront of the state capital and the bay. And this book, *Captains of the Sands*, is the existence of abandoned children on the streets of the capital city who go off to the most diverse destinies, children who tomorrow will be the men who will possibly direct the fortunes of Bahia.

I said above that I tried to set down the total life of my State. This was really an intention and I say so, even if it might be too ambitious for a young man less than 25 years of age to attempt what thus far no Brazilian writer has tried. Those writers never undertook an honest attempt to set down in novels the life, the picturesque qualities, the strange humanity of Bahia. Bahia is something mysterious and big, like India, or certain regions of Africa, or islands of the South Seas. That always escaped the few novelists who tried to write fiction with my State as the scene and its people as the characters. They stood before that fertile and strange humanity in a position of the most absolute lack of understanding. In their pockets they carried a standardized type of the hero of a novel (either an elegant and mannerly young man or an illiterate and oratorical backlands hero) and they never really tried to approach the people, never learned their customs except from some vague bits of information. There is no greater difference anywhere than between the Bahian figures in novels that have been written about my State and the real humanity of Bahia. In order to put these novels of mine (which may have many defects, but which have one quality: the absolute honesty of the author) together, I tried to seek out the people, I went to live with them, ever since my childhood on cacao plantations, my adolescence in cafés in the capital, my trips all through the State, crossing it in all manner of conveyances, listening to and seeing the most beautiful and strangest parts of Bahia's humanity.

I have always spoken of collected material and many of the

bosses of the Brazilian novel have criticized those words harshly. But in this series of mine of novels of Bahia, I have only given myself the freedom to invent, to imagine plots. I have refused to imagine either the customs of my State, or the feelings of its men, or the way in which they react to determined facts. All this, this going out to see how Bahians really live, I call "collecting material." I am certain that I was not doing the work of a reporter, but that of a novelist, just as I am certain that, even if my novels relate facts, feelings, and landscapes of Bahia, they have a broad universal and human meaning precisely due to the social character they possess, a universal and human meaning, doubtless many times greater than those of novels written in reaction to new Brazilian novelists and which are distinguished by their not accepting any local or social character in their pages, novels that basically do not go beyond intellectual masturbation, a sort of continuation of the physical masturbation that their authors practice every day.

Therefore, I will not admit any kind of comparison between my novels and others that have been written about Bahia already. It is not a question of literary pride. It is only the certainty that no one until today has dared look face to face with so much love at Bahian humanity and its problems. No one knows better than I, who wrote them, what the weaknesses and defects of my novels are. But, by the same token, no one can measure the sacrifice they cost me, the honesty that went into their making, the disinterest and pure love that made the novelist return to his people.

I know full well that this series of novels has nothing of genius or the miraculous about it. The work of a young man, it could not help but be full of defects. I do know, however, that there exists in it a feeling that has almost always been forgotten in Brazilian works of art: an absolute solidarity with and a great love for the humanity that lives in these books.

The novelist who set out to start this work at the age of 18 and who today, at the age of 24, sees it concluded, wishes to make it quite clear here that he wrote it with the greatest satisfaction. He knows quite well that writing in Brazil is still a sacrifice, that making literature in this country, with few sales, is heroic. But this novelist has had support from the public that few Brazilian writers have had, and he knows that there are many people in the country who have understood him and look upon him with sympathy and love. Free of any and all links of friendship with literary groups and forces in the country, this novelist went out to seek support from the public, who came to understand that they had a friend in him, someone who wished to speak with a frank and loyal voice. Furthermore, this novelist is happy to know that he made the suffering and life of the Bahian people known to millions of people in Brazil and abroad, making many hearts beat in solidarity with the drama of their brethren in Bahia.

This series of six novels of Bahia is only based on the love a young man felt for the suffering, the joy, the life of the people of his land. They were books written, if not with talent and literary capacity, at least with a desire for absolute understanding.

I dedicate these "Novels of Bahia" to João Amado de Faria, my father, as a token of love and great recognition. He was one of those men from Sergipe who came as boys to build a country in Bahia, a clearer of backlands, builder of roads, raiser of towns, and to him for his 40 years of daily work on the land of Bahia, for the strength of heroism and poetry in his life, to him, builder of the country of Bahia, this remembrance from his Bahian son.

JORGE AMADO

Mexico City, June 1937

BackAd TK

P.O. 0005527178 202